GW01071952

CLASSIFICATION: FICTION

This book is sold under the condition that it shall
not, by way of trade or otherwise, be lent, resold,
hired out or otherwise circulated without the publisher's prior consent in any form of binding or cover
other than that in which it is published and without
a similar condition including this condition being
imposed on the subsequent purchaser.

A CIP catalogue record for this book is available from
the British Library.

Printed and bound in Great Britain.

Paper used in the production of books published by
United Press comes only from sustainable forests.

ISBN   1-84436-092-X

First published in Great Britain in 2004 by
United Press Ltd
Admail 3735
London
EC1B 1JB
Tel: 0870 240 6190
Fax: 0870 240 6191
ISBN for complete set of volumes
All Rights Reserved

© Copyright Paul Eccentric 2004

The moral right of the author has been
asserted

cover artwork © Paul Solomons 2004

www.unitedpress.co.uk

Down Among
The
Ordinaries

AUTHOR'S NOTE

The following is a tale of sex, drugs and rock 'n' roll; betrayal, perversion and death. It is, therefore, unsuitable as a bedtime story for the under 5's.

I would like to thank the following people for their help and encouragement during the writing process:
Jonathan Pannaman, David Jordan, Paul Solomons, Derek Sansom, Beef Grant, John Dobinson, Charissa Botha, Lindsay Fairgrieve and Edward Tudor Pole.

For my mum and dad (sorry about the swearing).

CONTENTS

PROLOGUE

The rain fell effortlessly from the charcoal sky, soaking her midnight ensemble and adding an element of conviction to her own crocodile deluge as the two streams mingled to spatter in poignant unison against the polished mahogany lid of the casket. She snuffled indulgently into her black lace handkerchief as the six lugubrious pall bearers lowered her husband into the muddy pit that had been prepared for him. For it would rain again with the undisputed inevitability of death, but for this self appointed chief mourner, this melodramatic performance would be her swansong; the final act in her ultimately forgettable life story, for, (lets not kid ourselves) she had only ever been famous for being the wife of somebody famous. After today she would return from whence she had come, erased from the annals of polite society, wiped away like an incriminating stain from the crotch of one's trousers; cursed to a zestless future existence down among the ordinaries. From the wake on in she would be a nobody; not even a has been, because she never really had been. She had revelled in her fifteen minutes of spotlight, the image of her kohl smudged visage that had monopolised the tabloid leaders these past two months standing now as her epitaph; the distraught widow of the missing and now dead rockstar who took his millions to the grave with him.

She knew what was to come as she watched her capricious claim to kudos being buried before her in the nose to toe celebrity plot of Highgate cemetary. She dropped a single red rose onto the coffin and blew her restructured nose once again, her tears mingling with the dirt at her feet. Oh, she knew what was coming, I could see it even through her darkened shades. She had seen it happen before, to others of their circle; had even been a part of such wicked convention herself.

No. Her tears were not for Stephen, they were for herself, and all assembled (with the possible exception of the paperazzi) knew as much.

I knew what she was going through as I watched her hug my associate bearers one by one, eliciting platitudes of insincerity from each in turn as she worked her way towards me. You see, I knew what it felt like to be disowned, disinherited, disenfranchised. Oh yes, I knew better than most, that vilest trick; that cruelest fate of them all. I knew how it felt to be roosting in the uppermost branches when the rotten bows beneath me had come crashing down. I knew how much harder that fall the farther up that slippery ladder of success one had climbed. And how would she cope in a week or two's time when those same friends that even then I could hear offering their unconditional support as she sobbed against their already sodden shoulders, stopped returning her calls? How many bland answerphone messages would she endure before she finally placed that call to Telecom to check whether her line was working properly? And how many polite, yet formal letters would she receive informing her of certain amounts owing or possessions long ago lent, but now urgently required by their rightful owners, before she realised the true and horrifying extent of her new position?

Persona non gratis; persona not existant.

The rain rained and the mourners dripped. I waited patiently feigning interest in the intricately carved eighteen carat plaque that adorned the casket's lid, emblazened with a lyric from my old sparring partner's most recent hit single "What do I do now? make some retrospective vow, what a time to contemplate my faith?"

Prophetic or pathetic?

Rusty had done his bit and his indulgent bulk could now be seen waddling along the narrow pathways between the headstones in search of a direct route toward his chauffeur who, on witnessing the weather hampered progress of his employer, had begun to wave his cap above his umbrella as a marker for the fat boy to home in on among the line of similarly attired domestic servants, each also awaiting the return of their charges.

Morris was next, an over rouged dolly dimple sobbing perfidiously in his wake, pretending not to have noticed the row of telephoto lenses that had been tracking their every movement from behind the lines of the police cordon. Morris said very little. At least it saved him from lying as visibly as had Rusty before him. He was conserving his voice, he had said, for a performance that evening. Wouldn't want to waste his precious breath.

Lakhi smiled broadly from beneath his soggy fedora, cringing sympathetically while he muttered something non-commital and offered her his card. I saw her smile bravely as she accepted it, though she must have been dying to force feed it back to him, knowing as we all must have done that she would never have got past his PA, not even in an emergency.

Joe Munday should have been next. He had been the bearer directly in front of me, (I having been positioned on the back left hand corner of the box, the farthest from the eyeline of the BBC News crew and their cameras). But Joe had already buggered off. Having hung around just long enough to ensure that his mournful gaze would make it into the following morning's papers, he had gathered up his permanently stoned wife and sidled away in his Silver Cloud. (If, of course, it could be said to be possible to sidle in a Silver Cloud).

"Sly", she had said, acknowledging my presence for the first time that day. I think I smiled somewhat wanly, aware of the futility of an attempt at condolence when we both knew how much I had hated Stephen these past few years, and fresh out of mawkish verbiage in light of the fact that all the best lines had already been used at least once. No. Any reply at this juncture would have been an insult, I'm convinced.

She didn't hug me as she had the fawners, she just sniffed back the snot with the tears that we both knew were no longer necessary and pulled her drowning fox stole a little closer to her chest. "It's good to see you," she lied, her gauze veil lifting and falling over her lips with each breath, "Stephen loved you, you know, despite everything."

I wondered what, if anything, she would have known about love and how, in the face of the reason that we were even there that day she had the gall to presume to know her late husband's mind. I chose not to point this out, as surely she must have felt the congregation of Raybanned accusers, (each with their own wild theories as to why Stephen Twenty had taken his own life) glaring at her from afar.

The clever money was still on the grizzling wretch in front of me who had attempted unsuccessfully to divorce him on four separate occasions. She had been the thorn in his side that I had striven, but failed to be. She had wanted the loot, It was as simple as that, and that had been the sole reason that she had constantly put up with the kind of behaviour that lesser wives would have killed him for years before.

Ironic really, that he had taken it all with him.

"Feel free to come back to the house," she muttered. Not "You're welcome", but "feel free".

I forced the smile back onto my lips and handed her the card, inside which I had committed my thoughts and regrets (few that they were) with a practised eloquence that would have been muddled and misconstrued in verbal conversation.

She flicked a cigarette from its packet and pressed it between her blood red lips, bringing up her other, Zippo armed hand in reflexive response. She took a sharp lug into the depth of her lungs and then removed the cigarette, letting the laden hand drop to her side, her fingers flicking nervously at its ashen tip. She didn't offer the packet.

Asp like fumes curled from her lips as she spoke: "I wish they hadn't found him," she said, shivering in her flimsy satin dress and casting an anxious eye across the cemetary to where the police were attempting to hold back the fans from the departing celebrity mourners without losing their helmets in the process. I stood my ground while attempting to perfect an expression of a pity that I couldn't feel.

She came to a decision, dragging hard on her menthol weed; hard enough to inhale almost a third of its hit in a single in breath. (With lungs of that capacity, I idly wondered why she had never trained to be a singer). She dropped the remaining third into the open grave. "Ash to Ashes," she snapped and turned on her teetering stillettos to stalk back between the monuments toward her car.

"Stupid bastard," she muttered, and for a moment I was alone with my dead "friend" and unsure as to which of us the insult had been intended.

"See you in hell," I called to her receding back, not a retaliatory strike, you understand, merely a statement of fact. It was the last that I ever saw of her.

As I stood there by the grave side, my jet black hair plastered to my forehead; the barest hint of hair dye polluting the taste of rain, I pondered the point of burying a man who had already cremated himself a fortnight earlier. What would future archeologists make of their find when they attempted to exhume him in a thousand years time? Stephen might become famous all over again. Where was the justice in that when my own contributions had been forgotten even before my death?

" Selfish bastard," I scorned, as the petals of the rose detached themselves one by one from the severed stalk to float across the pooling puddle that now obscured the casket's legend and flow from sight into the slimy pit beneath. I turned up the collar of my Crombie for meagre protection against the biting April wind as I turned to follow the trail that my ex-friends had taken toward the Swains lane gates. The cortege had gone by the time I arrived, as had the bescootered paperazi in hot pursuit. If this had been the funeral of an ordinary then my presence might well have warranted a byline in an exclusives starved local rag, but it wasn't and it didn't. There were much bigger fish in attendance; people whose names still meant something to the uninvited hordes; the so called fans whose tacky tributes festooned the iron railings and the pavements outside.

I turned left out of the gates, deliberately garroting a pink nylon teddy bear with my cuban heel; an act of sheer spite for which a less twisted soul may have felt some inkling of shame, but for which I felt nothing but glee in a small measured dose. I was headed for Highgate itself with the sole intention of addling my remaining senses with the last of my cash, of mourning the loss of my friend in my own private way; where I could wallow to my hearts content in my own selfish pity as, with Stephen gone, I now had no one to blame for my own inadequacies.

I didn't hear her at first; the plaintive, mouse-like whitter of the girl at the bus stop. Only when she repeated her request with a little more urgency did I become aware of the subtle de ja vous experience that her persistence incited.

"I'm sorry?" I replied, asking for a third repetition of her request. It had been so long, you see, since anybody had even acknowledged me, let alone....

"Your autograph?" she pressed, "Please?" passing me a biro and a piece of folded card.

I stared down at it, recognising the barely legible scribble of "Rusty Rhine", the pseudo-aristocratic "MY" of Morris Yussof and the bold

italic scrawl of Lakhi Corner, the Oscar winning score composer -
(let's not forget!).

I snatched up the pen, trying desperately, but failing miserably in
an attempt not to appear too eager. It was like a narcotic hit for
me, or that addiction starved rush that you get from a post coital
fag. I needed this now - oh, I needed it alright!

As I scanned the page for a suitable space to flourish, I suddenly
realised just what it was that I had been asked to sign. "This is an
'Order of Service'!" I spat, recognising the oppulent motif and the
gold leaf lettering - (my copy of which now lay with its subject at
the bottom of a muddy pit,) revulsed by the girls brazenly petulant
disrespect.

"I know," she giggled, unwavering in her arrogant morbidity,
"Morris gave it to me. He didn't recognise me either."

"You're sick."

I looked up into her face, something niggling at the back of my
mind.

"You don't remember me Sylvie, do you?"

I stared right through her, long suppressed memories swimming
painfully into focus.

"What did you call me?"

"Neve?" she prompted, peering out from beneath the broad brim of
her black boater. "We shared virgin snogs!" she elaborated, "surely
you remember that? Leabridge juniors, 1962!"

"My God," I replied, my mind's eye hastily attempting to de-age the
figure before me to match the memory of her as a pigtailed five year
old, "My God! It must have been..."

"Twenty two years," she appraised.

"That long?"

"Since they blackballed me in favour of Lakhi."

The drizzle became a fully fledged shower once again, forcing a natural escape from what was about to become a rather uncomfortable
remeniscence.

"Please?" she asked again indicating the glossy pamphlet that dared
to juxtapose the licentious lyrics to Stephen's 'Last Temptation'
between 'The Lord is my Shepherd' and 'The Lord's Prayer' - (those
two all-time favourite - funereal-greats) and which currently held
the prized autographs of all but one of the surviving members of
one of the country's biggest selling groups of all time etched across

the sneering visage of the only dead one. "Could you sign it? It's the nearest any one'll ever get to a full band autograph again."

I scribbled my moniker, numbed by the days extraordinarily unpredictable turn, but with a little less artistic panache than I had originally intended. Still, it was legible, which was more than could be said for Rusty's.

"Look," she said, while she carefully placed the card into a re-sealable plastic bag, before poking it into her satchel, "Why don't we get together some time? You know, go over old times?"

"Why not," I replied, perhaps a little too quickly, while intending nothing of the kind.

She pulled a business card from her pocket and pressed it into my hand as she stepped onto the foot plate of a convenient route-master.

I watched her go, turning the soggy card over and around in my fingers.

"Neve Crilly Memorabilia" it stated, black on red beneath a mobile telephone number. I scrunched the card and dropped it into my pocket, wondering whether the wake might be worth a visit after all.

Chapter One
" Down and Out on the Vale of Health"

"Quickly Sylvie, quickly! In here!"

"We don't both fit," I plead prostrate, yet strangely aware of my grammatical faux pas.

"Hurry up Sylvie or he'll find us!" she urges, tugging urgently at the too long sleeves of the bottle green jumper that my mother had knitted me for school.

Neve, her fairy figure a full inch shorter than my own has succeeded in wedging herself horizontally into the old discarded sewer pipe that has been built into the artificial hillock behind the Wickstead playground for use in such games as "pirates" and "tag".

"'Ere'e is!"

It's Morris's voice, minus the now indicative smoker's burr and his latterly affected middle class accent. Neve twists herself around inside the pipe so that she is lying face up, her soapy white knees now stained with mud and leaf mould.

"Come on, Sylvie! I can hear him!"

"I can't," I plead, my head darting back and forth between the swings where I last saw our pursuer and my only embarrassing recourse.

"Lie on top of me," she giggles, "just for a little minute."

Terrified even more of losing the game for us and the humiliating ridicule of another defeat to that four eyed spanner Morris, I thrust my stunted body headlong into the pipe, my scabby white knees chafing her delicate ivory thighs; my weight on top of her forcing her blue and white chequered dress to ride up around her waist, thus exposing her grass stained knickers to Morris if he were to think of looking for us here.

She smiles beatifically back as my face appears above her own.

"Shush!" I whistle, pressing a shaking finger against her beautiful pouting lips.

She obeys my command instantly, though her chaste smile dips dangerously into a devilishly incorrigible grin that belies her obvious immaturity of body and makes me begin to doubt just how much of this is memory and how much a dream, tainted forever by the dubious hindsights of adulthood. Her freckle pocked cheeks begin to glow with a warmth that I can almost feel as I drown in those big round eyes that sparkle as I remember them with the proffered innocence of youth. I am seeing my best friend, the friend that I had always thought of as sister, for the first time. We have known each other forever, had played naked in that old rubber paddling pool while our mothers drank tea and gossiped, but never had I seen her so bare as I do now.

My heart is beginning to pound, releasing a sudden rush of endorphins that muddle my five year old mind. I have a hurt in my..... in my willy, but a nice hurt, an exciting hurt, like the one that I get as I climb the ropes in the school gym.

Neve giggles again as if she senses my arousal, wriggling like a raspberry blancmange beneath me, (or so my unadulterated imagination translates for me). I shush her again, hearing the scuffling footfall of our playmate as he searches the manmade hillock for our bolthole.

This time she reaches forward and kisses my sweaty finger, stoking the fire that has been sparked within my prepubescent loins. I throw confusion to the wind, lean forward and gently reciprocate. "Aha! Gotcha! You're it!" exclaims Morris, before: "Whatch you doin? Sylvie Quiggley?"

.....And then we are somewhere else; some when else. We are older now - I having earned the protection of long trousers and she having discovered eyeliner, stockings and braziers. Leabridge Juniors and indeed the 1960s are now, but a faded memory, as even those few summers past seem like ancient history to a thirteen year old.

Though seniors have parted us for the duration of the school day, Neve and I have remained every bit as inseparable outside of school as ever we were; even if time and hormones have made us a little warier of our equivocal bond. Nothing was ever mentioned of our "Virgin snog" again, not since specky Morris had made us the ridicule of the first year. And I have never tried it again-not with Neve - not with anyone, (a fact that is fast gaining me a reputation among my all male class mates) and it is to this end that today I have decided to introduce my new friends to Neve. (I remember this scene in perfect clarity as it plays out before me now, though, along with all of this, I had thought it purged from my memory forever).

I meet her at the gates of Saint Swithens and we laugh and joke all the way to the top rec'; that same recreation ground, though the pipes have long been removed after fat Tony got himself jammed inside for a whole night and had to be rescued by the Fire brigade. We are holding hands as we approach, an affectation from childhood rather than a property significator, I remind myself. And then she sees him for the first time, strutting across the tarmac like some kind of Eastend gangster, spearheading his wastrel entourage which consists of Morris, the tallest and least comfortable of the triad and Kenny Daniels (or Dan Dare as he is more commonly known, prior to his premature death during a game of chicken on the North Circular flyover in '73.)

Stephen Twenty, exuding far more confidence than any boy that I have ever met, is sex. From his Rod Stewart haircut to his Mick Jagger strut he is the boy that we'd all like to be.

Neve releases her grip on my fingers and my hand falls limply to my side. It will be a long time before she touches me again.

I catch sight of the smile that quivers at the corners of her lips, bulging her fading freckles into a parody of that look that I have seen only once before. Mute as he remains, awaiting introduction to his future mate, Stephen already has her under his spell. It is a spell that will last for the next seven years of our lives....

And then I woke up.

Recognising the dream for what it had been, a spontaneous regurgitation of old memories from the time before time, an era that I had long ago consigned to the great landfill of my conscience, a place never since visited and rarely acknowledged and probably only dredged through now because of the miasma of uncogitated emotions still churning through my shellshocked mind following the events of the recent past. I suppressed it. I had work to do.

It was a full eight weeks since we had lain my nemesis to rest, so why was I still so preoccupied with the issues that that tawdry event had thrown up?

It was beginning to affect my work, not to mention my sanity.

Everything I had written of late had been tinged with a melancholic morbidity that would be guaranteed to have my listeners reaching for their razorblades before reaching the bridge. I was becoming a blues man - a style that I had always reviled as musical masturbation.

The blinding rays of an un-characteristically bright early spring morning had dragged me from my wistful reminiscence like a bear being woken from its annual hibernation, in order that I might use the day while I could. I do not know why I had even been bothering to try to get my inspirational juices flowing before, when I knew all too well that I would never be happy with anything that I had written through the winter months. I am a summer person - I can't abide the cold and the damp. It depresses me. In years gone by I would have packed myself off for the duration to my retreat on Capri or to Joe's pad in Monseratt, but not any longer. At this point in my career an artistic retreat meant a pre beverage stroll around my acre and a half Hampstead reserve, mumbling into a dictaphone, conducting the air and causing more than a few contemptuous glances from the top deck plebeians on the passing buses.

But the winter months were never wasted - not even then. I may not have been able to compose, but I could still imbibe. I busied myself collecting stories; emotions and feelings - watching other people's actions and reactions toward one another. (Granted, in a more 'second hand' way than before, as of late I had had to become content with the scripted antics of actors and chat show guests through the medium of a television.)

I found that it usually took me a day or two of unfettered serenity to unlock this horde and to defrost the cogs and wheels that worked my award winning imagination; to release my soulful spirit on to the page and the tape. God, was I the consumate artist or what?

And this was to be the first of those days: a bright fresh April morning full of hope and inspiration.

Discounting the onerous debacle of Stephen's funeral - a mere social blip on the radar screen of society function- I had not left the safety of my razor wire topped, twelve foot high enclave with its anti climb paint and its infra red cameras for close on eight months. Not since my headline snatching handbags-at-dawn tiffette over lunch at the Savoy with Joe Munday. This fiasco in itself would not ordinarily have warranted such a lengthy period of personal her-mititude, not, that was, without the ensuing circus of a media starved of a royal exclusive now that everybody's favourite press darling was dead and buried. (She had a lot to answer for, that Diana: Her untimely demise having left her glitterati peers in a somewhat vulnerable and over exposed position.)

I felt safe here. Forgotten, but safe.

Pulling taught the cord of my black satin Kimono: a souvenir from a sell out tour of the Far East - the gown that had my name embroi-dered across the shoulders in stylised Japanese calligraphy (or at least - that was what they had told me) - the one that I had worn for the inner sleeve shoot for my first solo single, I stepped out from the west wing and tramped my way across the bluebell carpet toward the main gate. As I kicked my Wellington boots through the overly prolific bed of wild violet I let my mind drift from its post dream analysis and began to roll the words 'latent memory' around my pallette. Minor key, I decided; yet again - pensive, tristful, nos-talgic...bluesy. I elected to roll with it, disappointed that my sub-conscious had chosen to taunt my preconceptions once more, but powerless to pervert that seminal flow of inspirational 'sui generis.' My creative mind worked better on the move, (a fact that did noth-ing to improve my somewhat slipshod handwriting nor aid my inherent clumsiness.) By the time that I had reached the arrow-head railings of the burnished iron electric gate, (a priceless object d'art in its own right, designed to reflect my neo-gothic mood of the moment by the then up and coming sculptor Adrienne Beau - and costing me an amount in excess of the current market value of the suburban semi in Lea in which I spent my formative years) I had contrived the sketchy beginnings of a mood ridden melody, based around an eight note hook that strung together the only six words of lyric that I had conjured so far. (All of my hooks were of eight notes or more - due to the plagerism encouraging law that stated that up to seven consecutive notes could be lifted from any com-position without royalty payments or recognition being paid to the originator.)

I lifted the brass flap that had been set into the gates granite pillar, reached inside and retrieved my mail, the hook all the time running on a mental loop inside my head. As I turned to stroll back toward the conservatory and my mid morning tipple I tore open my solitary letter and began to skim-read its content, dismissing out of hand the unsuitably profane rhyme that had just occurred to me and threatened, if not rapidly forgotten, to break my concentration and tip the sentiment of the piece. Why were rugby songs so much easier to compose than love songs? And why when there were so many words that rhymed with 'hanker', could I only think of one?

'Dear Mr Quiggley,' it read, 'blah, blah, blah - it has come to our attention - blah, blah, blah - final warning - blah, blah - recover assets - blah - five hundred and eighty two thousand pounds and fourteen pence ...'

I stopped dead in my tracks, my rubber soles skidding me to a premature halt on the gravel drive and sending up a cloud of dust which threatened to aggravate my allergies. The potential hit that had previously been occupying my lobes suddenly became relegated to the depths of my unconscious, tagged by association to the narrative of the letter which, when later I would attempt to block from my mind, would be lost - probably irretrievably - along with it. My eyes tracked back over the letter heading : 'HM Inspector of Taxes'. How could I possibly have owed them more than half a million quid?

'Unpaid taxes for the years 97/98 and 98/99', it explained impassively. I was sure that I'd paid them! I even remembered signing the cheque that Andy had brought me. And anyway - What were they doing sending demands to my door?

That was half the point of employing an accountant! Andy would sort it out - there was no need for panic.

I pushed open the front door and strode through the marble hall, squelching mud and flower heads into the Chinese rug that ran the entire length of the main concourse.

I stamped on into the study, retrieved the cordless telephone and stabbed the keys "M" and "1", initiating an almost instantaneous speed dial of my accountants number.

"We are sorry -" began the dreary answering machine at the other end of the connection. I didn't wait for the beeps. I hung up and jabbed at "M-2", hoping to connect myself to the bean-counter's mobile. "We are sorry -" It repeated mockingly, and so again I broke the call - this time slamming the handset against its base unit with thankfully little enough anger to fully incur my tantrum.

My panic was interrupted by an impertinent chime from the entry phone beside my desk. I allowed myself a brief shower of relief as I realised that my financial friend and confidante had, as ever, been one step ahead and had already been en route having received a facsimilie copy of the demand with his own morning post.

"Andy?" I ventured, stabbing at the receive key and thereby accepting the call from the camera at the gate. But instead of the badly wigged, hornbilled little homosexual that I had expected to see squashed into the three inch square video screen, a sneering King Edward potato squinted miopically back, so close to the lens as to throw itself into a dizzyingly blurred focus, convincing me momentarily that I was indeed speaking to a sentient vegetable.

"Sylvester Quiggley, A.K.A.Sky Quip?" It mocked, with a little too much confidence for my own paranoid taste.

"Who wants to know?" I replied, sanguine from my fortress vantage point.

"Chisolm Reperations," spud face slurred back, "We're ere hon the hauthority of Munday Financial Services. Hi've got a repossession horda for 'ome hand contents hup to the value hof your houtstanding debt hof one hand ha quarter milyon quid."

said the human carbohydrate. (Whose speech impediment reminded me of Parker - the ex-con, butler from Thunderbirds.) He emphasised the word "houtstanding" in a way that made it sound as if he were genuinely himpressed by the amount owing, rather than to simply infer that the payments were now overdue. "You 'ave 'd three warnings, mista Quiggley, none hof which 'ave bin hacknowledged, so, has per the terms hof your hagreement wif mista Munday, we har now hempowered to henter the property to begin cataloguing. Now, you gonna open up, hor do we 'ave to take this bloody gate hoff?"

"Now you listen to me, cretin!" I answered too rashly, "You leave that gate alone!"

I was thinking on my feet, and for a man of my passion that was never a good idea. I could just about make out the sillhouettes of the rest of the sack, pacing like zombies on the scent of fresh meat in the background.

"Can you give me a few minutes," I pleaded rationally, stalling for inspiration.

"Too late, chum! You 'ave 'ad your chance to pay."

"So as I can put some clothes on, arsehole!"
"Five." He graciously conceded. I broke the connection and dived straight for the phone, hitting the redial and receiving the same dispassionate reply as I had before. I threw off the Kimono and kicked off the boots, the second of which upset a daintily impractical table, which, in turn relieved itself of its burden; a twelfth century urn that I had purchased at auction and had intended to use as a plant pot. The redundant antique split asunder, spraying the closest it had ever seen to vegetation (a year or so's worth of joint butts) across the already spoiled rug. I stumbled up the stairs, attempting to take them two at a time, but my wasted calf muscles resisted after the first landing and slowed my ascention to the leisurely pace that they had latterly grown accustomed to. On my eventual arrival in the master bedroom I was panting like a dehydrated dog under a desert sun. Adrenalin was no substitute for fitness.

There had to be something I could do? Maybe they *had* written to warn me. How would I know? Until that morning I had never opened anything that had borne even the barest hint of a frank of officialdom. It was always sent on to Greg. Greg, yes of course! Greg Hatch, my solicitor! I reached for the bedroom extension line and dialled 'M3' as I dragged on my leather jeans, breathing in sharply as they reached my hips in the hope that I could fool the press studs into believing that I was in fact a 32 inch waist and not a slovenly 34. I let the handset slip from its wedge beneath my chin as I recognised that same tired message informing me that both my options were conspicuously unavailable. I briefly wondered whether the "partners" were already on the case, perhaps having elected to save time by skipping the middleman-(namely me), but decided that this was probably wishful thinking and that they were more than likely on their "own" case in some seedy little short stay hotel. In a flash of uncharacteristic malice I also pondered the merits of informing their wives of the true extent of their "business partnership", but dismissed this thought as quickly as I had the last.

The entryphone buzzed a second time, indirectly causing me to snag my wrinkled belly in my protesting fly. My five minutes were up. Joe's bully boys were growing impatient. I accepted the call from the intercom on the landing whilst attempting to force my still unshaven chin through the neck of a chenille sweater. I caught sight of the result in the hall mirror as I passed and saw what a total pranny I would look if I ever decided to grow a real beard.

I picked furiously at the woollen bobbles that had velcroed themselves to my face as I clipped my reply: "What?"

"Ah....David Prink - representing the county court baliff?   Mister Sylvester Quiggley?"

"Apparently."

It had been decades since I had heard that name bandied as profusely as it had been that day.   I hated it more than anything in the known universe. Even more than I had hated Stephen - the git who had even been lucky enough to have been born with a cool moniker! It was my ball and chain, it was my anchor to the past - and even though it had been twenty five years since I had become Sly Quip it still came back to haunt me! Neve had changed it for me. Neve - that girl again.....

"I have an order of repossession - "

"Then form an orderly queue." I rapped, snapping off the connection and slipping into a too tight pair of winklepicker boots that I found at the top of the stairs. I stalked back to my room, cajoled through weight of numbers into flaccid submission, and pulled my battered gig bag from its perch on top of the wardrobe. I smiled for the first and last time that day as I opened the heavy duty cardboard, pregnant-briefcase and noted the neatly packed overnight assortment that Josephine, my Basque home help had prepared for emergency trips. I immediately set about retrieving objects that I considered of sentimental value. This whole farce would be sorted out by the morning. I felt sure, but I had heard numerous tales of similar occurencies in which it became impossible to be certain in a house of this size, just what had been taken and not returned after the event.

My old friend Reno had suffered just such a miscarriage of justice when his short lived pop career had taken a popularity nosedive at the turn of the decade. A similarly trumped up charge had been levelled at the French techno pop balladeer and, when the dust had finally settled, his home and hearth had been returned to him. But it was all the little souvenirs that had failed to find their way on to the baliffs inventory, personal effects which would later show up on the memorabilia markets or behind glass doors adorning the walls of celebrity sponsored eateries.

I dragged the case from room to room, removing pictures of myself with a succession of monarchs and world leaders, snatching presentation discs and paperweight award statuettes - cramming them all unceremoniously into the case like a cat burglar swiping pawnable swag. I paused for a moment, hefting my "Brit award" from palm to palm. It had been the loss of just such a meaningless piece of chintz that had driven poor Reno to fly his chopper into the headquarters of Eliptical records in Paris, killing himself, along with the entire staff of the pretentious little indie in one melodramatic blow. I put it back on its shelf and closed the toilet door on my way out. This wasn't another defeat, I told myself, recalling the disasterous chain of events that had led to that row with Joe that had seen me incarcerated on the Heath this year; the last vestige of nobility for the angel expelled from paradise; the final island of sanity above the sea of mediocrity and despair - No!. It was a tactical retreat! I wasn't *leaving* leaving, I was merely sending out for reinforcements.

Greg and Andy would sort it out. They always did. My programme for repatriation would not be forestalled, but merely postponed. I could still salvage some form of dignity from this temporary setback, but from out there, from the other side of the wall where apathy was the enemy of the falterer and indolence the friend of the loser. But I would not be alone in my quest. I still had friends.
I took a deep breath of clean and civilised air before launching myself from the conservatory doors and jogging out across the lawn, scattering browning daffodil heads in my wake. Behind me, I heard the rasping buzz of the intercom as the raiding party prepared for its assault. I fumbled for the keys to the DB7 as I ran, the weight of my case almost unbalancing me. I stopped amid the trampled flower bed and repeated my pocket slapping search, but to no further avail.
"Shit!" I cursed, glancing back toward civilisation, realising that the arrival of the second creditor would not stall Joe's monkeys for much longer.
Plan B. Behind the barn that housed my rather impressive collection of classic British sports cars was the potting shed and behind that I found my prize. Covered in suspicious looking greeny, snotty slime was a wooden ladder. I had never had a use for it before,

but in a sudden fit of inspiration had remembered finding it there after an aborted break-in a couple or three years before. With the change of plan came the need for a snap decision concerning the loot. I knew that I wouldn't get far in the degenerate world outside, weighted down with all the rescued clobber. I agonised for a few seconds before deciding to ditch my personals for the sake of both a lighter load and to make me a less obvious target for the yobs and mobs. Although I didn't realise it at the time, I would later praise both my ingenuity and my gift of foresight.

Amongst the winter debris I found my answer. A rotted stump that I presumed had at one time been an oak like its neighbours, nestled amid a crop of wild mushrooms - its hollowed interior almost, but not quite obscured by a filling of dried twigs and mulched leaves had attracted my attention. Without thought for my recently completed manicure I scooped out the detritus with both hands and unloaded my horde into a sack that I made from an Armani shirt, knotted at cuffs and collar. I squashed the designer bag into the hollow and recovered it with the shit that I had previously removed from it. I strapped my gig bag across my shoulders, straightened my emblem free black baseball cap - (I will not wear anything bearing logo or motif that I have not previously been paid to advertise) and wedged the ladder between the stump and the wall. I climbed nervously toward the razor wire summit, desperate to avoid a DIY castration as I straddled the wire and poised myself for the drop to ground zero. From here on, as I had expected since news of Stephen's untimely demise had first reached my ears, the only way forward was down.

I vaguely recall the smell of petrol as I pushed open the latched street door and stepped into the drably neglected stairwell of Haversham Mansions, allowing myself my first real breath in two miles of terrified scurry. Its beige tiled wiles, concrete steps and peeling iron banisters reminded me of the entrance to a run-down psychiatric hospital that I had once visited, (not as a patient, I might add), but even so, offered me a welcome sanctuary away from the stifling reality of the ghetto through which I had just passed.

I had kept to the main roads - a needlessly circuitous route, but in my panicked opinion - a surer one; avoiding the Heath itself and its somewhat dubious reputation as a haven for abusers and degenerates, passing Jack Straws on NorthEnd Way and following East Heath Road all the way down to the Heath Station.

I was aware by this time that my recent gulped breath was a breath too late and that if I didn't find myself a seat and begin to regulate my oxygen intake as my doctor had shown me, then I was likely to hyperventilate - thus risking brain damage in short shrift. My head was spinning, my fingers tingled and my breathing had become laboured and shallow - (this last symptom, a metaphor for the quality of my work of late). I leant against the plastic coated banister, relieved and secretly impressed as I counted my 'ins' and regulated my 'outs', that I had made it this far from home without incident. It had to be a mile at least from The Vale to South End Road!

I climbed the stairs slowly, controlling my intake and outtake in the measured doses that my vocal coach had schooled me all those years before, in order to neutralise the potential panic attack that so often followed exersion of the kind that I had recently partaken. I reminded myself that, although I had kept my boyish good looks through fair weather and foul, this body was getting no younger.

I left the stairs on the first landing, turned left and found the door to Greg's office ajar, as had been the street door below. My feet squelched on the twill tiles and I noticed again the pungent scent of petrol. I poked my head around the edge of the door that bore both my friend's name and profession in gold italics across the bevelled glass.

"Can I help you?"

The sudden break in the eerie silence startled me, coming, as the girl's voice had, from directly behind me. My previously stalled attack threatened an unscheduled return, bouncing my heart in its boney cage like a pulmonary yoyo on a string.

"Ah...!" I faltered, fighting for composure against my pitiful body's inefficiency to respond to stressful situation, "I'm looking for Greg ... or Andy," I elaborated, " either would do."

The girl chuckled to herself as if at some private joke that I had just reminded her of and disappeared, White Rabbit-like, back into Andy's office across the hall.

"Isn't everyone!" she left behind her as she rummaged noisily out of sight.

"Do I take it that they are out, then?" I followed, a tad sarcastically for my current position . I stepped warily in behind her and slowly began to survey the crime scene.

"It would tend to appear that way, wouldn't it!" She replied, with a wry malevolence, equal in affront to my own comment.

We had never met before. If we had then I felt sure that it would only have been the once. She had worked for Mafekin and Hatch for as long as I had known them and presumably a fair while prior to that. We had spoken over the telephone and I now saw that my mental image of the boys secretary had fallen much further than short of the physical mark. She was a much older; more care worn woman than I had previously envisaged. Her thighs were much heavier: cumbersome, even and she had what appeared to be a permanently etched scowl on a face uncommonly used to betrayal and disappointment. She looked like a traffic warden - maybe even a Jehovas witness traffic warden; well used to the frustrations that life could throw at her. I had thought her austere in our telephonic relationship, but had put that down to professional detachment, preferring to render in my minds eye the picture of a stern, but firm mid twenty.

I could count on the fingers of one hand the number of occasions when I had visited the boys at their office, preferring, as my station dictated, for my staff to visit me. But even though it had been some years since my last visit to Haversham Mansions, I knew that it should not have looked as it now did.

Both offices had been equally trashed. At first glance one could presume their state to be the result of a domestic's work to rule, but on double-take inspection it was obvious that a crime had occurred.

"You've been burgled?" I queried, ever more uncertain of the situation in which I had found myself.

The secretary: a 'ms' Arbuthnot, if I remember correctly, stopped piling her reclaimed files and with a flabbergasted sigh and an indignant pout turned to face me.

"Do you have an appointment?" she fired, wedging her saucer sized spec's back on to the bridge of her finely chiselled Roman proboscis, "I'm sorry, but I've lost track of the time."

"Er... no. Not as such, no. Just dropped in on spec' - but I know they won't mind." I added the last bit hurriedly as I saw the definite hint of a patience strained squint forming at the centre of her hairy brow.

"Mister...?"

"Quip," I affirmed, "Sly Quip." I waited for the name to sink through, expecting at any moment a humbled modification of attitude to seep out and replace her misplaced arrogance.

"Oh right," she said, indifferently, a slight smirk forming where awe should rightly have shone in its stead. I soon realised that this was the best kind of response that I could have expected from such a pitiably plain specimen and so decided not to push my advantage further.

"Well I'm sorry, mister Quip," she continued, "but you've had a wasted journey. Messers Mafekin and Hatch will not be in today."

"When -"

"Nor tomorrow," she interrupted, "nor the day after that." She turned back toward her work, then whipped back round again like a snacking emu. "Can you smell that, mister Quip?" she asked, indicating the air with a pair of wildly flared and bottomless nostrils, "Petrol!" she concluded. Well I had realised retrospectively, but at that time two and two had yet to make four for me. "This wasn't a burglary, mister Quip, it was an attempted arson!" She lifted an aluminium bucket from somewhere outside of my field of vision and inclined it toward me, revealing the scorched evidence of an attempted bonfire within. She must have read the frown of bemused consternation that my facial muscles were forming because she tutted and resumed her summary for the hard of thinking: "Andy and Greg," she spat, "they've done a bunk."

I laughed nervously to disguise my rising panic. This was not good news.

"No, no," I confirmed, "they wouldn't do that. Not to me."

"No, not just to you! Christ!" she cursed, unnecessarily, "What about everybody else? What about me? I'm out of a job! And unless I can find something incriminating on either them or you, then mother and I will probably starve! Now if you'd kindly bugger off and let me get on with it I would be most grateful."

I wanted to move, but my feet had grown roots and planted me in the dog-tooth check of the floor tiles. It had all seemed so simple this morning. Andy and Greg would sort it out. They would offer me a litany of encouraging clichés, take control and drive me home. I was stranded. I had nowhere else to turn. I couldn't face walking back through all those ordinary faces and even if I had, then back to where? This could not be happening to me. Not to me!

"They can't 've got far," I ventured lamely, wracking my pulsing brain for a more logical explanation than the one being offered to me by the embittered employee.

"Mister Quip," she began in exasperation, and I wondered momentarily if she had ever taught infants, "I don't work Fridays, which means I haven't seen them since Thursday. It's Monday today and there isn't an inch in the world that they couldn't have reached in that time. Especially considering what they stole from you!"

She passed me a buff coloured ring file labelled in smudged type with the name that I had been born with. (So she had known who I was all along!) I flipped through its loose leaf pages passing ancient tax returns, invoices, reminders and final demands. I even recognised some of them.

"I've paid these," I insisted indicating a pile of red letters amounting to the totals that had been thrust at me with my morning post. "No you didn't," she mumbled in mock apology. She was really beginning to get on my tits with her Mary Poppins attitude. Maybe she had forgotten just who it was who paid her wages. "All you did was sign the cheques," she went on, miming the scribbling of a signature in the space between us, "You left it to Andy to fill in the details."

"But..." I blustered, scrabbling for barely plausible excuses for the blatantly obvious, but finding none, "... Why me? And why now?"

She forced a look of incredulity, formed entirely for the benefit of my conscience. I refused to be goaded. "It wasn't just you," she chastised, "though they probably took more from you than they did anybody else. You were their last 'celebrity' client," she mocked, "anyone with any money had left them years ago." She smiled in a way that I could only interpret as condescention, but which twisted into a grimace of barefaced disdain. She turned back to her work, dismissing me with a waft of her hand as if she was some kind of royalty in the presence of an underling. "I thought I might spare you the grisleys," she continued, presuming me too stupid to work it out for myself, "but you're obviously too far up your own rectal passage to make sense of it for yourself."

She hefted another pile of plastic coated files from where she had stacked them down onto the desk, spattering droplets of petrol onto my trousers as they displaced the remainder of the fuel.

"Your career is over, isn't it; you're finished; washed up: old hat. Your funds are dwindling. They couldn't afford to lose you -they'd been bleeding you for years. So they took what they could *while* they could. Screwed everyone else in the process, if it's any consolation, but the crux of the matter is - it's your fault I'm out of a job! Now will you kindly leave so's I can work out how best to sue you."

I paused on the threshold of the outside world. Why did it all seem so daunting? I had lived there once upon a time; been a part, even, of such doleful monotony. What was it that I was really so scared of? Recrimination? The law of the jungle: survival of the fittest? Could I really learn to exist down here again? Or was I tainted? Was there no return to innocence once the taste of temptation had been sated? I dithered for a full and frustrating ten minutes before stepping back into the fray, having adjusted my cap and shades a total of fourteen times each while I deliberated over direction. I must have made a pitiful sight to any who may have been watching, but in my heart, my spirit was still yet to be broken.

It would have been of help if I had have had some notion of where I was headed, but I hadn't. I made a mental check list of my friends and crossed each through in turn as I considered their reactions to my pitiful plight. And just who *did* I still know on this level of the game? I felt a shockwave of regret begin to surge beneath my self pity, but I suppressed it before the faces and names of my long forgotten friends were able to shimmer into retributional clarity. I had made this bed from my own greed and vanity. What right did I have to expect alms from the pedestrian classes?

Ashes to ashes. Dust to dust. Everybody came from nothing and everybody eventually went to nothing. There were no exceptions. Well, no. That wasn't of course strictly speaking true. Stephen Twenty hadn't returned to nothing. He was bigger dead than he had ever been alive! To die while at the apex of one's career was to ensure unmittigated immortality. Look at James Dean, Marilyn Monroe, Marc Bolan, Henri Blutoe - to name but a handful.

I pulled my jacket a little tighter around my neck and chest, (in much the same way that I would have done a few years earlier when bustled from hotel to limo) and set off at a brisk pace in the general direction of town, steadying my pace after a few yards, wary not to appear conspicuously aimless. I wondered just how many others had passed this way before me, having lost their own precarious footings on the lofty plateau of success, tumbling back down to rejoin the herd. Where did they go?

Failure is the only crime that the successful will not tolerate. Deviancy, devil worship, addiction, prevarication and murder could all be absorbed : accepted, even, as quirks and eccentricities; encouraged in some quarters as saleable stock. But failure was failure. It showed a lack of ability - a lack of breeding, a fallible foible that if not eradicated at source could even undermine the dubious stability of those around you. If you weren't in - you were out!

As South End Road became Pond Street, my mind began to recap the unlikely events of the day so far, and in so doing unlocked the melody that I had been composing when the shit had first hit the fan. This in its turn linked me by association to the dreams that I had thought forgotten. Two of them, anyway. Probably the latter two. I remember reading an article in a Harley Street waiting room that the subconscious dreams three times over the course of a single nights unbroken slumber and that usually only the last and possibly the middle of these would be recollectable the following morning. I had made it a life's mission to be able to recount all three, having even once attempted hypnotic regression at the hands of an over hyped hippy 'dream doctor', but I was still yet to score that mythical hat-trick. Dreams, I am a devout believer, are the unconscious mind's way of telling the conscious mind what one is really feeling; they are the narrators of the heart: the orators of the soul and as such - my first and best source of lyrical inspiration. You can't hide anything from your subsconcious - all fears, lies and ambitions, though hidden through the use of mental compartmentalisation from one's day to day processes, come back to haunt you whenever you close your eyes. Perhaps it's better not to remember all three?

Snippets of these two dreams began to entwine themselves in flashed snapshots - images without cohesion or continuity. My childhood. My humble origins of Purlow crescent and Leabridge juniors. How long ago? How many years? How many lifetimes? I saw the faces of people whom I had once thought of as friends; people whom I had conveniently forgotten from the moment that favour had plucked me from the crowd and set me on the roller-

33

coaster of fame and fortune. I saw enemies; unrequited foes: those from whom I had escaped and for whom my immeasurable success had stuck in their throats with no less solidity than if they had attempted to swallow a billiard ball. I saw all these and more besides; phantoms from the forgotten past taunting me; goading me: daring me to acknowledge their part in my downfall.

As I attempted to deny their credance; as I fought to reel back the credit for my own personality, I felt a jolt to my right shoulder which unbalanced my undercarriage and sent me sprawling to the cobbled pavement.
" Arsehole!"
I heard delivered above the gabble and hue of the fashionable street cafés full of designer frocks and overpriced hair cuts, all chatting at odds into their constantly chiming pocket telephones.
I picked myself up quickly and dusted myself off melodramatically, casting an indignant eye in the direction of my usurper while warily scanning the vicinity for signs that I might have attracted unwanted attention. I needn't have worried. My misfortune had gone entirely unnoticed. There was a time (and not all that far in the past either) when a fall in the street would have made headlines. A time when any publicity had been good publicity. When an accident such a this would have reminded the record buying public of my worth as an artist, thus boosting my back catalogue sales and bumping up the advances for the next album. Sadly, though, those times had passed.
It had all happened so quickly, (my fall from grace and my fall in the street.) Six hours earlier I had been a 'resting' star. Within a quarter of a day I had become a nobody and a never-was: somebody to be bumped into and knocked to the gutter without a raised eye brow from anyone. Maybe there never had been a chance to retake the throne after all: maybe I really had died with my last album like Reaper had announced, only my body was yet to realise it? Perhaps I had only been fooling myself by staying on in the house on the Heath; denying the inevitable while all around me mocked my peers. I had fallen a lot further than just to the floor, but as yet, I had no idea how much farther I had to fall.
I decided that I had been thinking too much. Endless days alone in the house with only the odd 'paid for' distractions had often seen

me into ruminative trance - a state from which only an infusion of alcohol could ever seem to retrieve me.

Don't misunderstand me - I was not an alcoholic, nor was I ever the paranoid depressive that my rather jaded recollections of this time could well lead you to assume. I was just ... a manic melancholic. I set my sights on a 'one stop' convenience store that, due to its fashionable locale was ostentatiously masquerading itself as a 'New York style' Deli. I reset my shoulders and steered myself toward the counter, a part of me still desperately craving recognition while the sensible majority vote opted for a show of amiable indifference from the 'between jobs' male model at the till.

"Can I help you?" He minced, staring right through my cap and shades disguise, but making no affectation of recognition. In this part of town he had most probably grown used to the sight of vaguely incognito celebrities at his counter, either this or he was too young to remember my not-that-distant heyday.

"Cognac, please," I requested, inclining an eyebrow toward the well stocked shelves of alcoholic stimulants behind him, while I fumbled for my wallet.

"Litre?" he enquired, calmly, but reasonably.

The personal purchase of comestibles was not a custom that I was familiar with at this time. For some years that particular chore had fallen within the remit of Josephine, (my Basque home help, you'll remember) as was the translation of Federal European weights and measurements back into the now illegal British Imperial that my generation had all grown up with.

"A full one," I expanded sarcastically, careful not to reveal my ignorance, while pointing to the top shelf just above the assistant's Brylcreemed quiff, but the model stood his ground, refusing to be usurped by one whom he had obviously misconceived as an ordinary.

"Napolean, Calvados or 'French'," he listed, emphasising the cheapest of the alternatives as the one that he considered the most suitable for his foe.

"Napolean, thank you," I replied, reaching into the last of my pockets which, by the process of elimination should have yielded my wallet. I tried another round of my apparel, this time around with a little less decorum, but alas - to no greater availance.

"I know I had it ...," I began to bluster, while I wracked my brain for possibilities.

"Could you move over?" he responded dismissively, "while I serve this 'gentleman'?"

"But I had it when I left - the accident!" I blurted, suddenly realising what my yuppie audience had understood all along, " the bastard mugged me!"

My frantic pocket slapping search, which to the Deli's other customers must have looked a little like an epileptic Bavarian clog dancer's warm up routine, had netted me a measly total of four pounds and eighty five pence in loose change. Coinage! I never used the stuff! Anything less than a ten-pound note I had always just thrown away! That it should have come to this so soon, I thought, to be reduced to paying in cash; paying in buttons!

I waited for the pinstriped queue jumping banker to collect his change then slapped my own shameful collection of common currency onto the marble effect counter top, barely suppressing my mortification and failing completely to disguise it from the assistant.

"Not enough," he dismissed, moving tartly on to his next customer: a lithe, semi-naked teenager who had for some inexplicable reason chosen to wear the head of a fifties starlet for the occasion. She skated forward flashing her stuffed baguette, a crisp, clean twenty pound note and a mouthful of luminescant pincers.

"Chiou, Jace," she sang as he passed her her change, puffing out his disproportionate chest like a peacock on the prowl.

"Spare a penny for the guy?" he mocked, but I cut across her reply with my razor sharp return:

"Listen, *nobody*. Have you any idea who I am?"

I grabbed my chisel jawed opponent's striped apron and pulled him closer, removing my shades to give him a better view of my much photographed fisgog. "Do you?" I screamed, including the gum chewing roller blader beside me in my rant and noticing for the first time the delicate gold chain that dripped from her pierced naval and disappeared to God knew where inside her satin shorts, but which would feature prominently in my dreams for some months to come.

"Bad news, bud'," was his reply as he tipped a haughty wink toward the camera that had also recorded my famous face, "You're on candid camera!" he said, although he was far too young to understand why.

"Oh look," interrupted the girl as she passed 'Jace' her change, "Give him the bottle. It's not worth it! What if he hurts your face!"

Jace extracted himself from my grip, reached up and retrieved a 'litre' bottle of 'French' brandy which he slammed onto the counter scattering change this way and that.

"Run away quickly, little man. That camera's connected to the police station down the hill."

I picked up my bottle, thrust it inside my jacket and ambled out into the street, refusing to be hurried, but panicking all the same. I didn't thank my benefactor as I passed her, but I did snatch a second glance at her unique adornment, my mind entranced by the possibilities that it threw up.

On reaching the summit of the Vale of Health I dropped the case that I had brought with me in my escape; the case which bore inside it the sum of my worldly possessions, and sunk down into the long, damp grass beside it, totally and utterly deflated. My powers of reason had taken their leave of me at some point during my trek from the high street, leaving my motor functions at the mercy of my paranoias. (The act that I am about to describe to you may seem a trifle rash and possibly premature, but I can assure you that these next few moments form the pivot of a life altering event, one that I have at many times since that fateful day wished had not been curtailed by the timely intervention of Albert Edwardes. Furthermore, I will leave it to you, the reader, to decide whether I would have been better off all round had I never have met 'Prince Albie' at all.)

I stared out across the Heath and decided that I was far enough from the unforgiving sprawl of civilised urbania; remote enough, while still within the confines of the metropolis and, most importantly, the remit of The Evening Standard, and yet public enough for my final performance to achieve maximum effect. I had come here to this rural oasis; this arable magnet to London's cultured and perverted alike - to die.

It was typical of me. Every great decision of my life had been taken too late. Even this, my tortured suicide: an act that should rightly have ensured my position in rock history, would doubtlessly now be remembered as merely a poor imitation of Stephen's own glorious end. And if I had attempted to resurrect the band six months earlier than I had, instead of making that pompous attempt to get one over on Stephen first, then we would have at least have had his guitar track in the bag before the stupid sod had killed himself and my own career could well have been saved! And better still: if I had have got around to leaving that bloody yoke of a band one single earlier than I did, then I could have pre-empted Stephen's own solo launch and prospered despite him! What of all the ifs and maybes? If I had made my intentions toward Neve a little clearer before introducing her to Stephen...

Always too slow and always in Stephen's shadow.

I unscrewed the cap on my purloined bottle of cheap booze and tilted back my head, guzzling a generous dose of tasteless spirit which burned at the back of my throat. When this failed to make me vomit I took a second swig, convinced now that I was actually verging on alcoholism, despite my earlier potestations to the contrary.

I let my mind meander back to the day that I had first met Stephen. It had been September the fourth 1970. It had been a Wednesday - our second day at Rhampton boys grammar. Morris had introduced us. Morris and I had been 'mates' since infants, although I'd be hard pushed to identify a time when we had actually liked each other all that much. We had always lived within a few doors of each other and neither had ever found any real reason to dislike each other, until now. Now, with the benefit of hindsight, I could see one glaring reason to hate the bastard!

Morris and I had been separated by classes, he to find himself in the company of an unremarkable looking eleven year old whose renowned popularity had followed him from the juniors, and me to find myself alone in the crowd: a predicament new to me at that time, but one which would soon become a blighting precedent for the rest of my days.

Stephen bloody Twenty. I hadn't liked him very much to begin with. It had been an instant revulsion: an understandable reaction when taking into account my own lack of popularity at the time. It hadn't been his looks, although if I'm honest then I suppose I had been a little jealous of the density of the bumfluff already becoming evident even at that tender age. It hadn't necessarily been the fact that Stephen had hailed from 'the estate' and therefore quite obviously lacked both the brains and the moral integrity that Morris and I had been brought up on. No. His problem was something that I had recognised immediately and it was the one thing that the rest of the school had all noticed that I was sorely lacking in: confidence. Stephen Twenty had exuded it in bulk. And what other gangly pre pubescent would not have craved the same?

At Leabridge juniors I had been popular. After all , I had been the only five to ten with any first hand knowledge of the opposite sex which, for all the initial ridicule that this had earned me, had still reaped me a grudging respect from the sportsmen and the tough kids alike. But, as I had discovered on September the third - all past deeds were swept clean on entering the grammar. One had to earn one's standing from scratch. One had to learn to live in the immediate 'now' and not to revel in the exaggerated past.

It had been to this end alone that I had allowed myself to enter the Stephen Twenty set; albeit as a preferably proliferal member. I had tolerated Stephen, not wishing to appear fawning as so many other of his disciples had, but neither prepared to stand against his ego at this stage. In turn Stephen had welcomed me into his clique, quite openly allowing me a greater degree of individuality than he generally did his lemmings. Morris, on the other hand, had never developed the slightest comprehension of the subtleties and intracacies of the mutual power-play that was played out under his snotty nose for the better part of the next thirty years.

I brought the bottle back to my lips, an image of Stephen's mud spattered coffin crossing my mind; slipped, missed my target and chipped my front tooth, spilling piss weak brandy all over my jacket and sweater. I am a connoisseur of the swear word and I remember reeling off an entire thesaurus of curses aimed not solely at the offending article, but at my life and luck with equal vehemance. Ought I to blame it all on bad luck, bad timing or other people? Or should I look more deeply for the culprit that had led me here to die?

I was forty two years old, yet I felt no different then to the way I had done as a lovestruck teenager. The only difference was that with Stephen gone I now had nobody to blame for my inadequacies, my failings and my luck.

I am forty three as I write this epitaph. So much has changed in the year since I stood on the vale of Health clutching a bottle of cheap

spirit and a lighted match. I can see so much more clearly now; I
understand far more about myself than was possible back then.
There had been a wedge between us all these years, an insur-
mountable (or so I had presumed) dispute that had kept our relationship at the level of tolerance and misunderstanding, damning
us from ever developing respect and affection, though we were for
so long inextricably linked to one another through petty rivalries.
Such a shame that I couldn't know then what I know today.

As I wallowed in my hedonistic commiserations my thoughts
returned to the unknown fates of my contempories. What had
befallen them since their pop careers had run their courses? Where
had they gone to when their faces had stopped opening doors for
them? Was it possible to grace the cover of 'Smash Hits' one week
and then apply for a restart package from your local job centre the
next? They had to go somewhere.
Surely not every faded pop star chose to do the decent thing once
his haircut had fallen from favour? Perhaps there was a peculiar little village built into the coastal cliffs of North Wales full of odd little houses that looked like they belonged at the bottom of a fish
tank, where the tired pop stars of yesteryear wiled away their days
playing outdoor chess and competing amongst themselves for the
chance to call themselves 'number one'. And were they perhaps
kept there against their will by giant inflatable weather balloons; far
away from a world too embarrassed to acknowledge the fashions
and the hairstyles of the past? Maybe they occasionally escaped to
taunt their successors with revival tours of seaside towns only to be
rounded up and sent back as soon as sales figures for their 'greatest hits' anthology albums began to dwindle.
Surreal. And highly improbable. But they had to go somewhere!
What about Morrissey of eighties super group 'The Smiths'? The
man who had made national health glasses and deaf aids into
essential fashion accessories. But where was the Gladioli wielding
Manchurian now? Had he taken to market gardening? Had he
taken up psychiatry, specialising perhaps in the treatment of manic
depression? Where was he now? And Johnny Rotten: foul-
mouthed seventies anti-icon; self confessed anarchist and anti-
Christ? Perhaps social work had taken his fancy? Or the clergy,
even? Maybe he's doing voluntary work at his local hospice as I

write. And Kate Bush? How the hell could a girl in a chain-mail bikini just blend into the crowd? Perhaps she had just kept running up that hill until she had disappeared over the other side?

"Where are they now?" I screamed, panicking a small group of pigeons that had been amassing around my feet in the hope that I might have brought a picnic with me.

Of course, it's a lot easier for sportsmen. It is anticipated from the off that their careers will be finite. People actually feel sorry for them when they are no longer capable of past glories. They are helped into secondary employment, (usually to which they have no particular predilection), perhaps commentating on the measure of their heirs; advertising cosmetics or becoming panel game experts on sports that they have never even played. Some even worm their way into acting or even singing, for christs-sake, stealing jobs from the professionals by virtue of their commodity rather than their talents.

Retiring politicians are also spared the indignities thrust on the flailing muso, finding their oleic way onto the boards of the multi-nationals as overpaid, undertaxed and dormant 'advisors'. Some take pen to paper to become novelists, borrowing the sportsman's trick and succeeding by reputation rather than innovation, (though at least we have so far been spared the footballers' novel - all five cliched pages of it.)

Actors, of course, don't wane, they merely take 'character' parts as they get older. This, I am convinced, is the safest of all the public professions. But what of your common or garden pop star? It is undoubtedly the toughest of careers to forge. There are no schools for the budding 'Legend'; no specialist qualifications to study for, nor training sessions to guide one's path. It is just luck: pure and simple luck. Talent and determination also play their parts, but for every Elton John that makes the grade there are a million even more talented artists who just don't get the break. Maybe that's why they despise us so much; why we are always considered upstarts by our famous associates. Of course, there are those who are able to successfully cross pollinate.

Morris bloody Yussof for one; he having actually taken seriously the many spec'scripts that we had all been sent by producers hoping to flatter our names and faces onto celluloid and then call it a casting coup. Morris had been lucky. He owed his rising success to a director whose own career had begun with the directing of pop videos. She had a fashionable reputation and was well used to coaxing passable performances from talentless amateurs. He also owed a great deal to the writer of that 'made-for-television' film for writing a story based around the trials of a less than a competent bassest trying to break into acting.

Rusty had also found his niche during the 'Moonies' infamously disastrous hiatus period, taking the most obvious ex-pop star route - that of the producer/manager of the next generation of pop starlets. Once again, a career forged on a career rather than the utilisation of a particular gift.

And Lakhi had been lucky: a chance meeting with a Hollywood score composer while being interviewed for an American chat show having led him to success in a most unlikely field. That same composer must have since chastised himself nightly after Lakhi's debut attempt had pipped him to an oscar.

But these were the exceptions - it was just frustrating that they also happened to be my former band! Most of my peers had simply vanished into the ether - their names rarely to be mentioned again. And now I was to join their ranks - another loser set to enter the valley of lost souls. I dropped the screw cap onto the grass, held the bottle above my head and poured its remnants over my pathetic face and shoulders. I could hear them now, their ghosts calling to me across the Heath. Morrissey? Was that Morrissey, mournfully advocating the return of capital punishment for disc - jockeys? Or no - I could see him now! It was John Rotten, spitting filth and fury into the wind as he ran toward me.

I flipped open my Zippo and sparked it into action. The phantom still came. Closer now: close enough to distinguish features. Who was it though? Some jaded pop-star so obscure that even I had forgotten him? 'Hang the DJ' became 'Hang on in there' and then, just as I had brought the flame to my chin, the apparition hit me - head on - sending me sprawling back onto the grass. I felt the lighter snatched from my grasp and extinguished and saw the face of my latest attacker looming in above me.

"Bastard!" I rapped, angry that my impulse had been spoiled, knowing already the chances of my plucking the courage for a second attempt, "What the *fuck* did you do that for?" My anger chilled to frustration as I was inwardly relieved to have been spared a painful death, but still no nearer to forming any less lethal a solution to my plight. "If it's money you want," I blustered, "then you're too late! I've been mugged so many times today I've lost count!"

"Steady on, old chap! I don't want your loot - chap just can't stand about and watch a chap make a rather painful mistake."

"Oh you couldn't, eh? And what gives you the right to decide whose making the mistakes? What if it wasn't a mistake, huh? Maybe I wanted to die!"

"Well if you did, then you should have used petrol. Brandy will only flambé you! You'd have put yourself out long before you'd have killed yourself, and then you would have had to live with the burns!"

I realised that I had begun to cry. I pushed myself up into a sitting position, extricating my calves from this unwelcome Samaritan.

"Albert Edwardes," he said thrusting forward a rigid palm, "friends call me Albie."

"Well I'm not your friend!" I spat, although I did feel a pang of conscience spiting my fury as I stared him in the eye. (I would regret this later.)

The man who had introduced himself as Albie sat himself down opposite me and produced what appeared to be a solid silver cigarette case from within his immaculate tweed jacket, flipped it open and offered me from the row of semi-smoked dogends -some even stained with varied shades of lipstick.

"No thank you," I declined, smiling despite my predicament. Suffering still from a misplaced guilt I offered him my hand, though I bit back the urge to apologise to the tramp, "Sly Quip," I said, frowning embarrassingly in anticipation of the 'Wow! What *the* Sly Quip? That I had expected to follow. My condescention was, however, greeted with a simple: "Pleasure, Mister Quip, I'm sure!"

Albert lit himself the longest of his collection of castoffs, holding the soggy stump between the manicured fingers of his left hand as if he was doing the cigarette a favour by smoking it. I looked him up and down, re-evaluating this odd little fellow in his hand-stitched shoes and made to measure suit. His hair was thinning from the crown, which was unfortunate for his ears as they tended on the large side, but everything else about him spoke of dignity and breeding; nobility even. Everything except his collection of fag butts and the state of those handstitched shoes which had obviously not met with a polish buff in some time. A 'tramp' he certainly wasn't. I filed him under 'E' for eccentric as he exhaled a plume of blue smoke and asked me:

"So. Bad day, Mister Quip?"

"Bad day?" I repeated, emphasising Albert's understatement whilst inspecting the spent spirit bottle for dregs.

"So far today," I elaborated, noticing for the first time the dried blood around the lip of my bottle and touching a fingertip to the smarting area beneath my front teeth, "I've received two sets of bailiffs, each scrabbling for a piece of my estate; a tax demand amounting to more than half a million quid; discovered that two of my most trusted aides have been stitching me up for the last twenty years; been mugged and accused of shop-lifting - then saved from a well needed suicide by a well meaning, but blithering idiot. Yes. I'd say that today rates as a real shitter! "

I stared across at my unwanted saviour and he stared back at me like a christian massing an over used sermon to deliver in blind offence against atheist logic.

"How about you Albert? Can you match it?"

No. Maybe I was wrong. It was not brain dead conviction that I was reading on his face, it was submission. His eyes told me that his arroggance may have been a little hasty even before he had opened his mouth. He produced a silver hip flask from his breast pocket, presumably having been taken from the same gift set as had his cigarette case. It had a rather worn engraving of a fleur de ley on its flank and bore the inscription 'Ich Dien' , which reminded me of the tail side of a two pence piece.

He poured a generous measure of a urine coloured liquid into the cap - come - cup and offered it to me.

"Don't worry Mr Quip, I can assure you that it is of the highest quality."

I declined the offer, ironically, under the circumstances; considering my suicidal tendancies at the moment. Albert knocked back his shot with the aplomb of a professional drinker, refilled the cup and set it down on the ground between us.

I was beginning to warm to him, believing that whatever his burdening tale of woe, it would at least prove similar to my own. I felt some strange comfort in that I was not alone in this madness.

"Well," He began earnestly, yet resignedly, and I could see that whatever his plight - his dignity was still intact, "where to start, old chap?"

All thoughts of my own demise soon left the forefront of my mind as I urged him to pour out his heart. I took a tentative swig of the proffered drink as a show of encouragement.

"First of all, I relinquished my claim to the throne so that I could be with my homosexual lover. My mother then paid an enormous sum of money to a somewhat unscrupulous politician who claimed to be in possession of some kind of device that was said to be capable of breaching the dimensions to an alternative reality and allowing Sherman and I to begin a new life together in this parallel world. Unfortunately, my faked assassination sparked a world war that I fear may have destroyed my home world completely. Having settled here in your world, Sherman promptly stole all of our money and emigrated to the colonies leaving me destitute and alone -"

"You are taking the piss, right?"

"No, mister Quip, I most certainly am not! I am the prince of Wales-albeit from an alternative perspective."

"Fuck off!" I screamed through a thickening haze of inebriation, "Go on! Get away from me!"

"Am I to understand that you don't believe me?"

I stood up, putting my hands out horizontally to steady myself. Whatever had been in that last shot of Albert's it had certainly out-proofed my own supply. I looked down on the pitiable twat that had saved my worthless life and felt myself swaying in rhythm with the grass stalks. I spread my legs a little wider to compensate. Albert's body language shouted veracity and his hoity airs conveyed an ornery credibility that bred doubt to my intoxicated reasoning powers. The poor fellow's mind had obviously fled to greener pastures. Was this what I had to look forward to? How long would I spend in this wilderness of ordinaryness before my brittle sanity went the way of 'Prince Albies?'

Gravity reclaimed the fallen hero and returned me to my seat with a bump. I had offended him. I could see it all over his face.

"I'm sorry ," I conceded and flushed as I heard myself utter that most taboo of dictums. It was the drink, I told myself; I could deny it in the morning.

"I don't mean to offend, I'm a little stressed at the moment."

Albert's face lightened with the apology and after witnessing this effect at first hand I wondered why I had never thought to employ such a device before. I would definitely be using it again.

"Perfectly understandable, old chap. Been there - seen it!"

With this he began to loosen his tie, then followed this with the unpicking of his shirt's top three buttons. Revealed was a livid mark that appeared consistant with my expectations of a rope burn.

"It's what finally convinced mother."

"Elizabeth?" I cajoled, expecting him to deliver a reply consistent with my knowledge of the royal family.

"Good god, no! She's my grandmother. Queen Anne is my mother."

"But - "

"Different dimension old fruit."

"Right," I agreed, for a moment attempting to assimilate this new information into his previous story.

"They wanted me to marry to cement a pact."

"But you're gay, " I reminded us.

"Homosexual," He corrected. No better therapy could be bought than to listen to the insane ramblings of a certified fruitcake. Whenever things get on top of one it is always comforting to know that somebody else is always having it worse. Still. He seemed harmless enough. My therapist had actually advised me that there would be times when a mute ear could become my greatest friend. (I had previously presumed this simply to be her way of ensuring repeat business). But like an alcoholic, the insane were rarely cured, simply controlled. Doctors were far too shrewd to admit to anything more or less.

Right now, more than at any time in my life, what I really needed was that impartial ear; someone whose testement would never be endorsed - not even by a gossip columnist.

"So what do you intend to do?" I ventured, encouraging the man's delusions in the hope of gaining positive inspiration for my own predicament. "Have you thought about going back?"

"No can do, old bean. It's all been destroyed! Besides- " he whispered, and leant in closer, cupping his hand around his mouth conspiratorily, " I'm risking my life just telling you this. They watch us, you know."

"Us?" I asked, ignoring the more obvious question in order not to fuel his paranoias further.

"The 'relocated'," he replied; his eyes furtively scanning the open mound on which we were perched. "There are hundreds of us here and the same on my side. People from your world have relocated to mine. Popstars, politicians, anyone with enough money! But we'll all be killed if we give them away."

"And how does it work then?" My addled mind enquired; for one ludicrous moment seeing a glimmer of hope in the madman's tale. "How come nobody notices when these people go missing?"

"Ah!" Albert enthused, shuffling uncomfortably close in his enthusiasm, "That's the clever bit! You have to die first. Or at least appear to. Suicides mainly, or assassinations like mine. Then they nip over to the other side, nab your doppelganger if you've got one - and you swap places!"

Completely barking, I concluded: the perfect foil.

"Well I wouldn't worry too much, " I condoled condascendingly, "Your secret's safe with me."

"And what about you, mister Quip? What are you going to do? Don't you have any friends or family that you can stay with? There must be someone who can help you."

The only thing that gave any credance to his ridiculous story was the fact that he seemed not to have recognised me either by name or by face.

"I take it you are familiar with my work?" I asked, more to establish the depth of background that I would need to flavour my tale with than to ascertain the breadth of my fame.

"Should I be?" he replied, with uninhibited honesty, lighting himself another second hand dogend and replenishing our dwindling supply of alcohol.

"Some Young Moon," I explained incredulously, " the band not the cult leader?"

Albert frowned, showing no sign of comprehension.

"The biggest selling band of the nineteen eighties?"

"Not where I come from. " He countered.

"Eight platinum albums; six number ones-"

"So what went wrong?"

I could have cited any one of a number of good reasons for our decline - most of which would not have involved any kind of blame or fault being angled toward myself. For some peculiar reason that I still can't fathom I simply told the truth.

"I got greedy," I said and surprised myself so much by my sheer frankness that I sobered a few degrees in an instant.

"We were at the top of the tree," I explained, "We couldn't get any bigger! Everything we touched seemed to turn to gold. But once you've climbed that high,   where else is there to go?"

I remembered the first time that I had realised that particular truth. It had been right before an interview on 'Wogan'. I had been about to follow the weedy one from teeny bop flash-in-the-pan'ers 'Bros'. He'd been kicked out of his band for being irrelevant and, at the height of his fame, had given his final interview to the King of the cue card himself - Terry Wogan. And that had been it. He had left the set; left the studio, and one of the biggest names of the moment had simply vanished from history.

It could have been me! So fickle is this crazy world we call show business that any one of us could have had the rug pulled out from under us at any time. I began my first course of therapy the very next week.

"But I still wanted more!" I continued, with Albert now entranced by my monologue; I could tell, "I wanted to be the biggest," I told him, "and I didn't want to share my podium with anyone else. I was the front piece, I was the songwriter! I didn't need the others to prop me up!"

"Or so you thought?" he contributed.

I nodded gravely, acknowledging my own folly.

"People had advised me that if I was going to attempt a solo career then my best bet was to launch it while the band were still at their height. That way I had a safety net if it were all to go arse up. I approached Joe - ."

"Joe?"

"Joe Munday? Impressario extraordinaire? No, 'course you would-n't." For some reason I gained a swell of confidence in my discovery that as *I* wasn't famous in Albert's world - neither was Joe. I have no idea why that was important - I can presume only that it was the booze thinking for me. "Joe Munday was our manager," I explained. He was also our agent, our publisher and the sole shareholder of our record company. The Moonies were in every sense of the term - Joe's band. He had put us together back when we were all still at school. He had encouraged us; he had funded our rehearsals - he had got us as far as anybody could reasonably be expected to have got. "Joe wasn't keen at first," I said, taking a lubricative sip from our newly topped cup," not until he'd heard what I had written. We struck a deal. During the bands bi annual break, on condition that I still produced the material for the next Moonies album on time, we would release a solo single."

"Which failed?"

"No Albert," I chastised, suddenly feeling the true effect of my over indulgence as I felt my vowels beginning to merge into an incoherent slur, " it did not fail! I was a huge success! It outsold the Moonies' previous three singles put together! It was a classic piece of pop music history! Joe offered me an advance on the album - to be produced after the next Moonies album, but I was too impatient. I wanted to start right away."

"Advance?" he queried.

"Oh, it's an upfront payment in lieu of royalties that take years to trickle in. Anyway," I went on, "Joe eventually conceded and the band took an impromptu hiatus. It was the beginning of the end. I made the album and awaited its release along with the long overdue second single. But Joe held back. He had some great masterplan promotion up his sleeve. Unfortunately this plan turned out to be a running mate for me in the shape of Moonies' guitarist Stephen Twenty."

"Now that name I have heard of!"

Why was I not surprised?

"I'm sorry," he offered, having read my scowl at having had my flow interrupted again.

"It's not important," I lied, "not anymore. You see, we were compared. The one man in the world that I so needed to prove my dominion over and we were back head to head - the same poisition we had been in since day two of senior school!"

I saw Albert almost butt in with ' and he beat you, did he?' but then he thought better of it.

"Of course he won!" I admitted, "Stephen always won! He scored his first solo hit while I languished in the mid teens. Our albums were released on the same day. Mine sunk without a trace."

"But surely that's bad planning on mister Munday's part?"

"Not really, no. You see he would've been able to offset his taxable profits from Stephen's album against his projected loss on my non runner."

"So what did you do?"

" I went back to Joe and insisted that my next album was released ahead of Stephen's and you know what he said?"

No reply was offered.

"He said: 'What next album!' I begged him! I couldn't just sit it out and wait to see if Stephen would come back to the band. Besides. I had signed a two album deal!

"he did eventually agree, but only provided that I put up half the costs myself. And there was to be no advance this time round. Not 'til the previous one had been recouped."

I paused to wet my whistle on the final dregs of Albert's drink.

"And?"

"And he hated it! I remixed it. I took two tracks out and replaced them with two completely new tracks. He still hated it and he still refused to release it."

"And is that legal?" he asked, quite getting into my tale, "I thought you said that you had a deal?"

"It is and yes we did. He may have been technically obliged to record it, but he didn't have to realease it."

"But if you had paid to record it - couldn't you just have taken it to a different company?"

"That's not how it works," I told him, "he owns the rights - I'm not allowed to record for anybody else."

"That's most dreadfully unfair," he rallied.

"That's showbiz!" I replied. As therapy goes, this was doing me good, though my head was starting to resist my drunken attempts to strip it of its buried memories. I had mulled this era of my recent past until it had turned into wine - or was that until it had turned me to wine? This was the first time that I had gone through this stuff since my therapist had returned my rubber cheque.

"I waited. I waited until he was ready. And until, coincidentally, Stephen was ready with his next masterpiece!"

"The blighters!"

"Oh they assured me it wasn't personal. It was a purely business decision. And Joe did offer to lend me some cash until my residu-

als could catch up. As a show of faith he even took over my ..."
something had just dawned on me and I swallowed the urge to
vomit mid-sentence, " ... mortgage payments." Deciding not to
dwell on this new dimension to the overall conspiracy argument I
continued to orate:
"Joe even invoked some small print clause to get the band back into
the studio to help me reclaim my inheritance. But it all took too
long to come off."
(Morris - had finally found something other than hide and seek that
he was good at, Rusty had produced both of Stephen's albums and
was well into his third and Lakhi had moved to L.A. I didn't bother to bore Albert with the finer details - a gist was all he really needed.)
"They didn't need this album," I opined, "though it sure as hell
wouldn't have been a bad PR stunt for any of them! I was the only
one who needed it. Me!" I emphasised this point by jabbing at my
breast bone with my thumb, "I had set out to prove that I didn't
need them and look where it got me!"
I wavered on my feet, finally deciding to sit back down now the dramatic heart of the tale had been told.
"By the time we'd got a start date out of everyone Stephen had disappeared. We began without him. The rhythm tracks go down first
anyway, so there was no immediate hurry and Lakhi pissed us about
with his piano lines for weeks before he would finally agree on a
take. I was delivering my vocal when the news came in that
Stephen had topped himself. The selfish bastard whose luck,
charm and wits had been choking me since we were eleven years
old had slammed the coffin lid on my chances of revival whilst
ensuring his own immortality into the bargain!"
Albert lit his last two stubs and passed the longer of the two to me.
"Surely," he tiptoed warily, "with Stephen out of the frame, you're
free to prove yourself now? Isn't that what you wanted?"
I almost threw a retaliatory quip; a blustering denial of what I knew
in my heart to be the truth. I had wished Stephen dead, but not
like this. And not now! An overdose would have been better - an
irresponsible accident. Not suicide. And not at such an inoppor-
tune moment.
"How can I compete with a fucking dead man! " I spat, saliva and
vomit-trail spattering his baby soft cheeks. "I'm in his shadow - I

always will be! I'll always be compared to a man who can no longer put a foot wrong. The rest of us are just "Gary Glitters" waiting to happen, but not Stephen, oh no! He's immune from the tragedies of life now!

"And anyway Albie, I'm broke! They've all seen to that! Go quitely! That's what they expect of me - try not to be an embarrassment! Limahl didn't kick up a fuss when he ran out of hits, neither did Howard Jones!"

I felt sick, I had puked up my life story to a delusional down-and-out and now I was going to bring back the catalyst that had caused me to do so. I only wish I had choked on the chunder that followed this revelation. I wish I had never met Albert Edwardes.

Chapter Two
"Who's that girl again ?"

"Good news, Sylvie !"

"Good news? How the hell can you have good news? We've got the finals tomorrow night and Neve's broke her fuckin' finger ! Unless you've perfected cloning technology in the last two hours, Joe ..."

"As good as!"

"What are you talking about ?"

"I've found you a replacement !"

"Replacement ? Who the hell's gonna dep' for us at twenty-four hours notice ? How're they gonna learn the whole set by tomorrow ?"

"A friend of Morris's and ... a friend of Neves ..."

I look up from my pint of slops ; staring past the prematurely depilated dome of my manager (and at this stage my sociology lecturer) ; look past the acne packed and fluff free chin of Morris and right into the eyes of my second worst nightmare: Stephen bloody Twenty!

I haven't seen him for close on eighteen months - not since we all left school. I have heard enough about him though, from Neve. He has started an apprenticeship in motor mechanics while the rest of us decided to waste a few years at the poly. He has to fight off the job offers that most of us will never even receive. And, if all that she has told us can be believed, he could even go on to University if he wanted to. Bully for him!

"I didn't know you played," I say. It's the least offensive retort that my conscience will allow me to deliver.

"Neve taught me," he replies, "in return for a few lessons from me."

One day I'll kill him. I know this is my destiny. But right now, humiliating as this is, I also know that not to hear him out will be to throw away a whole year's worth of work - an unthinkable prospect and too high a price to expect the others to pay simply because I can't stand the thought of sharing anything else with the bastard! This is my band. This is my ticket out of the world of Stephen Twentys and this is also the only area of Neve's life that I still have access to.

"And you reckon you can learn the set by tomorrow?"

"Piece of piss! Practically know it already!" he replies, tipping a wink to Morris who blushes back as if caught by his mother in possession of a dirty mag. I sense complicity. I sense conspiracy. My gut reaction is to stand up and leave the bar - my dignity still intact; not to look back and not to come back with a Munday massaged ego in an hour's time. I look to Joe. I look to Morris. I look to that sly wanker Twenty. Mine is the casting vote. Shit! I know I'm going to regret this. We could still win the competition, but not now on the strength of my song writing abilities or my vocal talents. Not because of anything that I might be responsible for. No. If we win it now it will be because Stephen has saved the day !

"You'll play it exactly as I wrote it," I spit, defeat kept firmly in check and not allowed to taint my ability to command, "no deviation, no interpretation. Understood?"

"Fine. You're the boss, Sylvie."

"It's Sly!"

"Not to me it isn't! I gave you that bloody name ! You'll always be Sylvie to me ..."

Although I saw his lips mouth those words, the voice that I heard speaking them had a much gentler, more feminine cadence to it. I watched as his shoulder length raven hair became a sharp, jaw hugging blonde bob. His 'Never mind the bollocks' strategically slashed T-shirt slowly washed from banana yellow to white, developing bumps that forced the stencil of a rose patterned lace bra to show through the flimsy cotton mix fabric. His testes choking PVC jeans became an above the knee pencil skirt that left a little more to the viewers imagination. Overall Stephen Twenty suddenly looked a much greater prospect for the 'Moonies' revamped line up than I had previously thought possible.

"Sylvie," he/she asked, "You in there ?"

I opened my eyes a little wider as the angel lent in across me, staring into my strobing pupils like an optician searching for a lost contact lens.

"Where am I?" I asked, my head still convinced that I was on a fishing boat in a force twelve gale.

"You're in the one place that, even with all that money, you never managed to get ?"

"Heaven?"

"You're in my bed, Sylvie Quiggley, but you were too pissed to notice !"

"Neve ? Neve Crilly?"

"You stink, Sylvie. I'm going to give you five minutes to finish your dream then I want you out of there and into the shower so I can fumigate the duvet."

"What's going on, how -"

"You're a lucky boy, Sylvie. You've just been handed a second chance at life."

"Feeling any better yet ?"

Her voice hauled me back from my morbid reverie, back from a time when the future had seemed clearer and where the present had felt safer, though I doubt that that had been the way that I had seen things at the time.

"It's clearing a bit," I lied, still embarrassed by the advantage of her soberity. She re-entered the small lounge from the en suite kitchen bearing two steaming soup mugs full of hot sweet tea.

I had showered before crawling back into yesterday's trousers, (which I had attempted to sponge clean while I had been in the bathroom); borrowed a faded, baggy T-shirt from her airer and staggered into the lounge, collapsing aimlessly into her armchair where I lay foetally wound and belching. I accepted my first post alcoholic-binge refreshment with a whimper of all the pathetic vulnerability of a boiling lobster.

"How much do you remember?" She teased, flopping down on the mismatched sofa opposite and bringing her stockinged calves up beneath her thighs. I hadn't even the energy and co ordination to catch a brief flash of her knickers.

In truth I was remembering all too much, though probably not the kind of things to which I imagined that she alluded.

"Not enough," I answered semi-truthfully. I could remember the start of what I now knew to be the previous day: the bit where the sky had fallen in on me. I remembered my visit to Andy and Greg's and the feeling of betrayal that I hadn't felt since … and I remembered the distant past. I could recall with sarcastic clarity the events that had been plaguing me from the time before time; that existence that I had once considered purged from my conscience and my memory alike, but which had recently returned like a prodigal bastard to haunt and taunt me.

"I still don't remember how I got here," I said, sipping cautiously at my piping beverage, "I don't even know where here is."

55

She bent forward and plucked a twisted piece of card that had been gracing the ash try on the overloaded coffee table between us. She passed it to me, her low cut T-shirt revealing a tighter cleavage than I would have expected for a woman of her age.

"Your friend Albert found it in your jacket pocket," she explained. I recognised it instantly as the card that she had given me at Stephen's funeral two months previously - presumably the last time that I had worn that particular jacket.

"Albert?" I frowned, "I don't know an Albert."

"Well he seemed to know you. He called me from the Heath and asked if I wouldn't mind coming to collect you. He said you'd been trying to kill yourself?"

Oh, I remembered that, now that she had mentioned it. And himself. I turned the card around in my fingers and wondered idly how the royal fruit loop had known that Neve and I were acquainted. I hoped to a neglected god that I hadn't told him too much.

"Sylvie," she soothed, placing a presumptuous palm against my leather-clad knee, "why didn't you call me yourself? I could have helped you."

I wished that I could remember those final hours before waking in her bed as I altered my position and let her fingers slide away without showing my discomfort.

"Why?" I asked, dumbfounded that she would expect such a thing from me of all people. I searched her still beautiful face for signs of … what ? Sarcasm ? Revenge ? I don't know. But all I saw was that same Neve that the innocence of youth had seen all those years ago: "Why would you want to help me ?"

She flinched as I spoke, insulted by my assumption.

"I mean," I blustered, still too needy of her help to risk offending her and keen to get off on the right foot for once in my life, "Why would you want to help me after the way I treated you ?" (But I had dug myself in deeper.)

She stared at me as if the very notion of a grudge was anathema to her.

"But what did you do to me Sylvie ?" She soothed as she spoke, gently stroking my knee and in so doing sending my nerve endings into spasm. "That was over twenty years ago. Besides - it wasn't what *you* did, it was what Stephen did."

"It was Stephen's idea," I corrected her guiltily, "but mine was the casting vote. If it hadn't been for me, then you wouldn't be living here now."

"Oh, really?"

"You'd have been on millionaires row with the rest of us. Cars, boats, helicopters, holiday homes from Tanzanier to Tahiti. You'd have had a great life if it hadn't been for me!"

I really hadn't meant for that to come out the way that it had. Looking back now with the benefit of all that I have learned from my time on the ground floor, I can see how she may have been offended by my well intended, but tactless assault on her lifestyle.

She removed her hand from my thigh and sat back in her seat, collecting her cooling tea en route; her body language underlining my faux pas with obvious clarity.

"What?" I blundered further, misreading the situation and presuming that it had been my belated revelation that had garnered her sudden retreat, "You didn't know?"

"Of course I knew," she replied guardedly, sipping her tea as if the mug's presence at her lips would protect her from my too late confession, "in fact, I've always admired you for it. You wanted fame so badly that you chose to ally yourself with the person you detested the most over the one person who really loved you ! It can't have been an easy decision. You must have known that it would have to be broached sooner or later, but you chose the harder option."

"Neve," I said, dunking a custard cream as I wondered how best to explain her misconception, "It had nothing to do with your talent. Stephen wanted you out of the band because he'd found somebody else to share his lurid fantasies with."

"Oh, I know that."

"I cast my vote to -" I paused, unsure whether, even after all this time, I ought admit the whole truth to my old friend, "I did it to get my own back," I finally blurted; tense and prepared for the natural backlash which she had every right to unleash. I even welcomed it - deserved it for christsake! There had been enough lies and enough liars for one life.

She merely smiled behind her mug: a resigned smile that spoke of the wisdom of the intervening years.

"And what, Sylvie Quiggley," she clipped tartly, "gives you the right to presume that I wasn't happy all these years? What makes you so sure that I ever wanted the trappings of stardom, eh ? What's wrong with my flat? It's more than you've got. And at least it's paid for. I don't owe a penny to anyone. I'm safe. I'm secure. I've got friends - family. Where are yours ? When did you last speak to your father? What makes you think you didn't do me a favour?"

"Hold on a minute," I said, ignoring the embarrassing list of unanswerable questions just posed, "are you saying you knew?"

"Of course I bloody knew ! Christ Sylvie, I didn't give a toss about Stephen ! I only joined you're soddin' band so that I could still see you !"

"So why did you stay with him ?"

"Because he asked me and you didn't ! If you'd have said - just once: 'Hey Neve, can I take you out somewhere?' or 'Hey Neve - fancy a fuck ?" But you didn't, did you. You were too interested in that bloody band!"

For a second the tumultuous twister that serves as a mind for me switched itself off. For a scant moment the ever-spinning whirlpool of ideas, theories, plots and machinations went blank.

"And you know what?" she continued, before my automatic overdrive function could trip in and return me the power of speech, "I got over it."

She placed her emptied mug on the dayglo rug beside her, plucked a cigarette from the opened box on the table and struck a Swan Vesta against the rough slate edge of the fire grate. "I got a job," she resumed, more calmly, "I met Frank. We got married, bought the flat, had our daughter - two weeks abroad every summer. I forgot all about you for almost two decades."

I noticed that my throat had dried to the consistency of ancient papyrus. My mind, though still in a state of flux, restarted its cycle of torturous memories in an attempt to block out the ramifications of her speech. The taste of stewed tea felt sickly sweet against my tongue. I felt my stomach begin to heave as if some sadistic little imp had taken it upon himself to stir the volatile contents of my digestive system into a combustible pulp. I could taste a bitter regurgitated bile rising at the back of my throat.

"'Scuse me," I bubbled, dragging my resistant bones from the suspensionless armchair to stagger myopically into the bathroom where I proceeded to chunder a milky tea coloured discharge into the toothpaste stained basin. I sat myself on the rim of the bath. My head felt so heavy that I thought I might need to wear a neckbrace for the rest of my miserable life.

It's 1977 all over again and the annual 'Battle of the Bands' competition (sponsored by Leavalley Community Radio and the Lea
Herald) has been won by local press darlings: 'Some Young Moon'.
The crowd, which consists of four hundred odd, pierced and
spiked sixteen to twenty five year olds, who pack the sticky dance
floor of the Starlight ballroom, are on the verge of riot. One time
celebrity Tony Avalon is appealing for calm as gangly vocalist Sly
Quip steps forward to receive his trophy.
It's hard to believe that I was ever that young - a sentiment that I'm
sure Tony Avalon is appreciating as he passes me the golden envelope which contains our one hundred pound music voucher, (to be
redeemed at Fat Stan's musical pawn emporium) and the date of
our West End debut and 'big break'.
We are to play a support at the infamous 100 club on London's
Oxford Street: the punk HQ of the entire country ! The Banshees
had done their first gig there, (with Sid on drums, of course) and
the Pistols are regulars! This is it! The only way from here is up!
But there are to be some changes to our line up. Stephen's position will now be permanent; his impromptu solo during our ren-
dition of 'chew the cud' having been widely cited as the main reason for our unexpected accession over hot favourites 'Dawn Raid'
and our main local rivals 'The Organ Grinders'.
Joe has announced his intention to step down as our drummer in
order that he might manage us more effectively from the wings.
His replacement, in a deal struck backstage shortly after the win-
ner's announcement, will be Rusty Rhine, late of losers 'Dawn Raid'.
And Neve will be back, though this time with her keyboard rather
than her guitar. This is my idea - purely as a way of keeping her
close to me. Quite what we'll do with a 'synthesiser' in a punk band
I can't say, but it was better than a tambourine.
Six months pass and London proves to be all that it has been hyped
to be, with further opportunities following our support for 'The
Clash' opening up to us like a virgin lover discovering the wealth of
sensual possibilities attainable through a little imagination and a lot
of determination.
We receive our first NME accolade; the first of many, and begin to
be touted as hot property among the A and R reps.

I see our problem well ahead of its imminent arrival. Stephen has begun to discover himself on a wider stage, or, moreover, the wider stage has discovered him. We are four boys from the suburbs with mother hen Neve along for the ride, her mission: to save us from ourselves; to keep our heads on our shoulders, our feet on the ground and our cocks in our pockets.

She's going to fail, I know ... (I've already lived this life once - I hadn't expected to see it again. I know what's about to happen) True, Neve isn't the greatest pianist that the world has ever seen. She's no Elton John, but then who would want Elton John in a punk band anyway?

The motion is tabled that Neve be removed from the increasingly stifling situation - a motion seconded by the ever obliging Morris and thirded by new Twenty disciple Rusty. It is only vetoable by myself. (My single vote carrying the final word on any band decision.)

I reflect on my younger self's anguish as the bathroom wafts back into focus - an upward surge of sick and biscuit hauling me back to the present.

Things could have been so different had I not been such a revanchistic arsehole twenty years ago ! Had I had but an inkling of her feelings toward me, then I could have fought back; fought for her rather than acting in ignorant spite and damning our futures into perpetuity!

I fought to defend my decision, remembering all those times when I had had to witness that bastard's slippery fumblings in the back of Joe's transit; that look on Neve's face as he groped and gobbled her while I had looked on in homicidal torment. 'Damaged goods' rings like a mantra around my skull as I don my allegorical black cap and pass my judgment on the harlot and killjoy that had once been my friend. And in all the years that have passed since that fateful day, neither Sly Quip, nor Sylvester Quiggley have ever once considered the possibility that she may have been happier for the consequences; never once had I allowed myself to wonder whether she may have made a success of her life without me - *despite* me even! Never once had it occurred to me that she may have forgiven me! No. I had simply cut myself off from those memories: labelled them 'the time before time' and, as with everything else from my 'ordinary' past - consigned them to the far reaches of my mind, bound and gagged so as to avoid the legions of guilt that guarded the emotions that I imprisoned there. I never went back to Lea. I never saw my father or my friends there again. I had naïvely presumed that by denying the past it would simply cease to be, freeing me to better control my destiny.

But it had carried on existing. Lea was still there. Neve was still there ! And she had prospered without me! The past had forgotten me while I had desperately tried and failed miserably to forget it.

Neve had married. She had produced a child.

"Go on - get it out!" she said settling down beside me on the rim of the bath and placing her hand against the small of my back. "The consequence of the past has to be dealt with in the present before you can move forward into the future."

"What ... What do you mean ?"

"I mean," she ordered, "Chuck it up ! Get it out! I'll make you a nice bowl of soup."

This last statement proved to be the encouragement that my bowels had been waiting for.

I was awake. There had been no gradual elevation from dreamland to reality, just a sudden snap as my eyes had flipped open. In desperation I tried to hold onto the fading memory of my dream; to see if for once I might have been able to recall my entire night's adventures and thus understand the motives of my abstractive subconscious. But it had gone and not even a snapshot remained to decipher. I could usually remember something - if only a face or a name, but no: nothing. Had my demons tired of their torture? Had I perhaps been released from my guilt ? Or had I just not been asleep for long enough to conjure their images from my doomladen heart ?

The clock beside the bed told me that it was mid afternoon. But on which day, I wondered ? Was it the same day that I now remembered so clearly; the day when I had first awoken in this bed having been rescued from my not quite fatal suicide by my childhood sweetheart ? Or had I blinked and missed a whole twenty-four hour period from my life ? It was impossible to tell. I didn't remember going to bed. In fact, the last thing I did remember was throwing my guts into the bathroom basin.

I eased myself gently into a sitting position. My head still throbbed like a pulsing beacon, but by now more from my lack of hydration and sustenance than from an overdose of alcohol poisoning. I couldn't remember my last meal.

She had undressed me again. I was certain of this as my clothes were neatly folded and stacked on the chair in the corner of the bedroom. I must have passed out again. This was becoming a habit!

I dressed quickly and quietly and returned to the lounge hoping to find her and begin my apologies. (It's strange how missing time always seems to bring out this urge in people who were normally indisposed to this kind of self-deprecating behaviour.)

Of Neve there was no sign and a brief roundup of the flat's other rooms proved just as fruitless. She had gone out. To work maybe, I considered, though I couldn't recall her mentioning of a specific job while she had been listing her achievements the night before. I tried to imagine the kind of employment that she might indulge in, but gave up after discounting accountancy and the forces. I needed a drink. I have never considered myself to be an alcoholic - it's not as if I've ever been addicted to the stuff or anything. I just like to drink. I like the taste; I always did. And I liked the companionship that the bottle gave me back then. I liked the fact that its effects would occupy my mind in between the practical uses that I found for it.

I scoured the flat. The most obvious place to keep one's stash, (in a home devoid of either bar or cellar) is the kitchen, but the closest that I came to alcohol there was a bottle of white spirit which I found behind the u-bend under the sink. I searched the lounge - all twelve foot by ten of it, then the bedroom and finally the bathroom. This left me with only one other option: the locked room that I had encountered on my search for the missing Neve. I had, however, amassed a small change collection amounting to a princely five pounds and eighty-two pence. Enough, I thought, to buy me a quart of that homespun brandy with which I had marinated myself earlier. That would have to do, I decided, pocketing the buttons and returning to the lounge. I had no passion to get myself drunk. Not today - at least not until I had figured out where I was and what

I was going to do. I also needed to be sober in order to patch things up with Neve.

I reached for my jacket, but thought better of the idea, on catching a whiff of its in ground aroma. I put it back on its hook, pulled my Raybans and my cap from its pocket and started for the front door. This was the metropolis: there had to be an off licence within walking distance.

I turned the latch, but it refused to relent. I tried it again, checking for a safety catch that I might have overlooked on my first attempt. Nothing. The door was locked solid. Again I searched the flat, this time hoping to come across a spare key or a fire escape, but to no further avail. How could she live like this, I asked myself - aloud and unconcerned as to whether her neighbours might be able to hear me. It was a cell ! Desperation began to take a hold. I tried the windows in the lounge - the only windows in the flat, and although this did (on my further attempt) give way, I found myself no nearer an escape route. I was two floors up above a kebab shop, looking out across a busy intersection. I was trapped. Whether or not deliberately it was too soon to tell.

The time wore on with no sign of my gaolers return. I experimented with the television, though oddly only seemed able to locate four and a half channels. I scrambled myself a couple of eggs and succeeded in toasting myself two slices of whole meal bread without the luxury of a toaster, and, although both courses suffered a little from over browning, felt quite pleased with myself and my initiative.

It was six forty five and I was bored. I had been awake and dry since three eighteen and was in danger of becoming analytical if I could not find a way of numbing my senses very quickly.

I paced - considered the down pipe option - rejected it on the grounds that once down, (down there among the ordinaries) I would probably not have the strength to shimmy back up again - touched on the idea of attacking that white spirit - and for a second postulated death by hanging.

I tried the various bookcases that ranged the room, reading the spines, but finding nothing of even vague interest. I found her somewhat pathetic collection of compact discs and momentarily my spirits were lifted. They dipped again disappointedly as I discovered that she had nothing in her collection that I had even heard of. It was all modern stuff: trendy young Britpop. The kind of pap that I wouldn't even dignify by listing.

And that was when I noticed the picture. Incongruous really, just plonked on top of a pile of dog-eared old 45's. I picked it up for a closer inspection. The figure of Neve I recognized instantly. She had not changed at all since the snap had been taken. I also recognized the backdrop as that of the Eiffel Tower. The other two faces were unfamiliar, but I had no trouble in guessing at their identities. I presumed the male to be Frank: the 'husband' that until then I had conveniently forgotten the mention of. He was balding, mid forties - either Italian or Jewish, or both. The little girl that stood between her smiling parents would have had to have been about six or seven years old. She was blonde - like her mother, but her complexion seemed to match more to Frank's own (possibly) Mediterranean toning. Happy families. But where were they now ? Why were there no other references in the flat ? No toys; no second and third toothbrushes in the bathroom. I presumed that the locked room belonged to the child, which made me all the more eager to see inside. Could she have been locked in there just as I had been locked in the flat ? And where was Frank ? How would he react to find his wife sharing her bed with a much better man ? Maybe we had met the night before ? How else could she have carried me up to a first floor room ? But I decided not. I doubted that I would have forgotten a thing like that. That would have sobered me up in an instant.

I put the picture back on the stack and in doing so dislodged a silver key that had been blue tacked to the reverse of the frame. I wasted no time in my attempt to discover whatever it was that she didn't want me to see.

The key fitted the lock and the child's bedroom door came open. I stepped warily inside and switched on the light. (Children are not a hobby of mine and, to be perfectly frank - quite give me the willies).

The room had been decorated much as I would have expected it to be. The walls were a pastel pink; the sheets and pillowcases on the hand carved wooden bed having been chosen to match. Above and beside the bed, ranged on a succession of flat pack shelving units, sat row upon row of teddy bears. A family of six, more expensive and less loved bears, sat in a line on the bed with their backs to the wall, each bearing a Harrods logo and a date ranging between 1992 and 1998 on its out-turned foot. A pile of pre-school video cassettes had gathered a thick layer of dust, intimating that they had not been moved from their home on top of the half size wardrobe for some considerable time.

I was beginning to get a bad feeling about the room. It quite obviously was no longer used by its former occupant. Piled up from the opposite wall to the centre of the room was a city skyline of cardboard boxes - each marked both alphabetically and numerically. Piled behind the door was another tower of boxes, but these were made of an opaque plastic and were labeled with coloured stickers which read: 'Discs', 'mem', 'misc', and 'Tat'. All thoughts of Neve's mysteriously absent family dispersed as I crept forward and lifted the lid of an ex-banana crate marked with the legend 'D2'.

Understanding dawned as I delved into the box and pulled out one of the tightly packed cellophane files for closer inspection. They were photographs: A4 size; a mix of black and white and full colour, some overprinted with the logo of a film title and some bearing a fibre tip scrawl which may or may not have been the face in question's autograph. With the care that I imagined administered by a museum curator I gently peeled back the taped fastening on the back of my chosen packet and removed the set of pictures of Johnny Depp - the actor. Some were obviously publicity stills, taken to advertise particular films. There was a nice one of him in some kind of a 'Zorro' outfit standing next to an elderly Marlon Brando that had the title 'Don Juan de Marco' typed beneath it, black and white. There was a Johnny as 'Edward Scissorhands', a Johnny as 'Charlie Chaplin' from 'Benny & Joon' and a pile of airbrushed posed shots taken from various angles and featuring a variety of different hairstyles and facial adornments. I put them back in their sheath and wedged them back between DeNiro and arse nosed Frenchman Depardieu - more or less where I had found them.

A thought had suddenly occurred to me. I put everything back where I had found it, not forgetting to relock the door behind me and put the key back in the picture frame, then returned to the ashtray on the coffee table. The card with Neve's mobile number printed on it was still where she had left it earlier.

I dialed the number from the telephone in the lounge and was connected within two rings.

"Hello?"

"Neve! It's Sly -"

"Sylvie!" she exclaimed, almost deafening me with a treble heavy squeal of distorted air wave, "How are you? Feeling better?"

"Yes," I replied, relieved to find her in more jovial spirits than I remembered leaving her in, "Where are you?"

"Just coming up the stairs now." Two seconds later I heard her key turn the front door lock.

"I've been looking into your ... affairs," she announced provocatively, as if she were doubling as a private detective on the trail of a serial gigolo. She set the two plates down on the folding leaf table that she had had me drag into the middle of the lounge.

I stared down at her paltry offering and frowned in disbelief: an expression, though minus the internal sentiment, that Neve picked up on straight away.

"What's the matter?" she asked, sitting down opposite me and taking up her knife and fork to begin her assault on the smouldering meal laid before us, "Don't tell me you've gone off fish fingers? It used to be your favourite."

'When I was five,' I wanted to reply, but bit back my selfish retort. The truth was that I was starving and would quite possibly have eaten cat food if it had been served to me - cooked or otherwise. I had fallen a long way over the past few days, but I needed to remember that Neve Crilly had caught me one floor up from the basement. I should be grateful for whatever help she could afford to give me. For now.

"No, no," I blustered, slicing up my first fish finger, loading it with mashed potato and passing the smaller piece into my mouth, "It's just been a while since I've seen one - that's all."

As I chewed my breaded cod my saliva glands flew into over-drive. I couldn't remember food having tasted so good in ... years. Why had I stopped eating that stuff and when? I prepared for my second mouthful with a healthier relish.

"It isn't cordon blue, I'm afraid," she apologized humbly, "but I wasn't expecting visitors. Water?"

"Have you got any wine ?"

She swallowed her masticated mouthful and pouted sternly.

"You mean to tell me that you didn't search my home from top to bottom before considering the turps under the sink?"

I felt myself flush, but I don't think that she noticed; my more usual pillar-box palour having returned with the advent of a fuller belly. I didn't deny it though either, merely accepting the offered glass of highland mineral water and changing the subject.

"What did you find?" I asked hopefully, without, (at this juncture) even considering how she may have gone about her 'looking into my affairs'.

"You're well and truly fucked, aren't you," she said.

My heart sank at this affirmation of that which I already suspected.

"It did look that way to me, yes," I replied through salivating jaws as I gorged myself on the long overlooked delicacy.

"At least you had the sense to get out when you did."

"That bad?"

"Worse."

I reached for the tomato ketchup, suddenly, and almost too late, realising the one ingredient lacking from the ensemble.

"Joe lent you one and a quarter million quid which he secured against your house. I'm afraid he's got every right to repossess you in order to recoup his losses. He is after all a registered financier. But you were clever, weren't you? You'd already remortgaged the place a year earlier to the tune of eight hundred grand. Neither debts have been paid so technically they both have a legitimate claim on you. I don't know which of them has the legal high-ground, though."

"So I can't get it back?"

"Not unless you've still got all that money you borrowed tucked away somewhere."

I finished my dinner two bites ahead of Neve and noticed for the first time the two raspberry ripple mousses that she had stacked on top of the gas heater to thaw.

"Couldn't I declare myself bankrupt and start again?"

She finished her mouthful and downed tools, staring across the table at me with a look that I deciphered as genuine pity. She ought to have been gloating, but instead had apparently spent her whole day searching for a face saving way out of my self achieved predicament.

"You don't seem to have thought this one through, Sylvie," she elaborated, "You owe a further five hundred grand in tax ! You can't go
bankrupt from taxes. They have to be paid!"

"But that's a mistake," I pleaded, grasping at the slipperiest of
straws which promptly slid from my fingers, "that wasn't my fault! I
gave the money to Andy in good faith - it's not my fault if he chose
to snort it instead!"

"Somehow I don't think that's gonna' wash with HM Inspector of
taxes. You do realise you'll go down for this if they catch up with
you?"

My mousse had lost its flavour.

"Do you mind if I ask," she ventured, collecting up the crockery and
cutlery and heading back toward the kitchen, "What did you do
with all that money?"

I removed the chairs to their positions beside the windows, folded
down the table and pushed it back against the wall. I followed her
out to the kitchen carrying the ketchup and the condiments, trying
to think of a plausible answer to her impertinent poser.

"I'll wash, you dry?" I suggested fairly, hunting for a free surface in
the cramped anteroom that was, I noted, actually smaller than the
galley on my yacht.

"No," she corrected me, handing me a pair of yellow marigolds,
"you wash and you dry. I've got work to do."

As I loaded the discoloured plastic bowl with our sauce stained
plates I saw her pop a pill beneath her tongue, which she duly
washed down with the last of the mineral water.

"Are you going to tell me?" she pushed, passing me a squeezy bottle of super-market homebrand washing up liquid.

"You've never married; you don't have any kids; you're not a user.
Where'd it all go?"

I twisted on the taps with a little too much nervous vigour and succeeded in sloshing water all over my shirtfront and the crotch of my
trousers.

"You've not done that for a while, have you," she mocked, "slow
your flow - it's deflecting off the plates."

She leant in beside me and demonstrated the canny art of washing
the dishes to a man twenty years and a housekeeper out of practice.
I was suddenly affronted by a perfume that I had not tasted in …

"I can't help you 'less you tell me, can I?"

How could I tell her? I had trouble admitting it to myself.

"Look," I began decisively, reaching for the tea towel to mop my embarrassment, "I don't want to be a problem to you, Neve. I appreciate your helping me out yesterday, but I'll be out of you way as soon as I can."

My boundaries had been set. She snorted her derision.

"Where you gonna go, Sylvie? You show your face out there at the moment and they'll crucify you!" Check mate. "You can stay here for now. 'Til we sort you out."

"And is that alright with Frank?"

It *was* an innocent question. True: it was also an obviously indelicate one, but for all of her expert manoeuvering, she had left her flank wide open to my prying assault. I chalked myself an imaginary point, then rubbed it out when I registered the sudden change in conversational ambiance.

It was an innocent question. And one posed by a naïve ... no that wouldn't work, I knew. Frank was plainly no longer around - and neither was their daughter. I damned my arrogance and my ignorance alike as I prepared for her vengeance.

I watched her face lose its sheen and its vivacity as she stared me through with eyes that seemed to plead and blame in the same measure. It looked to me as if the mere mention of her husband's name had induced some kind of a post hypnotic suggestion. My poor sweet Neve. The idea that had struck me seemed preposterous in the extreme. For a father to gain custody of a child he would have had to have proved her unsuitability as a mother. All of a sudden I didn't want to know what had occurred between them, ill equipped as I was to know the correct words for any given situation.

And far from the happy-go-lucky woman for whom the years had been so kind, the Neve then stood before me looked every day of the forty two that I knew her to be.

"Frank's dead," she answered wistfully, "they're both dead."

"Oh God ..." I fumbled, longing for a re-wind button, "I'm so sorry - I didn't realize..."

"I killed them," she added, matter of factly. And she turned and left the room.

"You failed!"

I sidled into the bedroom, trying not to disturb her at her work. An hour and a half had passed since she had rushed from my sight muttering something elusive and improbable under her breath. Not another peep had been heard from either of us in all that time; she having encamped in front of her computer screen while I myself had duly marked time in the lounge mulling my worsening predicament and attempting to unravel this new conundrum without any of the relevant facts to hand.

"I'm so sorry, Neve," I pleaded, unsure whether I ought attempt to comfort her, claim my undying ignorance as a defence strategy or just pretend not to have noticed her shifted temperament. I realized then just how much of my recent time had been spent 'not knowing whether'.

"Leave me alone, Sylvie - I've got work to do."

I dithered on the threshold, feeling as if I had two hands too many. "I -"

"You what?" she snapped, turning from her flickering screen; her face bathed in its emerald light, showing me a side to her character that could not have been more alien. "You're sorry? Is that what you want to say? For what? An innocent question? Or you're sorry that I murdered my family? Or maybe you're just sorry I came to your rescue?"

"I -" I paused, momentarily thrown by her sudden barrage of questions and uncertain which of them to answer first.

"Or you're sorry that you're a complete arsehole?"

"Erm… what were the options again?"

"Piss off, Sylvie. You failed the test. There's nothing I can do for you - you're too far gone. Go on!" she insisted, "Go 'chew the cud!'"

I smiled, unable to stop myself at the mention of my first top twenty hit. I had never thought of that phrase in insult terms before, but on reflection I decided that it was an effective one.

"What 'test'?" I persisted, her second mention of the word at last soaking through the mire of my over indulged ego, "What test have I failed, Neve?"

She cued her mouse to transmit her e-mail, took off her oval spectacles and rubbed at her tear-reddened eyes.

"I wanted to see just how much Sylvie Quiggley there was left inside

'Sly Quip'," she eventually explained, her anger slowly abating. I acknowledged another new trait in the woman that I had wrongly presumed to know so well and that was her ability to shift mood at the touch of a hair trigger. I had seen this flaw before in others, though never in the employ of the rational. My brain began to flash 'yellow alert' behind my eyes. "I needed to know," she continued softly, "just how much of the sweet, gentle, generous and honest Sylvie Quiggley was still in there and how much was drip fed ego." I had no answer for her. Truth be known: I didn't know. I had never thought to look. In fact - now that I had considered the question, I knew that I didn't want to know the answer. I couldn't even remember Sylvie Quiggley anymore. He had died that day -

"Five pounds and eighty two pence," she accused, still managing to maintain her eerie equanimity, "That could have been all I had in the world," she said, "yet you had no problem just lifting it and saying nothing about it."

I fumbled the stolen change in my pocket; coins that suddenly felt like lead weights in my trousers.

"Don't worry," she went on, "it wasn't. I knew exactly how much was in the flat and where it was. And of course - in your quest for an alkie fix you couldn't possibly resist the only locked door, could you!"

"How did you ?" How had she known that ?

"Because I baited you, Sly. I couldn't have chosen a better name for you, could I." She paused for breath then added: "Tosspot!" with the aim of a truly professional insultress, "I needed to know whether I could trust you or not."

"Trust me? Trust *me*?" I rose, though well aware that anger would not at this point form a logical defence. "I'm damn near aristocracy!" I blundered, "I'm a fucking someone! I've met the queen ! My home's been on 'Through the keyhole!' Trust me? How fucking dare you ! I'm not some suburban dreamer, Neve, I'm the real thing ! I…" I realized that I had said too much and I didn't need the benefit of hindsight to realize that I had walked right into her trap. I had seen it before I had opened my mouth. I had seen her standing before me - net in hand, yet I had followed my tongue anyway, unable to resist her challenge.

"You 'what'?" she baited.

"I… I'm just an arsehole like you said. Sorry. I'll get my things." I wheeled right, turning on the spot and walked the length of the hall in three angry strides. In the lounge I found my battered gig bag tucked behind the stair door beneath my vomit impregnated jacket. I had no idea of where I might go.

"You don't have any 'things'," she mocked, entering the room behind me, her pose calm and faintly menacing.

"I still have my self respect!" I retaliated, though with a reduced fervour - the wind now merely trickling through my sails.

"After a failed suicide?"

I turned the latch on the door

"If you step outside this flat they'll bang you up."

"You saying you want me to stay?"

I had regained the baton. I had forced her hand.

"I … just needed to know if I could trust you."

"Question is," I retaliated, letting my hand drop from the latch, "can we trust each other?"

Paris in the springtime:

Snap happy tourists part their throng to allow us through. I smile longingly at my new bride and shrug my ample shoulders in a gesture that I intend to convey the expression: 'What can I do?' She returns the sentiment and adjusts her YvesSaint Laurent shades and matching headscarf, stepping gracefully from the jig, allowing only the most tasteful flash of thigh to tantalize the waiting press. I pass her the child, holding her aloft for just long enough to allow the morning's front pages to be planned.

I follow my family down onto the Champs Élysée. I tip the driver handsomely and show my appreciation to the horses: an affectation that I know will not be lost on the gaggling press hounds.

I doff a wink at a particular face in the crowd, pretending to recognize him; shake the hand of another while enquiring earnestly after his elderly mother. Then, taking the child's free hand in mine, I appeal to their sense of occasion and ask: 'no more pictures, please.'

Together we swing our precious jewel between us as we stroll past the bustling pavement cafés, brushing aside confetti and rice as it is thrown by my adoring fans.

She doesn't love me. I know this much. Her heart is promised to another; to her childhood sweetheart whom, though she betrayed, she can never forget. The child is what holds us together: the unconscious cementer of our unlikely union. I know that she still sees his face whenever we make love, but I can accept this. I know that I will never lose her for him. Not now. Not while we have little Neve.

"Where are we going, Daddy?" she asks as we board the lift at the bottom of the tower.

"To the top, darling. To the very top."

"I won't fall, daddy?"

"No, darling. Daddy'll protect you like he always has."

We step out onto the balcony, the wind whipping at our exposed faces and teasing our hair into miniature tornadoes. We can see the entire city below us; we can hear the distant ripple of applause as my admirers greet our audience.

"What's that, daddy?"

"That's the Sacré Coeur, darling."

"And, that?"

"That's the Arc de Triomphe."

And suddenly I'm falling; my little daughter still clutching my sweaty hand. I look up to see the face of my wife, calm, yet faintly menacing. I barely felt her hand brush against my back: I had imagined it to be a perfunctory embrace - a show of togetherness for the floating cameras. I had not been expecting the push that will carry me to my death ...

... And then I woke up.

"Tea?"

I flinched instinctively as my eyes rolled into soft focus on the figure standing above me bearing the wisping mug.

"You were out for the count," she said, bending to deliver my liquid breakfast as I struggled to extricate the dream from the reality. She placed the mug on the carpet beside my sofa bed and retrieved the overflowing ashtray into which a corner of my borrowed floral duvet had been trailing. "Sleep well?"

"Sort of," I replied, tucking my naked toes (my least attractive features) back beneath the cover and searching for the record stack through blurred eyesight for the photograph that had obviously inspired the backdrop of my nightmare. But it had gone. Neve was wrapped in a flimsy burgundy Kimono, tied loosely at the waist by its slim satin belt. She slunk discretely into the old and frayed easy chair opposite, managing to tuck her slender pins beneath her without revealing any more than she was prepared to exhibit.

"So what are we going to do with you?" she asked rhetorically, lighting what, by the length of her debut drag, I presumed to be her first cigarette of the day. I wasn't given the opportunity to respond: "You're a wanted man, Sly Quip."

She leaned forward and plucked the morning paper from the coffee table. My face, albeit a hazy and aged profile, took up two whole thirds of the front cover, leaving room only for the rag's logo and dual headlines; the first of which read: 'Bankrupt rockstar leads attempted heist - more dramatic pictures inside!' The second, even more humiliating by the fact that I felt compelled to follow its leader announced: 'Win a million in our fantastic new competition - see page eight'

"You realise what this means, Sylvie - don't you?"

"What?" I answered, nonplussed.

"Sly Quip has to die!" she replied as a matter of fact. "Come on - in the chair!"

"What?"

"You're too recognisable."

"I like being recogniseable. It helps me to be recognized! I don't want to be -"

"What?" she snapped, stripping back my duvet and offering me a hand out of my pit.

"'Ordinary', by any chance?" Well, Yes ! That was the crux of the matter, but after the last night's foot in mouth experience I opted for the silent repose.

"Come on. In the chair. It's just a temporary measure. Don't think of yourself as 'down' here to stay: think of it as a 'role'. You're just passing through. You're collecting experiences for your next album. And while you are here you've got to learn to adapt to survive."

"What're you going to do to me?"

Her shearing scissors glinted in the refracted strip light. I sat as I was told.

"Well the hair's got to go for a start!"

"Now wait a -"

I attempted to pull myself back up, but she was quicker than I was and she had the benefit of being above me; (easier to push down, than up.)

"It's my trademark!" I protested feebly, cautiously deciding against further resistance from an armed assailant who may or may not have cold bloodedly murdered her husband and child.

"Precisely why it has to go. They'll be looking for a forty two year old man with jet black hair, a permanent tan and eyes so Kohled he looks like a drugged out Cleopatra."

"Excuse me?"

"The eyeliner goes as well."

"Jesus," I moaned, but I really couldn't fault her logic, "leave me *some* dignity."

"Don't worry," she sniggered: (a most inappropriate affectation before commencing her strafing run, I felt), "you've been in need of an image change for years."

Another person's opinion is always a valuable asset in matters sartorial, but nobody likes to be told that they're looking their age! I had been using the same stylist for as long as I could afford him. I visited his Knightsbridge Salon fortnightly for a root touch, trim, facial and manicure. I trusted him implicitly, both with my grooming and my psychological needs. I knew that he would never forgive me for what this mad woman was about to do to his canvas. I knew that, regardless of the fact that I would probably never be able to afford his attentions again, I would never again be able to look him in the eye.

I closed my eyes after seeing the first lock fall into my lap. As if I hadn't sunk low enough already, the bloody woman wanted me to 'blend'! Street level; gutter level - how could this be happening to me ?

"Shit, Sylvie - look at these roots. You're almost completely grey under here!"

I hoped they were happy now: the demons; the heads that I'd stepped on in my clamour for the high life. They had been right to mock me in my dreams. I was a charlatan; a fraudster; a skin-deep hero ! Strip away the cosmetic support and all that was left was a hick from the suburbs with delusions of grandeur.

I heard an ominous click like the safety catch of a gun being disengaged followed closely by a droning buzz that sounded as if a swarm of electric bees had descended on my head. She pushed my head forward and I felt the cold steel of a pair of vibrating clipper blades as they connected with my nape.

"I'll give you a 'French crop'," she announced breezily, digging the unwieldy instrument into my skull as she worked, "and we'll have to do something about the beard too."

"I don't have a beard!" I told her vainly.

"You do at the moment - it's in all the papers."

I thought back to the dreadful CCTV pictures that had graced the morning's front page. She was right. I hadn't shaved in days.

"*I* know! How about shaping it into a goatee?"

"Absolutely not! Joe tried that once," I warned her, "-it looked like he had a fanny on his face!"

"You are such a charmer. Goatee it is then."

"Look", I ventured tentatively, "don't get too carried away! I really don't intend staying down here for long."

She forced my face to the side, nicking my left ear as she shaved too closely to my eyebrow.

"I hope not," she replied tightly, "You're the most ungrateful of patients! But pray tell: What's your plan for world domination this time?"

She switched off the clippers and yanked my head back to the upright, thus beginning a manic, apparently method free scissor assault on the top of my head.

"One, album," I replied confidently, "that's all it'd take. Just one hit album. I've got the material - I wrote a whole album for the Moonies' reunion!"

"But you're broke, Sylvie. What're you gonna record it with? Who's gonna pay the musicians? Who's gonna release it for you, come to that. You're out of contract!"

"Neve - I'm Sly Quip! Any number of companies would jump at the chance ! Besides," I added, hitting my stride, "Joe'd do it! It'd give him the chance to recoup what I owe him."

A brainwave struck her: "And if he refused, then you could always threaten to publish your memoirs."

I hadn't thought of that! I supposed that this was another of her attempts to barrack me, but never-the-less, the seed had been sown.

76

She moved around to face me and eyed my stubble over-eagerly.

"Hmm..." I mused, my mind flicking idly through the scrapbook of my past, "I would imagine there's a fair bit that Joe and the boys would rather the world didn't hear about."

"But that still leaves the problem of recording it, or are you intending to blackmail him into funding it as well?"

"I doubt I could bluff it that far, but if I had the album in the bag then he wouldn't be able to resist!"

"Piece of piss, then. How much do you need?"

I tried to reply through ventriloquism while Sweeny Todd jabbed away at my chin like a chainsaw sculptor at a woodblock.

"Ten, maybe eight if I pull in a few favours."

"Is that all?" she scoffed, "I think I've got that under my mattress!"

"You're joking?" I asked, but the irony was lost on her.

"Oh wise up, pillock! I can't get my hands on that kind of cash anymore than you can! This is the real world - Ooops!"

"'Ooops' what?"

"Hold still! You're wonky on one side, now."

"Have you done this before?"

"'Course I have! We used to have a Poodle. Principle's the same ... I expect."

"You've got to help me, Neve," I pleaded, pulling away as she lunged for a third attempt, "You're all I've got ! I don't have anyone else to turn to." (If only I had realised then how coincidentally propitious that statement had been.)

She switched off her clippers and squinted in at her handywork.

"Hmm...looks like you've got a fanny on your face. Still - not bad for a beginner. I could almost fancy you like that." She passed me a bone-handled mirror for my own inspection. Nervously I brought it up between us. Gone were my trademark black spikes that had survived the flouncy mullets of the eighties to be replaced with - virtually nothing on the back and sides and on the top - a half inch crop of grey fronds that washed out my skin and made me look at least forty. My chin was dressed with a light brown/flecked white and ginger fur triangle, which connected via two roughly symmetrical hair strips to a footballers moustache. I looked like Errol Flyn's dad. The only thing I was good for now was playing jazz!

"Well? Whaddayou think?"

"I look like Errol Flyn's dad."

"You look like a forty two year old version of the schoolboy I fell in love with. Take the earrings out."

I did as I was bidden. Resistance, as my ultimate fantasy female always said, was futile.

I looked up from my mutilated reflection and caught her eye. She hadn't changed. Not in all those years. Her face still moved in the same way that it had done the last time that I had seen it this close up. Her eyes still twinkled as they had done in the pipe ...

"Get yourself washed - I'll find you some clothes."

She returned a few minutes later and caught me staring at myself in the mirror, attempting to straighten the outer edges of the beard with a disposable bic.

"You'll get used to it," she said, depositing a hanger of men's clothes (which I rightly presumed to have once belonged to Frank) on the picture rail above my head. "Put 'em on," she ordered "I've got an idea."

"Don't be so bloody ungrateful! You asked me to help you, so I'm helping you !"

She crossed the kitchen in two Gestapo strides and bent in front of the oven to check on the progress of her masterpiece. "Have you any idea how to make gravy?"

My mind ran a hurried simulation based on observations it had recorded of other people that I have known working in kitchens.

"No." I eventually replied, deciding that this was probably not the time to stand up to her infuriating condescension with a stubborn display of hapless resolve.

"Look, Neve," I appealed, "I realise that you're only trying to help me, but there has to be another way. We haven't exhausted every possibility yet. Someone will lend us the money."

It was a futile plea I knew - I had spent the better part of the day begging my way through my address book and all to no avail, but the alternative was unthinkable !

"That isn't how it works 'down here', Sylvie. You have to earn your money; you have to work for it ! You can't just wait around for residuals on work that you did twenty years ago anymore ! Look," she said, her formerly indignant mood shifting into one of almost maternal concern, "I understand your misgivings, but there's a principal at stake here. There's a lesson to be learned. You'll grow through this. I promise."

"I'm not interested in growing, Neve. I just want to go home. Back to the real world."

"The real world?" she rapped back at me, feigning surprise, "you wouldn't know 'real' if it dropped its kecks and sat on your face! Can you make gravy? No. Can you wire a plug?"

I didn't answer.

"No," she decided. "Can you change a wheel on a car? Doubtful. You've got no standing in this world Sylvie - you're out of your depth. Nobody's going to help you - nobody's going to trust you. You've got no choice if you want to get yourself out of here."

"But manual labour, Neve. It's just not me!"

"You don't even know if he's going to offer you yet. Just bear with. Trust me on this one. I'm on your side!"

She smiled her most disarming of smiles and my bubbling brainstorm dissipated. She pulled a wooden spoon from a pot marked 'utensils', lent across the cramped single oven cooker and dropped it into a stainless steel pot that she then filled with water and sprinkled with a fine brown powder. She placed the pot onto the already warming electric hob and passed the spoon on to me.

"Stir that, slowly - while I nip and get changed."

Though I had had my misgivings about the plan since she had first announced it over breakfast that morning, of course she was right. There were no other options. If I was intent on my resurrection then I was going to need money. Lots of it. With nothing to sell and no vocational experience bar my ability to sing for my supper, (an ability that, in light of my dilemma would most likely hinder my recovery rather than abet it) my only option was going to be 'unskilled labour'.

Barry Tring: the evenings invited dinner guest, was supposedly the man to see. He was an old friend of Frank's - they had been through school together. Without Barry and his wife Shelly, Neve didn't think that she would have survived the loss of her family. I wondered whether I might uncover a little 'history' to fill in Neve's missing years as well.

Barry had a 'yard', whatever that was, where he often employed 'casuals'. (I presumed this term to refer to workers of no fixed repute rather than to the eighties fashion subclass of parka-less mods in Loafers and white socks.) I refused to consider myself a member of the vagabond set just yet and the term 'homeless' stirred connotations that I would never be able to deal with. Whatever my past indiscretions, I knew that I deserved better than this ...

"How do I look?"

Neve had re-entered the kitchen, her arse firming jeans and formless T-shirt now replaced with a red velvet shoulderless and backless mini dress, its bodice held in place purely by the resistance afforded its invisible elastication by her firm yet plentiful bosom. Behind me something fizzed on the stove.

"Take it off the heat!" she shrieked, but it took my mesmerised mind a second too long to interpret her words. Singed gravy began to trickle down the sides of the oven, pooling, cooling, then setting hard on the tile effect linoleum.

"Perhaps you're right," she grumbled, with not a small degree of applied sarcasm in her timbre, "You really aren't cut out for manual work. Go and get changed. They'll be here any minute. It's all laid out on the bed for you."

What I found 'laid out on the bed' for me actually turned out to be worse than the clobber with which she had outfitted me to match my makeover. I looked down at her dinnerparty choice - another fine selection from a deadman's wardrobe. As I buttoned myself into the personality robbing grey two-piece suit, over the starched pin stripe collar and the car salesman's tie, I pondered the lifestory of the ensembles previous owner. Who *was* Frank? What did he do? And what had he had that I hadn't ? (Apart from Neve, of course.) How did he die? I inspected the oxblood brogues that were supposed to compliment the outfit, but finally and defiantly decided to stick with my pointy boots. A line had to be drawn and it was here.

I heard the warped trill of the doorbell a scant second ahead of Neve's 'stand-by-your-beds' command. Buttoning, unbuttoning, then rebuttoning the snugfit jacket as I walked, I passed the open arch that separated lounge from kitchen and was startled to find my route impeded by a hand that shot out from within a cloud of chicken flavoured smoke and attached itself to my wrist. I halted in my tracks to hear Neve's disembodied voice whisper further instructions on behavioural etiquette in a tone that definitely suggested threat rather than warning.

"There's going to be wine on the table," she announced, as if to underline the occasion, "- if you get drunk - and that would be *my* definition of the aforesaid state - then I will personally turn you in at the nearest police station for tax evasion, burglary and any sexual charges that I can think up along the way. Is that crystal?"

"And if you don't get even a little bit drunk," I dared myself, knowing that with the deeper tenor of my voice there was a possibility that it could carry down the stairs to our waiting guests if I chose to up the decibel count even a fraction; thus rendering my host vulnerable for the first time since we had re-met, "then I might just have to make those accusations worth your while."

She released her grip and I opened the door to find that our guests had let themselves in, climbed the stairs and had no doubt heard our little exchange.

"Mr Moon?"

"Sorry?"

"Mister Sylvester Moon? Nevie's cousin?"

The penny dropped.

"Er, yes...Moon. That's me," I lied. Barry Tring, squatter and wider than his leopard print wife, thrust forward a hand that looked as if it had been made by a children's party entertainer from five red balloons twisted together. I received it politely, but cautiously; not wishing to burst it, while trying to remember Neve's hazily potted history of Sylvester Moon.

"Gonna let us in mister Moon, - 'fore I wither away?"

"Wither away," his pet wildcat repeated unnecessarily from beyond his shoulder.

Just a cursory glance at the formidable edifice that was Barry Tring was enough to convince me that 'withering away' was not something this bloater was ever likely to do. He could have died, been buried, then exhumed in twenty years time and still have been twice the man that I was.

"Please," I apologized, ushering the sweaty weeble over the threshold. His gold plated parrot followed meekly in his wake.

"Sylvie," Neve snapped, appearing from behind the balsa-coving arch that led to the sauna-cum-kitchen, "coats!"

"Nevie!" bellowed Barry, completely drowning out my half hearted: "Can I take your coats please?"

"Nevie," repeated Shelly, second in line for the bear hugging ceremony that played out while I disappeared into the bedroom and left her to make pleasantries with Mr and Mrs odious cockney wanker 1999. I flopped down on top of the duvet, Barry's fur trimmed camel over the one arm and Shelly's prostitution print fur on the other. I couldn't go through with it. I just couldn't do it. A thought occurred to me; a desperate, but better one. I sat up and opened the camel, fumbling for an inside pocket. Nothing. I tried the dead leopard, but came away just as disappointed. They may have been scum, I thought, having judged and condemned them much quicker than a man might fall in love at first sight, but they looked like loaded scum. By the time I sauntered back into the banqueting hall Neve and the Trings had taken their places around the dressed up fold down and were already engaged in tepid conversation.

"Come and sit down," Neve invited, "let me introduce you properly."

As had been my habit of late, I did as I was told.

I had been positioned next to Shelly and opposite the Michelin man, presumably deliberately, in order to facilitate our impending business 'chat'.

"Barry and Frank were at school together," she continued, "and he was our best man."

"Really," I replied, trying too hard to feign interest. Life could be so unpredictable. Less than a week ago I would have felt no shame at watching this man drown, but now, here I was, attempting to appear humbled in the 'barrow-boy-dun-good's' presence. I repeated Neve's sagacious words of earlier in the day: 'You'll grow through this' for moral support.

"Nevie tells me you've been away?" said Barry, this time with Shelly almost pre-empting the word 'away' and giving the sentence an almost ephemeral vibrato lift.

"Er...yes." I lied again, still not convinced of the plan to tell my prospective employer that I had been in prison. How was this a good reference, I wondered?

"Won't ask what for, good god no!"

"Ooooooh no."

"Point's not what'choo done, Sylv, but that you aint doin' it now. I'n' that right luv?"

"Right, luv."

I found myself flitting between the comedy double act as if watching from the touchline of a table tennis tournament. Neve's stoic - almost Vulcan expression never wavered.

"Clean slate, Syl," continued Barry, abbreviating my name pointlessly further than I had ever before tolerated.

"-slate," his wife verified, just in case I hadn't heard his sonorous vindication of my criminal past and very slightly missing her cue this time.

"Character building, is bird," he went on, seemingly oblivious to his wife's nerve shattering habit, or at the very least unsurprisingly numbed by it, "bit like national service I always say. If they aint gonna bung 'em in the army no more - then they should bang 'em up for a few years instead. Sort the men from the poofs -"

"-poofs!"

"What'choo say, Syl? Learn 'em all a bit of respect, eh? Teach 'em a decent trade ! Wouldn't get none of this paedophile stuff -"

"peedy..." That caught her!

"Knock it out of 'em afore they start wantin' to be 'airdressers, popstars and transvestites! What'choo learn inside Syl?"

"Learn?" Shelly mimicked over her freshly poured flute of 'Tesco' wine.

I gulped audibly on my own mouthful and looked across to my scriptwriter for directions. This was not an area that we had covered while trying to create me a felonious resumé.

"Rock breaking," I bluffed, "We did - done - a lot of rock breaking. And sewing!" I expanded, before remembering Barry's opinion of men doing 'poofy' jobs. "Mail bags," I added, "you know - tough sack cloth type sewing!"

"Sewing and rockbreaking, eh?"

Neve pushed her chair back noisily and stood up.

"Smells like the starter's ready," she announced, stubbing out her cigarette and smoothing down her dress, "give us a hand Sylvie."

I didn't need to be asked twice, almost beating her to the sanctuary of Cloud City.

"I thought I'd stop you before you told him you were on a chain gang!" she snapped through gritted teeth, "When I said to improvise I didn't mean from American films!"

"Well how should I know what they do in prison?"

"You will do if you foul this up, make no mistake!"

I sensed another agenda beneath her philanthropy. Why did she feel the need to impress the nobody? Here I was - formally one of the world's best loved artistes and she was speaking to me as less than her equal. Something about this friendship didn't ring true. Tring's hold over my friend was less than platonic.

"Look Neve," I whispered, as she doled out the homemade soup that I imagined she had whipped up especially for fatty to remind him of his happy times behind bars, " this is not going to work! I hate him already and she's getting right on my tits with all that ventriloquism stuff. Doesn't she have any conversation of her own?"

"She does," she said tightly, passing me two steaming bowls then collecting the other two herself, "but believe me when I warn you, you do not want to get her started!"

"And there's me thinking you w's gonna palm us off with some noncey avocado crap!" dribbled Barry, almost drooling into his nondescript broth, "shouldn't 'ave doubted you'd know a decent east end nosh, eh Nevie?"

"Decent nosh, eh?"

Deviation! Our Shelly was getting bolder, I noted.

"So what'choo do 'afore you went down?"

I looked to Neve for support, but received only a raised eyebrow. I had been ready to recount my legendary life of delinquency, courtesy of Neve's imagination (or experience?) and with a few inspirational touches of my own, but farther than that I was at a complete adlib loss.

"Prince of Wales," I blurted suddenly, the only trade that for some obscure reason I seemed able to bring to mind in that panicked instant.

"Landlord? Or barman?"

"Barman?" Shelly repeated, and for a second I presumed her to be judging my competence at wine pouring rather than simply parodying her husband.

"Barman," I bluffed, cursing my own stupidity, but grateful for Barry's lack of imagination, "serving drinks - you know - and …"

"Collecting glasses?" Shelly finished for me: her first independently orchestrated words of the evening.

"That's it!" I encouraged her, affirming her suggestion with the same two words.

"Not much of a trade, is it."

"Oh, I'm fully qualified," I rambled, but felt a sharp kick to my shin that was followed by a 'shut up' type glare from Neve.

"I'm happy to do ... most things," I lied, knocking back the final dribble of wine in the hope that it might anesthetize the brain that had processed and released such a masochistic statement.

"Hmm... leave it with me Syl old son - I'll drink on it."

After bruising my left shin Neve had left the table to begin the task of dishing up the main course. I followed her out to the kitchen, collecting up the soup bowls that the Trings had begun to use as ashtrays as I went.

"Quick thinking," Neve whispered, as I arrived at the sink beside her, "just don't get carried away. You don't need qualifications to work in a pub."

Chastened, I returned to the party.

Neve was not necessarily a bad cook; though I have tasted better, and tonight's offering: a slightly dry, tame, but palatable roast chicken with traditional trimmings was a perfectly acceptable endevour. Hers was a style that my taste buds knew well. They had grown up with it: it was my mother's. Neve's mother had died when we had both been eleven. My mother; Neve's godmother, had inherited the role of surrogate mother figure in her friend's absence. The similarities were uncanny. Even her vegetables had that melt on the tongue quality that I had been so eager to escape at sixteen.

The main course came and went without further mention of the evening's purpose; the Trings leaving nothing for the slavering vultures that they imagined to be circling above the table, thereby ensuring that the only sound to be heard was from the incessant scraping of their cutlery against Neve's worn china plates. Dessert was taken at a more leisurely pace and with a smattering of mutual anecdote which I assumed was intended either as some kind of territorial marking: a way of letting me know my humbled position in the proceedings, or of reacquainting old friends who, for whatever reason, had allowed a formerly close association to wane. For the most part I was largely ignored, although I couldn't help feeling that the stories were being regurgitated for my benefit. My appetite sated, I simply sat back and listened, gathering as much covert intelligence on the enigmatic Frank Capaldi as I could.

He had, it seemed, led a perfectly blameless life, but, as I was all too aware, hadn't everyone who had died prematurely? He had been a third generation Italian - (As tenuous a heraldic claim as Neve's was to Cork and mine to some nameless Viking pillager.) His family had apparently disapproved of his choice of wife and had disinherited him from the family business, though their claim on their grand-daughter had been something of a bugbear for Neve. Frank had run a market stall in Petticoat lane, selling end of season overstock, factory seconds and the odd fenced shipment care of 'Tring Industries'. He had been an ideal husband and father and best mate, and from Barry's poorly veiled complementation - could I presume something more? His demise had been tragic, but nobody had felt the need to extrapolate further, leaving me no nearer an answer to the burdening question of Neve's guilt than I had been before. But I did at least now have a mental picture of the kind of man that pressed her buttons.

I poured myself the dregs from the poorly fitted plastic tap set into the side of the cardboard carton of homebrand red.

"So Syl," Barry suddenly barked, hauling me back from peripheral view to take centre stage in his bombastic performance, "How d'you fancy a bit of light entertainment?"

Was this some form of jailbird code, I wondered? Should I smile conspiratorially, decline politely yet enigmatically, yawn and glance at my watch, or did protocol decree obsequience to the fatman for the duration of the evening?

"A drink?" the self-professed wideboy prompted, shaking the now drained wine carton to emphasize our dwindled stock. Neve, who I noticed had left the table on the cueing of the word 'entertainment', returned from her sojourn to the sink and I attempted to catch her eye as she lent across me to gather the remaining cutlery. Her expression remained irritatingly noncommittal.

Left to my own devices, and with my alcoholic appetite barely whetted I replied: "Why not?"

"Good boy," said Barry, stubbing out his half corona in his finger-smeared glass and turning to his suspiciously silent partner.

"Get the coats, Shell', first rounds on Syl' to celebrate his return to the employment fraternity."

I recognised the place as soon as I saw it. I had been there before - twenty years ago. In fact, twenty years ago I had virtually lived in pubs like the Britannia. This had been our world - playing for peanuts while the indifferent punters supped at their slops and aspiring novelists from the NME dreamt up new ways to rubbish raw talent. It hadn't changed much. The walls were still the same mucus green and the ceiling paper was still held in place by a cancerous sediment of nicotine and phlegm. The stage still occupied the same wall, its raised bier still cobbled together from balsa pallets and upturned beer crates and the house PA still gurgled like a simmering kettle, occasionally whistling as it came to the boil. But at least I finally knew where I was. This was the East End; a culture, though no more than thirty minutes drive away from The Heath.

And then I started to notice the differences. Where once photocopied flyers advertising forthcoming attractions would have been gaffered to the upright beams, chalk boards now pronounced the latest guest beer selection along with 'weekly specialty nites' which seemed to comprise 'pub quiz nite', 'non league pool' - using fluorescent balls, for christsake and 'karaoke nite', the latter of which, I noticed, was that very night. As I ordered the round using the crinkled twenty that Neve had surreptitiously lent me, a trio of plastered office types: their shirts stained with their lagered dribble and their ties loosened, yet at the same time knotted so tightly as to make escape an impossibility without the aid of the emergency services, clung scrumlike around the rooted microphone stand attempting a three part football chant style harmonisation of Cilla's 'Alfie'. I cast around the crowded bar, taking in the sights and sounds and behavioural patterns of the natives. Times change. Fashions come, go, come back again and blur, but the people never alter. So why did I suddenly feel so out of place ? This was where I had come from. These were my roots, as they say.

I struggled over to the bolted down table that Neve and her odious pals had managed to procure, losing the top half inch of each of their pints onto the tray as I was barged by those eager to avail themselves of my recently vacated spot at the bar.

"Not a beer man then Syl," Barry noticed astutely, as I dealt out the round. I was already a Scotch ahead of the pack, having bought myself two doubles, sinking the first while I waited for my change, and had mellowed enough not to need to revere him in quite such a reverent awe as I had earlier. I ignored his jibe and perched myself on the corner of the chequered benchseat, my hips resting snugly against Neves own.

Barry Tring felt it necessary to advertise his burgeoning testicles by guzzling his Guinness in a similarly single hit.

"Nice one Syl, more of the same?" I could feel that smouldering gaze of Neve's as it bore through my left cheek.

"No, I'm fine actually, Barry," I replied, sipping delicately at my lipstick smeared tumbler.

"I've got you a gooden!"

This was it, I thought - 'brace yourself'. The moment of truth: the offer that I could not refuse of degrading manual labour. I sipped at my scotch, eager, yet petrified in equal measure.

"You're doing Stephen Twenty's 'Not the monkey'," Barry dribbled, laughing uproariously at the picture that I knew to be my face, "I've got old blue eye's 'MyWay' and the girls are gonna do my favourite: 'Leader of the pack'. You're up first after the 'Everly brothers' over there."

It took a second for the mortification to set in. Barry had lined me up for the fucking karaoke!

"No way," I replied, the joke well and truly over as far as I was concerned. I finished my drink and placed my empty glass back on the froth pooled tin tray. I was serious - and not just because of the poor choice of material that the cockney fussock had chosen for me to perform. I had played to more people in more countries; sold more records and won more accolades in my career than Barry Tring had taken breaths in his pitifully insignificant life. I had performed for royalty; prime ministers; presidents and popes! I did not do Karaoke in a slime pit east end pub with the chance to win a 'pony' and a free round of drinks.

Barry merely guffawed a little louder at my display of obstinate defiance.

"Ave another drink if you're scared," he goaded, "It'll be a laugh!"

"Laugh!" Shelly squealed without removing her brimming Marlbro. "For whom?"

"F'rus, you great nonce! Where's ya' sense of humour?"

"No way!" I repeated.

"You want the job, don't ya? Well get up there and sing f'rit! I can't employ no-one without a sense of humour, Syl. You wouldn't last a day!"

"A day."

"Y're up, Syl. Go on, my son - knock 'em dead."

I made my way to the stage as the balding, bowtied MC called his halfwit audience to applaud the arrival of the next contender. He passed me the gob encrusted microphone and pressed the reset button that cleared the hazy monitor screen of the previous victim's lyrical prompt.

"And now!" he spat, too close to my ear for comfort and sounding like a Seventies referee at a Saturday afternoon Wrestling derby, "The Britannia presents: mista Sylvester Moon!"

A ripple of drunken heckles segued the embarrassing pause between Stephen's indulgent introductory solo and the on screen pointer's indication of the start of the melody.

"I must complain," I began self consciously, inwardly berating my old rival for leaving such awkwardly long gaps between his lyrical phrases, "apportion blame," ... I rhymed, "seek recompence ... and I won't rest until I've spoken to the man at the top. I will accept ... heartfelt regret ... and while I wait ..." I took a deep breath. Stephen's original vocal had been double tracked ! There was no way that the next line could be delivered without a mid word pause for breath - and that just wasn't professional! (Who was it that told the little shit that he could write songs!) "You'll compensate me for my losses mister big shot at the top ! Are you listening to me ?"

An earsplitting howl of feedback coursed through the antiquated sound system, thankfully blotting my failure to reach that high 'E' at the end of the chorus. It didn't, however, disguise the audience's baleful reaction to my impromptu impression. I heard the burlesque croak of the MC as he reset the machine and garbled across my attempts, less than thirty humiliating seconds into my performance.

"And that was crap, mate!"

He said, wincing as the PA shouted its own chastisement for my failure, "Stephen Twenty would turn in his bloody grave ! Ladies and gentlemen ? A round of abuse for mister Sylvester Moon! Next up - a warm welcome back for last weeks top turn : 'Horny' Abigail Horner singing 'Some Young Moons': 'Stuff the beaten track'."

I returned to the table to find the Trings close to a syncopated cardio seizure, while Neve attempted to hide her rubicund jocularity behind a sopping beer mat. Inside my temper boiled, but I was determined not to humiliate myself further by apparently taking it too seriously.

"Don't give up the day job?" Barry guffawed, with Shelly reiterating the words 'day job' in order to insinuate herself in the hilarious gag.

"So just what is the 'day job', Barry?" I asked, hovering in front of the table, too rapt to sit.

Barry smiled and plucked a fresh cigar from his top pocket. He unwrapped it, bit off the end; spitting it onto the threadbare carpet, and jammed the remainder between his bloated guppy lips. He took his time lighting it, looking across to Shelly and Neve as he did so to ensure that he had the whole table's undivided attention.

"It's a management position," he eventually revealed, acknowledging my gradual muscle relaxation with a smirk that instantly tensed me up all over again.

"Waste management," he elaborated.

I lowered myself onto the bench seat and reached for the fresh whiskey that had been my promised reward for my humiliation.

"And that entails?" I ventured, imagining a quiet, paper shuffling position, well away from the rougher of my new employer's employees. Barry lent forward and as I moved to follow suit he exhaled in my face.

"Shit shoveling," he said, breaking into a self-satisfied rictus, "emptying out the chemical Kharzis."

Shelly suddenly released a cackle that would have put a pantomime witch to shame. Neve tried, but ultimately failed to contain her own amusement.

I didn't think - I just acted on impulse : just like they do in the adverts. I stood up and with a single jerked flourish emptied my glass into the big man's face. Barry's response was quicker than could have been predicted for a man of his limited movement. A single butt, though one loaded with the power of a rutting stag caught me clean across the bridge of my nose ; the momentum throwing me backward onto the swill coated floor. In less time than it would have taken to zip a fly, the fat, bearded, wannabe-gangster had the table ripped from its rivets and was above me with a four inch blade chafing my windpipe.

"No, Barry! Leave him! Please don't hurt him!" : Neve.

"Hurt 'im ? I'll fuckin' kill 'im! Do a fucker a favour ? You wanna learn your place, Sylvie ol' son!"

"Fucker!" I heard Shelly reiterate from somewhere beyond my limited field of vision.

"I'm gonna cut you a break, sunshine. Just 'cause you're our Nevie's shag. But I see your face again …"

He left the all too obvious conclusion hanging in the fetid air.

"Coats, Shell'." Was the last I ever heard of Barry Tring.

Chapter Three
"Waiting for a bright idea."

"Oh Sylvie, I'm so sorry! I didn't mean you to get hurt."

"OW!" I squealed as she dabbed at the deepest of the four contusions on and around my swollen and misshapen nose with a lavender oil soaked cotton wool ball.

"There was nothing I could have done!" she soothed, attempting to placate my fermenting ire with a patronising attempt at coquettishness; a ruse which failed miserably in its attempt to re channel my energies, "It was Shelly ! She saw through you straight away."

"Nice of you to mention it. OW!"

"Sit still! I've got to clean these wounds."

She dabbed again at my disfigured visage, her face betraying what I took to be concern for the sheer extent of my defacing. "I didn't know 'til we got to the pub," she said, "Shelly's a huge 'Moonies' fan. She talks about little else. That's why I told you to avoid conversation with her - but I promise you I didn't know then that she had you sussed."

"I think it's broken."

"It isn't broken. It's just swollen. You know," she continued, discretely altering the subject to keep me from the truth of my fortune stripping injuries, "It was Shelly that first gave me the idea for the business."

"Business?" I queried, not having considered her hobby along those lines before. She failed to find offence and continued her explanation: "Frank told her that I'd played for the band when we were at college. After that she begged me to get her all your autographs."

"I don't remember that."

"You wouldn't. I went straight to Joe. I reckoned he owed me one after the way I was treated."

I licked the still seeping blood from the rim of my burning nostril. "You couldn't have told me this before I made a total tit of myself!"

"Oh, I don't know," she replied, smirking coyly as she surveyed her reparations, "I think it took a lot of guts to drown poor Barry like that. He could've killed you!"

The thought had crossed my preoccupied mind, though not soon enough to have been of any precognitive value.

Neve tore the backing strips from a flesh tone waterproof plaster and fixed it to the bridge of my nose.

"Mind you," she added, repacking her first aid kit as she spoke, "I think it's about time you thought up a new offensive. It's one thing drowning a camp impresario in the Savoy, but if you're gonna try it on a gangster in an East end pub then you've got to be prepared for the backlash."

I laid back on the bed and blinked my aching eyes. How did she remember something as trivial as my break up with Joe, I wondered, even to the point of naming the restaurant ? It hadn't exactly been stop press news. I'd forgotten it myself until she'd mentioned it and yes - she was right : there is a time and a place for everything.

"Do you think he'll grass me up?" I asked, watching the rippling movements of her velvet dress as she sat down beside me on the bed.

"Not his style," she replied confidently, "If he'd have wanted you hurt he'd have done it while he had the chance. Besides - he doesn't know you're staying here."

I pulled myself up to face her, resting against my elbows. "So how did you get yourself mixed up with the likes of the Trings?" I fished surreptitiously.

"Oh, they're not that bad. They can be good friends so long as you stay on the right side of them."

I looked deeply into her soft jade eyes, but remained wholly unconvinced.

"And they're pretty much all I've got," she concluded, and I sensed a wary reluctance on her part to be grilled further on the subject.

"So why are you doing this?" I asked, holding the gaze that I had instigated and searching those mesmeric orbs for the telltale sparkle of an untruth, "Why are you helping me?"

Neve Crilly smiled back, apparently content to dally with the opening gambit of intimacy.

"Old time's sake ?" she tried, then gave herself away with a shrinking blush which enhanced her faded freckles and reminded me of an age long lost. "No - I don't know." She shrugged. "When I saw you at the funeral I just wanted to run to you and hug you. You looked so tired; so pathetic - as if you'd suddenly realised that what you'd striven so hard for was not worth having after all. I wanted to wrap you up and make it all better. Silly really," she decided, breaking our occular connection to massage her stockinged toes.

"I get a bit sentimental sometimes."

"But you didn't," I reminded her, and as she turned back toward me I noticed a slightly sequestrated frown underlying that piquant sentimentality.

"No," she replied, somewhat wistfully, "I thought I could still see Sylvie through Sly; I thought that despite what I'd seen on the telly and read in the papers - some semblance of Sylvie Quiggley might still have survived. But when I spoke to you I realised I'd been wrong. I wanted to hit you. I wanted to shout all the things I should have shouted twenty years ago!"

"You hid it well."

"It was a funeral! Our friend's funeral!"

"That didn't stop you from using the situation to your advantage," I accused her, but regretted my misplaced arrogance before I had even finished my sentence, accepting her tempered rebuttal: "Pot-kettle-black!" With my hands held high in exaggerated submission. She punched me 'affectionately' on the thigh, effectively moving our flirtation to a higher gear.

"You never even liked him," she added, rubbing it in with: "What was it ? Good PR?"

"Still doesn't answer my question," I prompted, trying to re-establish our eye to eye contact.

"Don't be coy - it doesn't suit you ! You know why. We had a bond, you and I; something that transcends the here and now. We were as close as siblings for all those years - especially after my mum died." She reached her hand toward mine and as we touched, my body convulsed as if I had inadvertantly poked a live wire.

"I never stopped loving you, Sylvie. Not during Stephen - not even after the vote. I'd have been there any time you needed me. All you had to do was ask."

"I didn't know -"

"You forgot all about me."

"No!" I snapped, surprising myself with my sudden vehemence, "No I didn't! I didn't ever forget you Neve". (Which was true): "I tried to. God, I tried! I tried to deny everything before our success, but no matter what I did I still couldn't forget you."

I couldn't believe my frankness - honesty has never been a natural attribute of mine. Perhaps it had something to do with my recent deposition? Maybe I was telling the truth. "I've never met anybody like you Neve and to be honest -"(in for a penny, in for a pound) "I've never even bothered to look."

She laughed in my face and I was unsure whether she believed me or not, or was simply incapable of absorbing a compliment.

"Sylvie!" she trounced, "Your sex-ploits are the stuff of legend! How many bastards are you supposed to have spawned ? It was eighteen last time I looked!"

"You read too many papers," I chastised, not at the time registering her precision, nor doubting its innocent intent, "If you must know, (and quite why I felt compelled to tell her this I will doubtless never fathom): I'm still a virgin."

My honesty was received with a total lack of respect; Neve suddenly recoiling on the bed while she laughed in a way that I found impossible to distinguish between disbelief and relief. She realised that I wasn't laughing with her and sat back up to face me.

"You're serious, aren't you!" she eventually giggled.

"Deadly," I said, "I'm a voyeur; a pervert, if you like. I watch, but I don't play."

She hadn't needed to know this and I failed to comprehend my need to extrapolate.

"Jesus," she replied, "Why?"

"I'm yet to find the right person?"

"Oh, come on Sly Quip? you were a bloody millionaire! Voted World's most eligible bachelor - Cosmo' '88 and '89; World's sexiest man in 'Girl' 1990! You could have had royalty!"

"I didn't say I didn't have chances." I replied, flattered by her photographic reminder of better times past.

"You're not -?"

"Gay? No, I'm not. Nor am I impotent, before you ask."

"So what do you 'watch', then? Girl on girl? Or girl on boy?" she teased, "Or worse?"

Needless to say I was not feeling particularly comfortable with the direction she was taking with this.

"Do we have to do this?" I pleaded, reaching for her hand again. She didn't resist me.

"Yes," she answered cooly, "We do."

I hesitated, watching the change in her set and realising that my embarrassing secret was turning her on. My conscience whispered softly in my ear, reminding me - as if I'd never been here before - that this was in fact the last polite exit point from a rapidly deepening dalliance. I shushed it silently and it retreated, to return later with a 'you were warned' admonishment. I realised also that it was turning *me* on. I continued: "Girls," I said nervously, "on their own."

"Kinky. Not couples, then?"

"No."

"You like to watch girls playing with themselves?"

"Yes."

Her eyes had begun to sparkle like those of a five year old's on Christmas morning, eagerly anticipating the opening of the big present. She pulled away from my grasp and slid from the bed; slinked across the room and came to a halt in front of the wall mounted sound system. She selected a CD: Louis Armstrong's greatest hits; loaded the disc and dimmed the lights.

She turned back to face me and ever so slowly began to tease her red velvet dress up over her stocking tops, following the slim back straps of her suspenders until she had revealed the shiny black triangle of the briefest of thongs. The dress ruffled further until she reached her diamond studded naval.

"Don't do this Neve -"

"Don't tell me what to do Sylvie, I'm not you're hired 'tom'."

She turned around and bent forward, keeping her legs straight as if intending to touch her toes. The baby smooth skin of her thighs and cheeks tightened until I thought that it might burst, as the thin black string of her thong resolved into view when her cheeks reached parting point.

I fought to quash an impulsive urge to break into sweat, filling my head with mundane thoughts - anything but what I was watching being performed by my childhood sweetheart - all grown up.

When she returned to the upright I noticed that she was holding a bouquet of silk scarves in her left had while the fingers of her right were sliding up and down the satin straps that joined stocking to belt. She moved closer to the bed and reached forward to slip a pink silk noose around my wrist. She fastened its other end around the iron bedstead and pulled the binding taught, moving on to repeat her action for my remaining three limbs.

With my body spread-eagled and securely fastened in place, she lifted her right leg, placed her foot against the bed and proceeded to slide her stocking down her thigh, off her calf and over her painted toes. She repeated the manoeuvre for her remaining stocking, and then dropped both redundant items to the floor. She reached her hands behind her back, all the while her eyes never leaving my own. As the opening violin assault of Louis', 'We have all the time in the World' slowed the pace of her musical accompaniment, she unclipped her lace suspender belt and, in a movement that belied professionalism and put to shame the girls of 'Hushed Escorts NW3', reached up and unzipped her dress. As it fell to join her discarded lingerie on the shag pile carpet, my eyes were distracted by the two reasons why it had required neither shoulder straps nor a bra to hold it in place. And this woman was forty-two? All this time I had been wasting my money paying excess for the under twenty fives! She crossed the room, her near naked form as pert and toned as a women half her age. She leaned across me, her rigid nipples wafting mere inches from my parched lips. She dug her hand beneath the pillows and pulled out a bone-handled knife. Its blade - all six inches of it - shimmered in the candlelight.

My pulse began to race as my mind swam with possibilities. For just how many years had I longed to see inside those knickers? But then fear suddenly overtook titillation and I tested my restraints, Why would anyone keep a Bowie Knife under their pillow? I was reminded of Sid Vicious' pathetic defence when charged with the murder of Nancy Spungen. Of course it was *possible* that she had simply rolled onto the blade during the night ...

"No pain!" I begged as she ran the steel point over my shirt and trouser, "I definitely don't do pain!"

Neve smiled, obviously relishing her domination of the proceedings. She climbed up onto the bed and stood between my open legs, her bare feet close enough to my crotch that I could feel her toes against me. She passed the knife behind her back and sliced the waist cord of her G-string. It buckled and released the pressure on her final cloth covering. She brought the knife forward and held it against the flat of her tummy, point down between her legs.

A globule of salty saliva escaped my lips as I watched her inch the blade down behind the silk triangle until its razor tip point had pierced the apex. Then, with the flourish of a magician revealing flowers from his sleeve, she sliced the knife forward, stripping herself bare before me. She let the weapon fall to the floor and I felt a brief sensation of relief wash over me; brief, because in the next instant she dropped onto the bed between me and began a rabid assault on my belt buckle, fly and shorts; in no time at all releasing me from my self imposed shackles and exposing my glory to somebody other than my mirror reflection.

"Hmmm," she mused, studying my equipment like a mechanic would inspect a smoking engine, "not gay and definitely not impotent." She edged her way up my body using her knees for traction until she straddled my throbbing horn; the warmth radiating from her organs causing my own to self lubricate.

"As you've not done this before," she whispered, leaning hard against my hair free chest, "I think I'd better lead".

She hoisted her pudenda, hovered momentarily as if locking onto target, then sank down on top of me, slowly, tightly and deeply.

Even the shock of an ice cold shower couldn't break the spell that she had cast so well that night. I had waited an unreasonable amount of time in order to savour the experience; an experience that I had known my whole life long could only be adequately sated within the arms and thighs of Neve Crilly, (though 'adequate' was an insult both to Neve and to the experience of Neve.) I had saved myself for that moment, even though I had never expected it to happen, and every nerve, every sensibility of my mind and body told me that morning that it had been worth it. Worth every day; every week; every month - every decade ! And, even though I know that this all sounds about as corny as a Stephen Twenty lyric - I felt as if I had tasted heaven.

Nothing in my life to that moment could match it. My first number one paled into pathetic insignificance beside it. My first gold disc was worth nothing next to a single heartbeat inside of Neve. Even the thrill of seeing Michael Aspel step from behind the Palladium's velvet curtains with his big red book tucked nonchalantly beneath his arm - even that was cheap compared to last night.

I stepped from the shower and toweled myself down, still mindful of my bruised and scabbing face and even more tentative around those areas that were suffering from a severe bout of repetitive strain. Life was beautiful. Life was exciting. For the first time since Stephen had died, my life was worth living!

She had already left the flat by the time that I made planet-fall. I spent my morning tidying up after the night before, or as Neve would later so tactlessly point out : 'putting things in piles and moving them about the place.' But despite my lack of adherence to a pre-set criteria that she really couldn't have expected me to fathom in such a short time - the thought had been there. I had wanted to do something for her; something for someone other than myself.

Maybe I'd learned something from my dethronement. Maybe the universe was teaching me a long overdue lesson in humility?

It took me a perplexing fifteen minutes to find the 'on' switch on her vacuum cleaner. It was an ingenious design, I eventually marveled, though, as a note to the designers, - if both the 'power' and 'shiftgear' functions are to be operated by foot switch, then it may, in future models, prove prudent to colour code the afore mentioned controls. My patience was wearing a little thin by the fourth time that I had switched myself off instead of folding myself down, but on the whole I found the experience quite invigorating. There's something unusually fulfilling about tidying one's surroundings. I remember making a mental note to take more of a domestic interest when I returned to the Heath.

On reaching the 'spare' room I was not surprised to find its door securely locked, probably imagining itself immune from my spontaneous spring clean. I backtracked to the lounge to retrieve the key that I had utilised on my previous sojourn into her maternal shrine, but was surprised to find that it, and the picture frame that it had been tacked to were missing from their usual resting place. I searched the room, then searched the flat, but drew a total blank. I wondered why she might remove the only visible reminder outside of the locked room of her former life - her late husband and child. Was this perhaps, I pondered, her first post-widowhood tryst? Had she maybe suffered the pangs of post coital guilt as she had hidden away the picture, and with it my only access to her past?

Unable to complete my self appointed chores, I retired to the kitchen and toasted myself two slices of wholemeal bread under the charred and rickety overhead grill. I picked up the note that she had left for me before leaving at just after seven. For the first time that morning it began to concern me how little I now knew of my former friend. My own life was a well-documented affair; I never had the need to relate anything to any new acquaintances that I might have picked up over the past few years. Everything bar the frequency of my bowel movement had been recorded and presented in one medium or another for the terminally bored populace to peruse at their leisure, but of Neve Crilly, (previously 'Capaldi'), I knew relatively nothing.

Where did she go to all day everyday ? Presumably she had a job of some kind other than the collecting and selling of autographs. (I still at this point had a problem with the ethics (or lack of them) in such an endeavour). Did she have any friends other than the Trings? Was her father still alive? Had she a lifeplan ? Any ambition? I thought I should know - now that we had crossed that taboo border into virgin territory (or out of it in my case).

I read the note that she had scribbled for me on the back of an empty fish finger packet. It was a shopping list with a postscript advising me to keep my head up, my shoulders back and to avoid eye contact at all costs. Beside it she had left a spare door key and two cash dispenser fresh ten-pound notes. There was also a hastily scribbled map of the immediate vicinity and with these things - something even more important to me : her trust.

I turned left out of the flat and followed Bethnal Green lane for fifty or so yards before reaching its junction with Brick Lane. It was at this point that I noticed a 'p.s' at the foot of the cardboard memo to remind me that the weekly market closed at one p.m. I checked my Rolex; noted that it read twelve fifty two, pepped up my pace and pulled down my sweatshirt sleeve to conceal my rather out of place timepiece.

I found Neve's recommended 'fresh fish' seller just inside of Brick Lane, but on smelling the stench which seemed to emanate from his pitch, decided that this title was something of a misnomer. I reminded myself that it was just past noon on a too hot June Sunday, but just to be on the safe side I elected to ignore Neve's primary order and set out in search of an improvisational alternative. She had been right to warn me, as most of the stallholders that I passed were busy loading their unsold wares into the backs of suspiciously non descript blue or white transit vans. Nobody noticed me, or if they did then they failed to recognize me in my shabby cast off attire and working class crop. My bruised and bloated face probably added further credence to my borrowed identity as I counted four passing locals sporting similar tribal markings among the market stragglers.

As I proceeded further from the relative sanctuary of the flat and ever deeper into what I still considered enemy territory, I felt my passion bolstered bravado begin to waver. Was it me or was it true that the farther South one went - the shadier, dirtier and uglier the punters became ? Of course, this wasn't my first visit to the east end of London - far from it, but it had surprised me how easily I had forgotten the culture that had created me after all those years on the Heath.

I took a right turn opposite a Wholesale leatherware shop and crossed into Sclater Street, passing an oily looking eastern European type selling counterfeit Jaffa cakes and disposable razors from the back of an old Bedford H.A. I followed the line of the road until it opened onto an area that, judging by the surrounding architecture, had at one time been a row of identical terraced cottages, but which was now a concrete landfill dotted with tatty red and white striped market stalls. I followed my nose, though with hackles raised and fingers sweating around the damp bank notes that I still held firmly inside my trouser pockets. I had split them up, putting one in each pocket on the unfathomable assumption that a potential mugger would only demand the turning out of a single pocket. (Well it had seemed logical at the time.)

My furtive eyes alighted on a refrigerated truck with a fold out shopfront built into its flank. The legend: 'East End Prime' ran along the remainder of the vehicles exposed side, not quite obscuring the lettered logo of its previous owner, which had been painted out using not quite the right shade of grey. Beneath the eye-level counter and behind a wall of condensated glass was an ice packed, tiered display of raw meat. While I ruminated my choices, a cleaver-armed butcher in a blood spattered apron sold a pound of minced beef to a fossilized woman in a hat. I tried to imagine how the cuts on the shelf might look on the plate. I think I had still been a student the last time I had seen raw food.

"Yes mate! What's it to be?"

"Oh, er … nothing … mate," I mimicked, intending a show of camaraderie rather than offence, "I'm just ... browsing."

"Well don't take all day," said the shaven slaughterer, embedding his weapon in a mound of red flesh as he spoke, "We're closing up."

"Er ..." I dithered, no nearer a solution and now beginning to reconsider my original instructions. I was out of my depth. Pathetic, really - I know. I wondered briefly how I might cope in the wake of an international eco-disaster, having to catch and kill my own food, when I couldn't even buy it in a market without losing my nerve ! "What ... er ... what would you suggest?" I offered meekly.

"Well," the butcher replied, snatching up a lethal looking hand held pitchfork and impaling a long dead slab of red flesh in the under-counter tray, "Nice bit a' sirloin - cut you the pair for a fiver; throw in a couple a' lamb chops for tomorrow - call it eight quid!"

"Er ... is that good?"

"Alright! Call it seven fifty - I'm robbin myself with that!"

"No, I wasn't haggling," I defended, sensing the tension of the hard sell, "I mean - oh I don't know what I mean ! What about those ?" I said, pointing at two semi-circular chops, half crowned with an inch thick wedge of rind.

"Pork chops? You want chops? 'ow 'bout four chops and a quart a' kidneys to wash 'em down - call it a fiver - no - to you sir: four fifty!"

"Fine. Are they easy to cook?"

"I'm a butcher not a bleedin' chef!" he replied, spearing the chops and dropping them into a plastic bag which he twirled once before thrusting into the taping machine, "just stick 'em under the grill," he said, receiving my proffered ten pound note by its driest corner and jamming it into his back pocket, "ten minutes a side - dab of apple sauce - bob's your jolly old'."

I reached up and took my prize, inwardly reviling at the touch of the cold, malleable slabs in their polythene jacket. I thanked the man and explained away my stupidity with: "I've been away for a bit,": an explanation that the butcher accepted with a nod, a wink, and a tap of finger to nose.

The procurement of the vegetable accompaniment was to be a far less taxing affair, though the greengrocer's directions for the prepa-ration of the apple sauce had gone way above my head. Realising just how un-self-sufficient I was for a man of forty-two and for the first time in my life beginning to feel 'less' than the people around me, I decided to cut my losses and return to the flat. I had no clear idea of how long the planned meal would take to prepare and I didn't want to appear flustered by such a relatively 'simple' task in front of Neve, so I elected to give myself as much time as possible to master the long forgotten task before me.

As I walked back past the spot that the butcher's mobile abattoir had recently vacated I noticed an elderly, snowbearded afro-Caribbean man piling banana crates full of tattered second hand paperbacks into the back of a buff coloured Ford Escort van. I paused beside his final wallpapering tressle and scanned the spines of his literary jumble.

"Looking for anything particular?" the old man asked, replacing his spectacles over his eyes from where they had previously been resting against his forehead.

"Do you have any cookery books?" I ventured whimsically. The bookseller lifted a gnarled index finger, signaling that I should wait while he rummaged through a box that he had already packed away. He reappeared a moment later with two possibilities, one held in each ancient hand.

"'Vegetarian Stroganoff - a healthy alternative," he read, indicating the left handed volume, "or 'Madur Jaffries eastern delights'?"

"Thanks anyway."

"No problem."

"Ooh!" I exclaimed, suddenly noticing a name that I recognized among the dog-eared hardbacks which packed a box marked 'bargains', "'The Immortal Henri Blutoe'! How much?"

"All in that box : fifty pence," he replied, readying himself to heft that final box into the back of his van.

I fished out the exact change, made my purchase and set off back along the route that I had followed on my outbound journey; my mind suddenly ablaze with the germ of a plan: a plan that I honestly thought would be an easy route back to my plateau.

I knew the story of Henri Blutoe well. I was a huge fan of his music, his style and his wit - had been for as long as I could remember. He was a modern day legend and, like all legends, his tale was a tragic one. But I hadn't bought the book for a refresher course in celebrity suicides. What had inspired me to part with a little more of Neve's money was the 'idea' of the autobiography. Blutoe had been a genius; not only as a vocalist and songwriter, (though that fact, I must insist, ought never go unmentioned in any analysis of the man's life), but equally in the area of self-promotion. I remembered the circus that surrounded the publication of the book which now bobbed unceremoniously among the brussel sprouts and the carrots in my plastic carrier. It had been launched in a blaze of publicity a mere week after its author's spectacularly public suicide, which he had detailed explicitly inside the already printed tome itself. Blutoe had been honest, brutal and vulgar in his literary assassination of his peers and associates. The book had been banned and stripped from the shelves inside of a week, pending four separate counts of libel from his glitterati targets. Its publishers had been arrested and charged with conspiracy for failing to report the impending suicide in order that they might cash-in on the gruesome spectacle.

Henri Blutoe had striven for immortality. He hadn't been content with mere success in his lifetime - he had wanted his work and his story to transcend his mortality. He would never be forgotten: That much was certain. And neither need I, I thought, wracking my brains for material and trying to think of a simple gimmick that didn't involve my premature death.

My own career may have been floundering, (temporarily) but those of my ex-shipmates most certainly were not ! And who was more qualified to sift the drugs, the sex and the rock 'n' roll lifestyles of my former friends than myself? No-one! Lakhi Corner: the Oscar Winning score composer and the Japanese minor whose parents had had to be paid off after a particularly deviant sexual stunt had gone horrifically wrong. Well wasn't dear Lakhi in line for the next Disney epic ? And Morris Yussof, currently hotly tipped as the latest megalomaniac adversary in the next James Bond. How lucky he had been eight years ago to have escaped the trafficking charge that had seen poor roadie Diz breath his last breath of freedom for five years. And Joe Munday - a contempory Oscar Wilde! I could go on! But there was no rush. As Louis said: 'We had all the time in the World'!

She arrived home a little later than I had anticipated to find me dozing over the Blutoe book that I had devoted my afternoon to. Her eyes swept the room taking in the subtle changes that I had deliberately made in order that she might notice my domestic handywork without the need for me to point them out. I smiled up at her disarmingly.

"What is that smell?" she demanded, off loading her shoulder bag and following her aroused olfactory senses toward the scene of the crime.

I had time just to respond with: "Ah ... don't go in the -," before she did go into the kitchen, replying to my warning with: "Jesus Sylvie! What the fuck have you done to my kitchen?"

"I ... I was hoping to surprise you." I explained feebly, arriving beside her in the archway and cringing as I looked again at my earlier mistake.

"Well top marks, mate," she snapped, somewhat sarcastically, "Your cunning plan succeeded beyond your wildest imagination!" She turned back to face me, her expression reminding me a little of Jack Nicholson's in the Shining. I was reminded spontaneously of the knife that she kept beneath her pillow, "Now tell me," she continued testily, "What the *fuck* have you done to my kitchen?"

I held my position as she moved into the cramped galley, staying what I judged to be a little over the extent of her swing.

"The ... er, the brown things on the side there were chops ..."

"Chops," she clipped, and the word sounded more like a punishment than a description, "and the green slush that's welded to the bottom of my nonstick pan?"

"Not quite sure on that one," I replied honestly, "could have been either sprouts or cabbages."

"Looks like puke. And the orange sludge on the lino - I suppose that's 'carrots', yes?"

I hesitated before saying: "No, it used to be a mixing bowl."

"Tell me the white goo that's all over everything is potato?"

"No," I said again, reflexively indicating the scorched ring on the ceiling with a tip of an eyebrow, "It's melted polystyrene."

"And I'm suppose to be what Sylvie: impressed ? Compassionate ? or homicidal?"

"Look Neve," I began lamely, but it was all that I could think of to say, "I'm really sorry. I just feel so useless sitting here while you do all the work -"

"You've noticed then."

"Yes," I said humbly, though in retrospect I'm not sure that her reply wasn't sardonically laden, "and I'm truly sorry for being such a total waste of space."

"For being 'what'?" she goaded, and I sensed a gradual metamorphosis back into an approximation of the Neve that I had woken up with that morning.

"A sad, pathetic, clueless, arrogant, ignorant, egotistical knob end who can't work a vacuum cleaner or cook a pork chop!"

"Nor make gravy," she added needlessly. She looked me up and down and smiled ruefully. "Did you hurt yourself?"

"Just a graze."

"Let me see," she snapped, ripping off the plaster that I had stuck across my cheek to cover my latest wound with unconcealed relish. "You don't cover burns, pillock! Did you run it under cold water?"

"Warm ...ish."

"Needs to be cold. Brings the temperature down. That'll scar, you know."

I squinted into the fat speckled mirror above the sink. Already a blister the size of an old ten pence was pocking my blemish free skin and ensuring that the only front cover that I would grace from here on in would be 'The Lancet'.

"Still. It's good to see that you've woken up at last. There's hope for you yet Sylvie Quiggley. Fancy a Chinese?"

Back then I had mistakenly decided that she had been trying to teach the supercilious popstar that overdue lesson in humility. I had thought her plot to be altruistic in intent. But then I still had so much to learn about life in the big wide world.

"I'll get my jacket," I offered, but she stopped me in my tracks, flicking her stilettos from her toes and pointing toward the floor with a ruby fingernail.

"Not yet, you won't. You've got some groveling to do first. On your knees, doggy, kiss my feet."

I complied, grubbing around on the filthy kitchen lino as she dictated her demands.

"Properly. Good dog. Now. Ankles, calves, thighs ... that's right."

And that was the thing about Neve. I should have spotted it sooner really. I never quite knew what her reaction was going to be in any given scenario. The frequency and duration of what I would come to label her 'swings' were erratic and unguageable. Her verbal, (sometimes caustic) could equally be encouraging or flattering. There really was no way to tell until it hit. She was a powder keg. A time bomb. A coiled spring. I should have run away then while I still had my dignity, or at least while I still *thought* I had some dignity.

Neve lifted her skirt to reveal an identical black G-string to the one that she had slashed the night before.

"Take it down," she ordered, "With your teeth!"

I've pondered over this one for some considerable time. (When I think back over this period of my life I still find it rather difficult to distinguish the various warring elements of my psyche; to understand exactly what was going on in my mind at that time; to separate friendship from lust; logic from fear; need from greed.) I can't say with one hundred percent certainty just whose brainchild it was -sometimes I like to think it was my own, but in other less lucid moments I prefer to lump the blame onto her. I don't really like to think that I could have been manipulated into conceiving the idea myself - (which is in essence a combination of the two possibilities), but for the sake of continuity in this account I will say that it happened like this:

I had waited until breakfast on the third day after our one and only sexual encounter, (although obviously at that time I wasn't aware that my first would also be my last) before plucking up the courage to broach the delicate subject of her working day.

"Work." Was her answer to my question of: "So what are you doing today?"

It was an innocent enough question; not too prying, not too pushy, and at this stage in our relationship not, I felt, unexpected.

"But what is work?" I followed, sensing the raising of her guard as she replied with: "Something one does in order to procure remuneration. A bit like standing on a stage getting off on teenage girl's hormonal frustrations. Though not quite."

Was that supposed to have been a dig or a wry witticism? Either way, it was certainly a subtle warning that I shouldn't pursue that particular line of questioning any further. For the time being anyway.

"What about you," she countered, as I cursed my sliding confidence scale for regurgitating the knife under the pillow scene for the umpteenth time, "I notice you're up ahead of lunch today. Any plans?"

"Yes, actually," I clipped, recalling her comments on my enthusiasm over the Blutoe book from the evening before, "I'm going to write an autobiography."

"In a day?" she mocked, "And who's your subject?"

"It's an auto- Oh very funny! No. I mean I'm going to *start* it today." She didn't need to say anything. Her face said it all. It was that same expression that she had reserved for my ideas since we were kids. That all too smug: 'Yeah, right' that the Americana-overdosed youth of today were all too fond of using, only without the need to open her mouth. She had always done that, right from the first time when I had confided in her my ambition to become a popstar; back when every one else was ridiculing me for dyeing my hair black and trying to squeeze sovereign rings onto the fingers of my permanently leather-gloved fingers. That look. That: 'You think so, do you?', self-satisfied smirk that always made me work even harder to prove my ... I hadn't thought of it like that before. But now that I had - maybe that was how she had done it; how she had convinced me to write the bloody book while all the while imagining it to be my own idea! Ingenious.

"Look," she said, setting down her coffee cup and placing the tips of her fingers against my exposed forearm in order to communicate her shift of tone from flippancy to genuine concern, "I don't want to sound negative - I'm glad you're looking for a positive way out, but ... well, the Blutoe book says it all. He's only been dead two years and the most exciting premise ever for an autobiography is already in the bargain bins for fifty pee!"

She bent forward and kissed my forehead condescendingly, rising from the table as she did so, "I'm sure you've had a fascinating life babe', but who's gonna want to read about it? You're yesterday's news."

(Yes. The more I think back on it now, the more I'm able to appreciate her machinations.)

"The bastards I take with me for a start," I snapped back.

"You're serious about this, aren't you?"

"Very."

"And you can prove it all? All your friends sordid little secrets?"

"Can they prove that I can't ? And anyway - mud sticks."
She smiled mischievously as she opened the door that led down to the outside world.
"Let me see it later. I want to know what those bastards really are."
And with that she was gone.

Where to start. Two hours had passed and all that I had accomplished had been slightly burnt tea and toast.
The idea was sound - of that much I was solidly convinced, (still am for that matter,) but how to achieve it? Should I write my life story as Blutoe had done, with special attention spared for the defrocking of my detractors, or should I just cut to the dirt and present a warts n' all exposé of the seedier side of Some Young Moon? Which approach was the more interesting; the more readable; the sexier? And which of these options was going to be the easiest to write? How should I go about either ? Ought I imitate Blutoe's first person account, showing my own feelings and vulnerabilities; offering my own jaded opinions on my associate's nefarious misdeeds, or should I simply list the facts in standard news stand presentation ? Should I keep my revelations succinct and inferred, allowing my readers to draw their own conclusions, or should I write it for tabloid minds and hammer home my tits out message ? And I would have to list my own inadequacies - few that they were, for fairness sake. I would of course have to appear better than my colleagues, but not too angelic. Popstars were supposed to be rebellious, belligerent and carefree. It was what was expected of them. I needed to approach this from an angle which didn't appear patronizing or moralizing, but which still somehow managed to liberate my peers of their dignity while elevating my own reputation to greater heights.
I needed a plan of attack.
I tore out the page of schoolboy doodles that comprised my sole output thus far, crumpled it in my fist and lobbed it ashtraywards. I smoothed down the next leaf of Neve's borrowed jotter and wrote myself a heading:
'Stephen Twenty'.
I stared at the legend for a further ten minutes, harassing my memory for inspirational titbits. I wrote the number '1' in the margin and underlined it with a jaunty flourish. I looked at the clock.

Well, there were the drugs of course, but Stephen's vices had never really been a secret. In fact, now that I came to think of it, Stephen's vices probably accounted for the greater part of his charm. They imbued his character with that spontaneous, fearless, devil-may-care / devil-may-take allure which, while wetting the knickers of the pre-pubes', brought out the maternal instinct in those fans actually old enough to have one. For Christsake! The man's drug abuse had become a marketable commodity!

I put a deeply grooved slash through the subheading 'drugs' and wrote a fresh '1' beneath it. This was going to be harder than I had imagined.

When Neve arrived home at a little after eight P.M she found me slumped and napping amongst a mountainous pile of scrunched paper balls, which was only being kept on the table by the ring of soiled teacups that surrounded it.

"Reached your downfall yet?" she enquired sarcastically, peering over my rounded shoulders to sneak a preview of my day's toil. I guarded my work with my arms like a schoolboy hides his essay from prying plagiarists. "'Munday is a Wanker!'" she read through a crack in my barricade, "Is that it? Hardly groundbreaking stuff, is it. Do we really need a book to tell us that?"

"All right!" I rapped, my brain drained from a day spent pouring through all those painful and rarely visited memoirs, "you win! It's never gonna' hurt them. The worse they are, the better people like them."

I was unaware that she had moved up behind me until she dug her fingers into my stooped and aching shoulders and began to mould me like a potter at her wheel, one hand either side of my neck. She arched her hands, then gently, slowly, but firmly worked the knotted muscles in my neck until I started to purr like a pampered Persian.

"You're just not looking hard enough," she encouraged, "everybody has a secret. You've just got to find it. And if you can't find anything sordid enough, then elaborate on what you do know. It's all just a matter of perspective after all."

"I thought I'd just string some anecdotes together," I offered unenthusiastically, "you know: show them the way the crew see them, rather than the public."

"Boring," she berated, digging her thumbs deeper into the joints of my shoulders as if doing so might instigate a spark of inspiration in my tired mind, "It's got to be seedy; it's got to be damning. Think 'News of the World', think 'Jim Reaper'."

"Ow!"

"Sorry, you're not relaxing. Stop clenching."

"You're suggesting I do a 'Public Eye' on them?"

At the mere mention of the epitomous scandal mag 'Public Eye' my massage abruptly ceased.

"If that's what it takes," she replied noncommittally, suddenly losing interest in both the state of my muscles and my waning confidence alike.

I considered the suggestion for a frightening moment. Had I really sunk that low! This book was supposed to have been about me; the tragic story of my rise and fall, with my former associates receiving 'credit' purely for their contributions to my inauspicious demise. Instead I was being tempted to enter the realm of trashcan journalism: a blight that until recently, and along with every other public figure in western civilization, I had attempted to steer clearer of than Park lane with two hotels on it. Public Eye was to Journalism what Celine Dion was to easy listening. As a student of journalism, albeit briefly back in the mid seventies, we had learned to despise such cheap and transparent tactics.

'Public Eye', for those of you unaware of its poisonous reputation, is the definitive celebrity stalker magazine. But unlike its middle shelf paparazzi influenced rivals that glean their share of the crowded market from the abundance of wannabe somebodys who like nothing more than to snoop around the kitchens and Kharzis of the mildly famous, Public Eye's readership owes a little more to Sunday tabloid culture and the terminally plebian appetite for scandal and sleeze. In actuality, the publication that has made winning friends and influencing people into an extreme sport for the glitterati, (along the lines of bungee jumping and Russian roulette), tends to fall somewhere between the two camps. It does indeed like to show the insides of its victim's abodes, but rarely the areas that have been spruced and dressed for the occasion. Public Eye doesn't employ bored little daughters of influential families to interview their targets, they employ escorts and private detectives to worm their way into some poor sap's confidence with the sordid intention of revealing the truth behind their rival's own exposés.

It is a situation that reminds me of those all too obvious traffic speed cameras that proliferate our highways and byways.

They don't actually stop people from speeding - in fact often the reverse, in much the same way that Public Eye doesn't stop the elite from having their fun. Just as the wily driver learns to spot a 'hidden' camera or even to anticipate the likelihood of such by the camber of the road, adjusting his speed for the duration of the marked trap, then reverting to normal once confidence has been restored, so the wary starlet learns to spot that bogus groupie while still in control of his or her faculties. And just as the sneaky traffic cop with an unfulfilled ticket quota positions himself and his radar gun behind a tree a few yards past the marked trap, so Public Eye has learned to lure, trap and kill its intendeds with similarly sly tactics employed.

I asked myself again: Had I sunk that low ? I tried a different tack. How easily had I slipped back into life among the ordinaries? Could I ever be truly happy here? Could I live with second best? The answers to these questions confirmed my fear. Yes. I had sunk that low.

"Cheer up," she called, reappearing from the kitchen bearing two plates of oozing fish and chips, "Rome wasn't built in a day."

"True," I replied sardonically, "but the walls of Jericho came down in less."

"Eat your dinner," she said with a pseudo maternal lilt that confirmed a return to the mood that she had arrived home in. She smothered her wetly battered cod with a rather liberal dosing of malt vinegar. "I've got a chance for you to earn yourself some cash," she said, piling a steaming forkful of soggy chips into her erotically wetted mouth, then smiling as if in possession of some lascivious secret.

"Not another Barry Tring," I countered, perhaps a little unfairly, as I filled my own palette with a generous portion of working class fare, "'cause I couldn't go through that again." The bridge of my nose still ached from Saturday night's spanking, although the weald had begun to congeal. She ignored my pessimistic flippancy and said simply: "No Barry Tring," between mouthfuls. "On Saturday I'm going over to Camden to do a memorabilia fair: selling autographs and stuff. I was hoping you'd come with me; give me a hand. I'll pay you," she added, obviously interpreting my rapidly upwards-accelerating eyebrows.

"Neve!" I whined, picking a fishbone from my molars, "I am a star! People ask *me* for my autograph! You can't expect me to sit at a table selling other people's! Its ..."

"What? Demeaning for someone of your thoroughly reduced status?"

"It's immoral for a start!"

"So is living off a woman's earnings."

I took umbrage with this particular comment, my male chauvinist instincts calling arguments and counter-arguments to dispute her unfair and technically wrong accusation, though I stopped short of voicing them. I still didn't know what she did to earn her money.

"Anyway," she continued, as if morality issues were far beneath her concerns, "It's lucrative. It also requires little or no manual or mental strain. It's easy money." Neve finished her chips and pushed her knife and fork together on her plate. "Your choice," she said, "but I can't see any easier way of making money. Not unless you're ready to consider prostitution."

I picked at my remaining chips, all of which were now stone cold, and rediscovered another long forgotten childhood habit: that of dunking in tomato ketchup. It was just a small thing, but two decades of eating the right things in the right way in the right restaurants had all but stripped me of my appreciation of life's simpler moments.

"Look," she interrupted, attempting to clear away the plates before I had finished my pickled gherkin, "I'll do you a deal. Come with me tonight while I speculate and I'll let you keep your profits."

"What are you talking about?"

"Get your coat and a hat: we don't want you giving yourself away."

I wiped away the trail of pickling vinegar that had seeped from my lips and swallowed my last chunk of marinated marrow.

"Where are we going?"

"South bank," she replied, carelessly running the soiled plates under the hot tap, then dropping them into the plastic bowl full of suds and mugs, "London studios. Cameron Shah - the actor - is doing an interview with Parkinson."

"I thought he was dead."

(I don't quite remember whether her eyes really glinted at this point, but for arguments sake we'll say that they did.)

She smiled impishly.

"Not quite," she said, adjusting her comportment in the kitchen mirror, "It's his first interview since his triple bypass - and it's his only one - on doctor's orders. We might not get another chance to catch him."

So cool and calculated. I wondered just how many of my own fans had considered my life expectancy before passing me their autograph books.

I returned to the lounge suitably attired for clandestine encounter, still outfitted in dead Frank's castoffs.

"I've got to do something about these clothes," I moaned, having shoehorned my middle aged bulk into the much smaller man's weathered denim jacket and jeans.

"Well then," she congratulated herself, "perhaps you'll see the need for the expedient procurement of Wonga."

We left the sanctuary of the flat and followed along the same route that I had taken the day before: left into Brick lane and on toward the leather shop with the grammatically incorrect name.

Passing the point where I had turned right toward the market we continued down the east end's most famous lane and turned left a little farther on, arriving in less than ten minutes at Shoreditch tube station.

"He hasn't made a film in years," I eventually noted as we stepped out onto the district line platform, "surely he can't be worth much?"

At this point I was still labouring under the naive misapprehension that actor's signatures were only worth as much as their most recent hits, as I was about to discover in spades was the rule for pop stars.

"The autograph market is a shrewd one," she answered mechanically, as if leading a school party around a museum. The doors parted on the newly arrived train and we stepped inside our carriage.

"There are a lot of variables."

"Oh?"

"Such as how popular the artist is; how accessible they are; are they A list or B list; how approachable they are and, most importantly, how alive they are."

I decided to cut to the chase. I found it uncomfortable to think of the ageing thespian in terms of commodity, but Neve was right:

needs must.

"So what's he worth?"

"Today? About forty quid - if we're lucky."

"And I suppose 'lucky' means 'if someone's prepared to pay it'?"

"You're catching on."

"So how much do you make in a day, then?"

(Keep going, I thought, while she's prepared to divulge. Who knew when I might get another chance?)

"Well Camden's usually a good one," she replied, a little more candidly than she had when I had quizzed her about her other ventures, "we should do a couple'a ton. I've got seventy five in advance orders that came in over the net this week for a start."

"And they would be for the good Mister Shah, right?"

"God, no! We might be stuck with them for a while, yet."

(If I had imagined that sanguine glint earlier, then I certainly wasn't imagining it now.)

She turned to face me and smiled coquettishly, saying: "But then again ..."

The leathered visage of a sympathetically lit, yet still air-brushed Cameron Shah stared out at me from the page, his supercilious monochrome scowl advertising his unquestionable suitability for whichever dastardly role was currently on offer. Shah had played everything from vampires to mummies, from jackbooted nazi warlords to cannibalistic serial killers. He had even been cast by Brannagh as an unlikely Moses in his luvvy remake of 'The Ten Commandments': a part for which he had so obviously not been born to play. His face was that of nightmares. Those hollow eyes, sculpted cheekbones, and eyebrows so feral that no amount of pan stick could make him look more like a ghoul than the good lord had already intended. So it had been with piteous surprise that I had noted just how innocuous and frail the poor old sod had looked in the flesh. True, he had been the victim of ailing health and frog-marching years, but I had seen nothing remaining of that heart stopping terror that celluloid had so effortlessly projected, in the eyes of the mustachioed Egyptian.

I had followed my lieges instructions to the letter, approaching the actor slowly, but purposefully as he had stepped from the side door of the studio, aided by his 'virgin sacrifice' PA and a vat bred studio security blimp. I had been politely insistent, as I had held out the two 'A4' black and white prints that she had given me from her file. 'No dedication', she had insisted, just get his name and make sure that he dates it.

Shah had been nothing short of a gentleman as he had bent to sign his name for his nameless fan, putting me to shame as I recollected my own customary arrogance in similar situations in the past. He had thanked me for my concern over his health and had assured me that he would be back on the set of 'Leachman II' within the month. He had chastised his grumbling assistant as she had led him to his car, herding him into the night as if it had been twenty years earlier, when the night's fan base would have consisted of rather more than one soul.

He hadn't recognised me and for that I was grateful. We had met only once before - I believe in 1985, when he had given a cameo performance in one of The Moonies over indulgent promo' videos in our attempt to out camp 'Duran Duran' and 'Adam and the Ants'. For the first time in years I had felt pity for somebody other than myself. I had also felt oddly humbled in the presence of what I considered to be 'a real star'.

I had watched them go, his PA rather unsympathetically forcing their speed across the car park, and had therefore been witness to the old roués final death scene; clutching his chest and dropping quite pathetically to the tarmac just beside his blacked out Mercedes. And although he had died much more spectacularly a hundred times before, the blood curdling shrill of his assistant more than made up for his ham demise in sheer melodrama alone. The blimp had dropped his charge and grabbed for his walkie-talkie, punctuating his SOS with panic stricken bellows for 'help' from the few passing stragglers still leaving the Festival Hall along the road. I had been moving to their aid when I had felt the instant pull of an arm that had locked itself beneath my own: Neve's arm, and with it the sensible 'not quite the kind of publicity you need, Sylvie. Time to go.'

I had remonstrated indignantly at the time, but in retrospect I suppose I knew that she was right.

The following morning's breakfast news had carried the story as its leader with initial reports blaming Shah's sudden expiration on a spontaneous heart attack, probably brought about by the shock of seeing a pre-publication copy of the forthcoming edition of 'Public Eye' magazine taped to the window of his car! The front cover in question had featured Shah himself in a none too flattering pose strapped to some kind of DIY 'rack' with nothing but a boxed exclamation mark to cover the actors indignity. The headline had promised a tour of Shah's Monte Carlo home, paying special attention to the 'dungeon' and the literature collections. The Police had appealed for witnesses, but although Neve had confessed to me that night on our way home that she had seen everything from her vantage point on the opposite side of Upper Ground; up to and including the mystery figure that the security cameras had also recorded taping the offending article in place, she had adamantly refused to call the special hotline for which an emergency number had been flashed across our TV screen.

"How much?"

"Sorry?"

"Your 'Cameron Shah'?"

I focused on the fat, sweaty mound of anorak that was obliviously threatening to flatten my precariously set tressle table in The Camden Centre, Kings Cross. I prayed that her calf muscles were sufficiently reliable to hold her unfeasible weight for just long enough for her to waddle on to the next stall as I dragged my mind back to the matter in hand.

"Hundred and twenty," I replied, turning my peculiarly popular prize to face my prospective punter. "It's the last picture he ever signed," I waffled on, "it's dated, see?"

"Such a tragedy," the beanbag replied, "but then - I don't think he's really dead, do you?"

I winced at the thought of Shah's final moments on this mortal coil. I still felt like the angel of death a week later. I was, after all, the last person that he ever met. "Well if he wasn't *then* - he will be now after a week in a deep freeze." I snapped, understandably touchy, I felt, about the incident.

"No," she whispered, conspiratorially, winking an eye that was in danger of disappearing into her bulging red cheeks, never to be seen again, "I mean - I don't think he was ever really alive."

I looked at the fruitcake as she loomed across the table, her udders brushing against my display and dislodging a signed cricket ball that bounced onto the floor to disappear among the hordes of misfits that crowded the memorabilia fair. I had spent an entire morning manning the stall, fending off the terminally lonely and the day releasers who seemed to treat the poor, anchored traders as if they were attending some sort of psychotherapist's convention; ranting total bollocks about this film and that television programme and its affect on their quite plainly disturbed lives. Who gave a toss whether Bogarde said 'play it again Sam' in 'Casablanca' or just 'play it again' ? Who gave a flying fuck whether Julia Roberts used stunt tits in 'Pretty Woman', or from which episode on Captain Kirk started wearing a toup'!

"Are you buying or not?" I asked reasonably

"Eighty."

"What ? No. A hundred and twenty."

"Ninety."

"Are you deaf as well as ugly? It was his last autograph ! You can wait around all day for his resurrection, love, but I've got a sneaky feeling you'll be wasting your time!"

"Ninety five."

"One ten."

"D'you take Visa?"

"No. Cash only. It says so on the sign."

"Well I'll think about it. I've still got more to see."

And she left.

"Tea, Sylvie?"

"For Christ sake Neve," I rounded, "Where've you been? I've been getting my brains sucked out by morons for hours!"

She passed me a sticky polystyrene cup, not quite full of piss-weak tea and stepped around the table to join me, placing the Botham autographed ball back on its podium.

"Just checking out the competition," she gloated, scanning my sales pad for results, "How're you doing?"

"I've sold a Babs Windsor and an Obi Wan Kenobi."

"Oh, well done. How much?"

"Sixty for Obi Wan, and haggled over a fiver for Babs."

"Not bad. Any interest in your Shahs?"

"Don't." I warned her emphatically, "Everyone wants them, but no-one's willing to pay. D'you think if I told them I killed him they'd be more interested?"

"Patience," she soothed, stroking the back of my hand with hers, "We're too near the door for early sales," she took a tentative sip of her tea, "they barge in, do a couple of circuits, then when they've sussed out who's got what they start flashing their cash. And remember," she added, poking me with a gloved finger, "No deals before noon."

"I don't like it," I said, gagging on my first gulp of the beige water and screwing up my face instinctively.

"Sorry, it was out of the machine."

"Not the tea," I spat, though she knew perfectly well what I meant, "I mean this!"

I gestured a little dramatically around the room.

"This whole caboodle," I ranted, "It stinks! And so do the punters."

"'Ordinaries'?" she mocked, but I was ready for her sleight.

"These aren't ordinaries," I corrected, (knowing her opinion on my less offensive title for those people not of money and style; those that the impolite of my class would have simply called 'proles' and been done with,) "There's nothing 'ordinary' about two blokes walking 'round in broad daylight wearing nylon wigs, plastic pasties stuck to their foreheads and insisting on speaking nothing but 'Klingon'! These people are sick, Neve. And what we're doing is even sicker!"

"How so?"

"Cameron Shah is barely cold and we're already trying to profit from his 'fortuitous' death! Shit. If I didn't know better I'd think you'd planned his heart attack just so's you could hoik the price of his scribble!"

"How much?"

My speech was interrupted by the return of the bubble woman.

"I told you!" I shot, still angry with my foisted partner, "It's a hundred and twenty quid. Sterling! Not intergalactic credit!"

"I'll take it," she said, rolling forward a wad of crisp twenty pound notes and snatching up her prize before I could change my mind. "It's a bargain," she extolled, "there's one over there for two hundred!"

I cursed under my breath as my satisfied customer waddled away with her picture. Neve just smiled, accepted the cash and passed it to me.

"Don't worry," she said quietly, "he's a friend of mine. I put our second Shah on Damon's stall and we've got his second Elvis over here. That's how we set the prices. 'Makes them think they're getting value for money."

"I don't like this atall, Neve. People sign this stuff in good faith. They don't expect it to be sold on for profit."

"Everyone's got to make a living."

"But this isn't your living, is it," I replied, seeing a possible opening and finally having the balls to use it, "This isn't all you do, is it." (I took a second swig as I composed myself,) "What do you do?"

"How much?"

A tall thin 'man' with long, straight, (obviously dyed) jet black hair and trousers so painfully tight that his bollocks stood prouder than the baubles on a Christmas tree, had stopped in front of our stall and picked up an old vinyl LP that I had not previously seen and was dangling it by its corner between his fake fingernails. It was an autographed copy of Henri Blutoe's 'Everything You Call A Flaw'.

"Sixty pounds, sir," Neve replied, spontaneously rescued from my leading question.

The deviant pouted and placed the record back on the table.

"What about this one?" he enquired, hoisting what turned out to be a White label copy of 'Some Young Moon's' 'Torn Shirts EP'. Splashed across its psychedelic front cover I was surprised to see my own autograph in slightly smudged royal blue marker. Neve avoided my gimlet glare.

"I'll do it for forty if you take the pair," she said, still not catching my eye.

"What if I only want the Blutoe?"

"Sixty. Take it or leave it." He looked across at me, but I kept my expression as implacable as possible in an attempt to mask the broiling indignation within. "I'll think about it," he eventually minced, returning the disc and slinking along to our neighbouring stall.

"I'll get us some sarnies," I heard her squeak, as she disappeared yet again leaving me none the wiser.

Chapter Four
"Ask The Family"

"It's up to you, Sly," Joe challenged, passing the onus for the decision back to me, "Your vote carries two, as per the charter. It's your band. If you think we'll do better with her, then I'm behind you all the way, but you've seen Lakhi play - he wipes the floor with her!" Joe was right, of course. I knew that. But this was Neve's future we were talking about. There was no doubt in my mind that this band was going to break the big time. In one week's time we would begin recording our first single. This was it. This was what we'd all been working for. We were going to be rich ; We were going to be famous. Could I really cut her out now? All right, so Lakhi Corner, the keyboard genius from 'The Plants', could knock spots off her dubious talents, but so what! What did we need a keyboard player for anyway? We were a punk band! Neve was a sodding guitarist and a better one than her other replacement: Stephen bloody Twenty! We didn't need Lakhi. I didn't want Lakhi in the band. But what could I say? If I said that we didn't need a keyboard player, (Which was the truth) then I was condemning her anyway. 'Deadweight' Stephen called her, but of course he hadn't said that while he was fucking her!

True, she had started to cramp our style with her mother hen attitude toward post performance lig promiscuity, but was that any reason to cut her out? Stephen thought so, but then wasn't that just a guilty conscience on his part for having been caught with his knob out in the back of Joe's transit? Why couldn't she have just left of her own accord after that sordid little incident? But if Neve Crilly was anything, it was stubborn.

I couldn't do it. I couldn't sign the warrant. She was my friend and … and I loved her. I had done ever since that first stolen kiss, and I loved her despite the fact that she had given her innocence to … him. As it so often did when faced with a decision of any kind, my mind returned me to that July afternoon when we had all finished our last day at school. (I hate this memory in particular and even now, after all that's happened this past year, I am still haunted by its spectre.)

It's 1974. We're all supposed to be meeting in the rec' at six o'clock, 'Wavy Line' carrier bags chinking with bottles of Woodpecker cider for our party. I arrive early, hoping I might catch up with Neve before Stephen arrives and wedges his tongue into her delicate mouth for the duration. I'm in luck. I can hear her giggling on the other side of the artificial mound. She's probably brought that little blonde with her that Morris fancies. I wriggle to the crest of the hill on my belly hoping to surprise them and peer down the other side to the spot where that old sewer pipe used to be. She's there all right, lying on her back in the dandelions; her white lace knickers dangling redundantly from her stilettoed right foot. Adele isn't with her, but Stephen is. He's lying on top of her, one grubby hand thrust beneath her school blouse, groping her budding breast; his spray on black jeans loosened just enough to reveal the crack of his hairy arse as he pumps like an overworked steam piston, filling her virgin body with his raison detré.

She sees me watching and is instantly embarrassed. She tries to struggle free, but her spent beau still has a few press ups to impress her with. Then he sees me and he begins to laugh, slow to replace his angry organ: seemingly eager to show me the true extent of his power over me. Neve recovers her modesty and buttons her blouse, but it's too late. I've seen it all and I'll never forget what I saw; like staring at a loved ones innards during a life saving operation - some things just aren't meant to be seen.

The only good thing that came from this experience was that I finally realized the limit to Stephen Twenty's dominion and it was a turning point in our relationship. He had no power - only the power that I gave him. Neve was the pivot - she always had been. It was Stephen's hold over *her* that was disempowering me. Without her we were equals. And that was when I knew what I had to do.

I stared at her across the crowded bar of the Fiddler, watching the pulse of her tight little arse as it wriggled with her giggles inside her skin tight PVC trousers. I watched her as her left hand snaked down beneath the waistband of Stephen's leathers; I watched him turn and tweak her crotch; saw him drip his slimy tongue into her multiply pierced ear.

"OK", I heard myself say, as I took a long gulp of bottled lager, "but

I'm not going to be the one that tells her."

"No problem," my manager replied, "You won't regret it!"

Joe patted my shoulder paternally, put his jug back on the bar and moved to intercept his quarry.

"Just get it over with before I wake up," I added and turned away, those regrets already acknowledged in the pit of my stomach.

Did she know, I wondered? Had she any idea how it had really happened? Did she realize that I had sold her out because I couldn't stand seeing them together; seeing him ill treat her and abuse her in front of me while I stood in impotent silence, too weak to intercede; to tell her how I really felt about her? Had she had any idea of how I had felt about her all those years ago?

And if she hadn't, then should I enlighten her now and risk the fragile alliance that we had only recently achieved? What had I to gain by doing so, but a little belated self-respect; a slight easing of the conscience with which I had tortured myself for over a quarter of a century?

I shifted on the uncomfortable dining chair and tried to refocus on the page in front of me, realizing that, yet again, I had allowed my mind to wander from the job at hand.

I was still a lifetime from completing my book. Over the past few months I had tried to discipline myself, rising with Neve, to shower, breakfast and be sitting pen in hand in front of my work as she left the flat each morning at 7:45, but although I had scribed a lifetime's notes into two exercise books, I was still to uncover the secrets of focus and anchor. I had begun with a single stream of consciousness; a list of memories, jumbled and only half-baked, but as I had worked, so a game plan had slowly started to evolve. I had set my memoir into vague chapters: one for each member of the band, one for Joe Munday and one; a kind of prologue that I intended as a potted history of The Moonies, (as related from the inside) that would chart the bands rise from the halcyon days of mid seventies pub punk to our stadium filling, chart topping status of the late eighties /early nineties. I was also planning an epilogue of sorts, detailing my own ignoble demise and admitting my own greed inspired folly that had brought down the band at its peak. I had to. I couldn't leave my own record unblighted - not if I intended my work to be taken seriously and not just to sound like the bitter diatribe and desperate attempt to cash in on my associates success that it so clearly was.

Apart from the plan, which took up a bare ten sides of ring bound notebook (if you discounted the many crossings out and torn out pages) I had fleshed only one chapter in any detail and that was headed 'Morris Yussof'. Morris and I went back a long way. All the way, in fact. Our parents had introduced us as far back as primary school - our fathers having shared an office all those years ago.

Character annihilation had come easily, as, although we had known each other for a lifetime, I don't remember ever having counted the little shit among my friends. He had just always been there, like a big red birthmark on your face that you can do nothing but learn to live with - he had always been no more than a skin away!

Morris was a snide: a trait that seemed to have developed as an antithesis to his angelic, even cherubic, pre-thirteen year old face. All blondes look angelic at that age, particularly the ones with the round cheeks, button noses and freckles, and it doesn't take the genius amongst them long to realize that that look can be their passport to unchallenged innocence. With the arrival of puberty, however, his naïf qualities had upped and deserted him overnight to be replaced with what I had always considered to be a meritous dose of oil and acne. His effeminately overlong eyelashes, which had won him the hearts of every mother in town, had been hidden behind a lazy-eye patch and a pair of skyblue national health spectacles. Morris had become the man in the iron mask. Justice had been served. But despite the loss of his unfair advantage; this presumed air of holy virtuosity, Morris had still somehow managed never to be the one caught in possession of the incriminating evidence. Just once would have been nice! Just to watch the bastard squirm! But no - it was like some kind of 'superpower' with him: the ability to always have the perfect alibi.

His second greatest flaw was of course his ability to be led. I will never forget Joe's biting remark at his audition that Morris could not be any more easily led if he could have been saddled, bridled and hitched to a hay cart. (I liked that one, but if it was going to make it into the book then it would have to become my own observation.)

I could list the instances of our (barely adequate) bass player's professional snideyisms for days, but this was to be a single chapter

assassination, not a biography, and so I opted for the crime that would tip the scales for the majority of the jurors. I read back what I had written thus far:
'In relating this particular tale it is necessary for the reader to be familiar with a few things about 'the tour'.

1)   Before embarking on 'the tour' the road manager must complete a 'carnet'. (This is an inventory, which must list every single item of equipment that is to be transported from territory to territory for use by the band and its crew.)
Customs officials at each border passed are obliged to check this manifest in order to ensure that equipment is not being transported for the purpose of trade or the avoidance of duties. (Needless to say, this legal formality is rarely enforced and even if it is - is rarely thorough.)

2.   It is the responsibility of the road manager to ensure that all equipment is checked, maintained and counted prior to and after each performance.

In September 1991 'Some Young Moon' were completing the last leg of an exhaustive nine-month world tour to promote their album: 'Chicken Feed'.
On leaving Amsterdam on the 15th, bass player Morris made a complaint to long-term Moonies road manager Roger 'Diz' Gillespie about a 'buzzing' noise that he had noticed coming from his amp. When the problem was not instantly rectified Morris, sent out for a new one to replace the troubled unit and was duly 'reprimanded' for causing a carnet discrepancy. Diz insisted that the old amp be dumped before crossing what was probably the strictest border control in Scandinavia, but Morris refused to leave his trusty 'Orange' behind and had it loaded back onto the lorry against Diz's wishes.
The tour moved in to Denmark; the carnet was glanced at by Danish customs and the amp was duly forgotten. It would probably have remained so too if it had not been for the fact that, on arrival back in England, both Stephen and Morris, along with two roadies and five British army reserves, were taken into custody and charged with affray, following a drunken rampage that had lasted almost the

entire eighteen hour ferry crossing from Esberg to Harwich. As a consequence the band and crew were also held by British customs while the carnet and corresponding kit were checked with a fine-toothed comb.

It was at this late stage that Diz remembered the amp discrepancy and pointed it out, hoping that his honesty would help to placate the officious scrutineers. But instead, on closer inspection of the broken equipment, British customs officials discovered a cocaine haul that was later rather publicly overestimated to hold a street value of half a million pounds inside the gutted machine. As the amp's owner, Morris was questioned, but, as ever, his subliminal innocence saw him released when he convinced the court that he was merely a 'user' and that Diz was in fact his dealer. Stephen, rather spectacularly, chose this moment to reveal his own insatiable habit for the white powder and also lied under oath to protect his colleague. Roger Gillespie spent the following eight years in Wormwood Scrubs for a crime that everybody knew he did not commit. As ever, our boy Morris came out unscathed, (though he has admitted to receiving a more stringent than necessary body search every time he re-enters the country.)

Was it enough, I wondered? And where was my proof? I had seen the mechanically incompetent Morris, (the man who I'd once heard call a roadie to untangle his DI lead for him) poking around inside the aforesaid amp' with a screwdriver on the day of its reported death, but without a corroborative witness or a photograph I suppose my tale could be considered libelous at this early draft.

I decided to rewrite it anyway. I could spice it up a little, perhaps drop in a mention of Diz's staunch anti drug stance, (a reputation that his counsel was keen to impress during the trial, but which any witness wishing to stay in the employ of the Munday corporation had been quick to rout.)

And was it formal enough?

This was a whole world away from songwriting. Had I the style to sell my message, or was I going to need a ghostwriter to smooth my delivery?

I decided not to worry too much at this stage. The important thing was that I should get the relevant details out of my head and onto the page. Any interested publishers could tweak my style at a later date - after I had cashed my life saving advance !

As I picked up my pen to begin the seedier draft, I found myself startled by the sound of a key turning in the locked front door. My eyes flashed toward the chintzy carriage clock on the mantelpiece above the gas fire. She was early. An extremely unusual four hours early.

The door squeaked open to reveal the shape of a man; and not a young man, flat capped, donkey jacketed and heavily listing to the left - presumably due to the weight of the 'every little helps' carrier bag that was whitening the knuckles of his left hand. As I searched my memory bank for a possible name match for the age worn gent that I almost recognised, he suddenly broke into a broad and gap toothed grin.

"Sylvie?" he enquired somewhat hopefully, "Sylvie Quiggley?" The faded Dubliner accent gave him away the moment he spoke my name.

"Mister Crilly ?"

"Fergus."

"Fergus. How the devil are you?" I ventured, unsure whether a protocol existed for greeting the sire of a lover.

"Well, son." Fergus Crilly replied, pumping my hand with his own free hand as if winding the starter on an antique car, all the while dripping rivulets of rainwater from his dusty jacket onto the newest of Neve's carpets. His turf accountants mind matched two and two, calculated the form and offered him reasonable odds for his next assumption: "So," he announced, smiling paternally (I felt) and holding my fingers in a 'Welcome-to-the-family / Watch-your-step' kind of vice like grip, "You two finally got it together then?"

He chuckled to himself and released my numbing hand. "Feck," he laughed, "I wish I'd taken that bet of your father's back in '64! Jesus! You look terrible! 'Beard looks like a twat!"

"Thanks, Mister Crilly, I really needed that."

He hefted his shopping bag onto the table, scattering and crumpling my loose leaves indiscriminately as he tried to persuade it to sit upright.

"I'm wrong, aren't I?" he corrected himself, his nicotine stained smile waning as he scrutinised my reaction, "she's hiding you, isn't she? I read the papers Syl, son; you lost your job, didn't you."

Thoughts of Morris Yussof quickly evaporated as a new thought struck my opportunist mind. I replied by way of a gurn, not ready

to commit to either suggestion nor to deny them while I attempted
to plot a game plan for information retrieval.

"I'm not using her, Fergus - if that's what you're thinking," I insisted. "I love her; I always have done. Just took me a long time to
admit it."

"Glad to hear it," he said, his smile shifting once again, "I think this
calls for a drink and I don't suppose we'll find any in here. You'd
better come with me … son."

"So when did you last speak to your father?"

Fergus supped at his Guinness, then, wiping away his white froth
moustache with the back of his hand, dared me to answer his question. I refused to meet his gaze, staring instead through the mirrored tiles on the wall behind the bar until my reflection began to
morph into that of the man that I had renounced all those years
ago. Or was that what I really looked like now ? Were those world-
weary eyes and that alcohol beleaguered complexion really mine
and not the man's who had driven my mother into her too early
grave? The lips moved, though I wasn't aware of the sensation as I
heard him impart the only useful snippet of advice that I had ever
heard him render: "Learn a trade, son", he had said, "as a fallback.
Just in case you don't make it as a rockstar." I bet the old bastard
was laughing now. I had taken it as a lack of faith at the time and
left the poly' the very next day. I wasn't going to start doubting that
decision now. I formed the mental construct of a cartoon safe and
locked my memory back in its box. I squinted at the image, but it
refused to become my mind's eye vision of myself: the young, successful, self made me that had hung on so many bedroom walls,
what - a lifetime ago?

"Nineteen seventy five," I eventually replied, quite defiantly pro-
voking his challenge, "at the funeral."

"Wasn't the last time he saw you, you know."

"Really, Fergus," I said dismissively, although I have to admit that my
interest had been slightly piqued by this unexpected tidbit, "I
appreciate your interest, but as far as I'm concerned - I buried them
both that day."

He raised his hands in surrender and smiled resignedly, saying: "fair
enough, son. Fair enough, but I'd 've never forgiven me self if 'n I

hadn't at least 've tried. Now," he began provocatively, ignoring his previous line of enquiry as I had vehemently suggested that he ought. I surprised myself with my own unanticipated disappointment that the pensioner had not put up a better fight. "How is my daughter?" he asked.

"When did you last see her?" I countered, outwardly quite innocently, but inwardly clutching at a chance to cross-examine our new subject.

"Ooh..." he pondered, tapping his yellowed stubby finger against his lip, "six months - no - seven?"

Shortly before my own demise, then. My suspicions were confirmed. For some reason I felt inclined to trust the old man over his daughter, though I couldn't have explained my reasoning. I could recall at least four occasions over the last couple of months when Neve had 'just popped round' to see her dad. I had had no reason to question her honesty ... until now, though I wasn't about to trust him quite that far.

"I didn't take to the Italian," he explained, walking straight into my trap, "fella thought he was mafiosa." He chuckled into his diminishing pint and I fished around in my trouser pocket for the loose change with which to replenish it.

"Frank?" I prompted, snaring a two-pound piece between thumb and forefinger and passing it across to the barman, inclining my eyebrows toward the Irishman's dwindling reserves by way of an order.

"Tha's the fellow. Nasty piece of work was Frankie."

"Violent?"

Fergus narrowed his eyes before replying, as if reciting his answer from a pre-written script: "Of the tongue ... mainly." He exchanged glasses with the barman and I sipped cautiously from my tumbler, all too aware that I couldn't afford a second shot.

"'Made her feel like turd in his treads," he continued, warming to his theme, "'don't know what my Nevie saw in 'im. Slimy little bastard - didn't deserve her."

"So what happened to him?" I pushed, but regretted my failing patience as soon as I saw his expression.

"She didn't tell you?"

"No. Not really."

"Hmm..." he considered, then belched quite proudly in that way that the over seventy's believe they have a war weary right to, "maybe she doesn't want you to know."

I didn't know how to phrase the explanation that she had given me. On the one hand it seemed a trifle insensitive to discuss over a pint, (if indeed it was true), and on the other it seemed a little ludicrous if it was, (as I expected) an out and out lie.

I examined the set of my opponent, attempting to weigh possible parries against probable counters. I knew that I might not get another chance to find out about my friend's missing years and knew that I had to chance my luck or forever wonder.

I have always been of the opinion that in any given situation there is a perfect combination of words that can tip the balance of an argument to one's favour. It's simply a matter of finding them. Unfortunately, and despite this fervent belief, the right set of words in the right order rarely enter my head at the right time.

"She told me she'd murdered him." I said and edged back a touch while I gauged his response. Fergus supped noisily at his Guinness, betraying his knowledge by his simple failure to respond. He removed his cap and wiped back his non-existent hair, replaced the cap and cleared his throat. "Alright," he said, "me'be you've a right. As I said: Frankie Capaldi was a bastard. She married him too quickly. T'was a rebound thing, y'know. She was getting a name for herself as something of a 'groupie'. All them amateur popstars she'd been seeing - that 'Twenty' bloke - never took to him neither. So she switches to amateur gangsters and carves herself a new reputation as a wannabe moll.

"Oh, he was a charmer alright. Could've charmed the Virgin Mary out of 'er kecks, that one, but he was an evil git. Pulled her down to his level, so he did, then, once he'd got her where he wanted her, he stripped away her confidence. She wouldn't even breath without the say so of Frankie Capaldi - couldn't even fart without his consent. You know," he said, staring at me through narrowed lids as if the fault for his daughter's degradation lay with me, "after little Sylvia was born -"

"Hold on?" I interrupted, holding up my flattened palm like a whistle baring Italian traffic cop, "'Sylvia'?"

"Their daughter," he explained, "You didn't know?"

"I... didn't know her name, no."

"Ah. Well, after Sylvia came along Nevie was diagnosed with acute

postnatal depression. Personally I didn't agree, mind. I'm of the opinion that the depression was more the result of Frankie's mother moving in to help with the baby. Consequently, my Nevie spent the first nine months of her daughter's life in a psychiatric ward."
While he let me absorb this revelation Fergus absorbed the majority of his remaining beverage.
"Shit 'im up a bit, that - Frankie, I mean. After she came home he calmed down a bit. Couldn't lose his rag in front of his precious daughter. That was when he got himself in a spot of bother."
"Bother?" I queried, now well and truly gripped by the old man's tale.
"Stolen gear. He was fencing for a mate of his, ooh-what was his name? Fat bloke; wife like a parrot -"
"Tring."
"Tha's the fellow. You know him?"
"We've...met."
"Hmm. Well you see, Frankie was something of a drinker."
Fergus punctuated his point with his empty jug slapped against the bar top. This time I made no move to replenish him and discretely indicated my own empty shot glass.
"Sorry, son," he apologised, "forgot about your... ´circumstances`."
He pulled a crisp twenty from a battered leather wallet that he kept in his shirt, beneath both a waistcoat and a jacket. He hailed our host then continued with his story: "Of course, you'll understand my Nevie's feelings on that subject - (What with her mother and all), So,"
(I felt the switching on of a few more bulbs as I listened on, "Not a bright spark our Frankie, never was one to know when to shut his mouth. He gets talking to a couple of wide boys in his local - starts making out he's a bigger fish than he really is. It's the drink talking of course. Trouble is, see, those wide boys were CID.
"Well Frankie shits 'imself. He sings like your proverbial canary and your fella' Tring gets his collar felt. He takes to the bottle big time after that and the verbal gets physical soon after. Nevie plays her trump card and threatens to tell Tring who grassed him if he doesn't stop hurting her. That's when he breaks her arm. Poor Nevie. Poor kid was desperate. She thought Tring's boys would rough 'im up a bit, you know: teach 'im a lesson. So two weeks go by; Frankie comes out one morning, gets in his car. Straps little Sylvia into the

back; keys in ignition: Boom!" Fergus gestured with his outflung arms, inciting a few heads to turn further down the bar.

"Shit," I said, not quite anticipating the story's explosive conclusion and wiping spilled Guinness from my jacket collar.

"Mild, Sylvie. That's why she thinks she murdered them. Spent the following two years back on the psycho ward."

"And when was all this, Fergus?"

Fergus finished his pint and stepped down from his stool.

"Ten years? Ten years come October. But she's put her life back together now. It's all behind her. Look after each other, son. You've made an old man very happy. Oh," he suddenly thought as he rebuttoned his donkey jacket and straightened his cap, "When you're ready, he's still where he always was ..."

Chapter Five
"If You Can't Beat 'em"

The dreary twilight of early autumn had given itself up to a premature nightfall as the gnawing, whipping wind heralded the onset of
another downpour. I hastened my pace and turned up the collar
of Frank's fur trimmed camel frockcoat for meager protection
against the conspiring elements as I scurried back along Bethnal
Green road toward my appointment with a bowl full of Maris
Pipers.

Fergus Crilly had declined my generous offer of dinner with myself
and Neve; particularly generous on my part considering how little
money I had managed to accrue from my now regular Sunday
morning stint on Neve's celebrity autograph pitch in old
Spitalfields market, citing the need to return home before his wife
- a sentiment that I could empathise with as I felt myself fumbling
with the lock on the street door. Not that I expected to be chastised
for my mid afternoon tipple - not that I thought for a moment that
Neve would be angry with me for spending my own money. No. It
was just that I didn't want her to think that I had been slacking. I
didn't want her to think that I'd become too comfortable. I hadn't,
god help me I hadn't! I just found it so difficult to show gratitude
for her unconditional support in this most difficult of situations
and honour - yes honour - decreed that nipping out for an afternoon jar was taking the piss.

I dallied with the idea of telling her about my meeting with her
father. Part of me thought that it might - I don't know - bring us
closer together ? She had coldly refused my sexual advances since
that first night, though we still shared the same bed at this point,
and I secretly craved that initial intimacy in this, my hour of need.
As I reached the top of the stairs, though, my mind was made up. I
didn't trust her anymore, not completely anyway. Not because of
the Frank thing - I couldn't blame her for that, no. It was that niggling doubt over her working day and now nights too, (since
Fergus had blown her alibi) that just wouldn't go away.

"Where've you been?" she snapped, without looking round, as I entered the flat to find her stood pouring over my morning's work in the lounge.

"Just ... nipped out for some fags." I bluffed, presuming that she had beaten me home by mere minutes as she still had on her coat and hat, and the Chinese takeaway that she had obviously brought in with her was still sat steaming in its bag on the kitchen worktop. She could never have known how long I had been gone, I reasoned - sound thinking, except for one minor detail.

"And a drink," she guessed, "With my dad!"

I followed her gaze toward the spilled carrier bag that Fergus had forgotten to call back for and my heart sank. I had lied and she had caught me out. How could I now accuse her of dishonesty with me? For a moment I was tempted to continue with some futile prevarication, but I could sense the coming of one of her tidal mood swings and so opted for a pre-rage lashing that could be more easily rectified later.

"Yes or no?"

"Is that a problem?" Question with question: a politician's response: Don't allow the spectre of blame to settle too easily.

"But you weren't going to tell me?"

She'd played this game before, but that didn't mean she was going to win.

"What makes you say that?"

I pulled a cigarette from its packet without revealing its solitary comrade and thus exposing my original lie and lit it between my teeth.

Neve turned back to face my work and I jumped in with a pre-emptive parry: "I invited him back for dinner," I said, presuming her potential anger to have been quelled by my quick thinking, "'didn't think you'd mind -'"

"I don't," she rapped, "so why lie, Sylvie? What did he tell you, eh? What was it that your tiny mind couldn't cope with ? 'He tell you about Frank, eh ? How he drove me into a nuthouse ? And Sylvia ? Did he tell you how I killed my baby?"

"He, er ..." I blustered, taken unawares by her sudden attack, "he touched on them, yeah..."

"I bet he did ! So now you know, huh? Now you know all about me? And after all I've done for you - you couldn't have just let me be; let me tell you in my own time - if and when I'd decided to trust you?"

I had lost control of the situation by this point; I'd touched a nerve. I had unwittingly lit the metaphorical fuse of her disproportionate temper. This would have been a good time to back down, possibly, in retrospect, to get out. But oh foolish me.

"Now you just wait a fucking minute!" I countered, my own diva tantrum puckered and poised, "I haven't pressed you to tell me anything that you weren't ready to tell! Like," (go for broke, I thought - or rather I didn't think), " Where you go all day; how you earn your money ! You told me you'd murdered your family. Did I run away? Did I press you for information ? Eh ? No! I trusted you ! -"

"You didn't exactly have a choice, as I remember!"

She pulled off her hat and tossed it onto the armchair, slid her arms out of her coat and let it fall to the floor. She ruffled her brim marked hair like a dog would shake itself after coming in from the rain.

"I don't have to explain myself to you, Sylvie Quiggley. This is my home - I'm the one holding all the cards here ! If you don't like that, then you know your options. Now get the plates before my dinner goes cold!"

We had eaten in silence, neither of us apparently having anything more to add to the boundary-marking dispute that would change the essence of our relationship from that point forward.   The evening had dragged in front of the television set, Neve flicking between banalities every time that she thought that I might be getting into some working class game show or mind numbing sitcom that she had alighted on; neither of us prepared to break the impasse and admit to the need for sleep. It was as if the longer we could each stay awake, the more it confirmed our positions. To accept the weakness of fatigue would somehow be to accept defeat in the eyes of the other.

I forced my lids to remain open, even as I felt myself drifting toward unconsciousness. I could not afford to let her win this battle. I was better than her. I had achieved. It was bad enough that I had to accept her help, I would not let her treat me as an inferior.

"I'm going to bed," she suddenly announced, lobbing the television remote in my general direction as she went, "You coming?"

"In a minute," I said, cursing myself for my stubbornness and feeling that she had somehow turned her eventual defeat into a win, though my sleep deprived brain was unable to offer a satisfactory explanation for the phenomena at this juncture.

I allowed long enough for her to fall asleep before joining her in what seemed these days to be too small a bed. I slept fitfully, my mind unable to leave our argument to rest. By the morning I had what I felt to be a solid case for the defence and, with the plaintiff suitably rested, all I needed was the chance to reel it out. I waited, biding my time. The perfect moment, I decided, would be five minutes before she was due to leave for work. That way she would be too pushed to answer rashly and would have the rest of the day for my point to absorb.

The kitchen clock read seven fifty as I heard her pulling on her coat and jangling her keys. I prepared myself while I filled the sink with hot water and watched the suds rise to the level of the draining board. I opened my mouth to ...

"Right," she said, stopping in the archway beside me while she pulled on her gloves, "The 'honeymoon' is over. I can't go on earning for both of us," she continued reasonably and by the sound of her - as well rehearsed as I had been, "You're gonna have to start bringing in some cash."

My heart jumped, (again) causing me to lose my slippery grip on one of the previous night's dinner plates, which duly slipped back beneath the foam to connect sharply with its twin. I retrieved both plates to check them for chips as I hurriedly composed my reply.

"I thought we had a deal?" I heard myself whine, "Once I've sold the book rights I'll pay you back two fold. Ten fold once I've secured enough loot to do the album!"

"If you sell the rights, Sylvie, and *if* you make enough to record an album! Besides," she gloated needlessly, fully aware that she had taken me by surprise, "I think you're getting too cozy here -down among the ordinaries - anyone'd think you'd settled in!"

As I ran my finger around the rim of what had been my dinner plate I felt the incision, then the tear as I located the damage to her crockery. I whipped my injured extremity to my mouth and sucked on the seeping blood.

"Why don't you start with Morris," she suggested dispassionately, removing the security chain from the front door as she spoke, "you've got enough on him by now. You can work your way through from there. And it'll give you an incentive to finish the book." She opened the door and stepped through onto the small landing beyond.

"Look on it as research."

I hurried to the door as Neve began her descent to ground level.

"Hold on!" I demanded, my throbbing digit still wedged beneath my tongue and causing my words to garble and a line of dribble to run along the back of my hand.

"That's blackmail!"

She stopped two steps from the street door and turned back to face me.

"Not necessarily. You don't need to threaten him. Be subtle. Just remind him of what you know. Tell him you're writing your memoirs - that ought to shit him up in itself."

"I can't just -"

"You have to, Sylvie. If you want to stay here and keep your cover, then I'm going to need to see that you're really trying."

"*That's* blackmail!"

"Yes," she replied, as she turned the latch on the street door, "That *is* blackmail, isn't it. Oh," she continued, almost as an after thought, "and I expect that'll need a stitch."

"Mister ... Sylvester Moon?"

"Hmmm?" I replied, waking with a start, images of a fox-like Morris Yussof attempting to outrun a pack of scandal hungry press hounds fading quickly from my mind's eye.

"You're next, Mister Moon," the effette, vaguely Scandinavian nurse who had triaged my wound damn near a quarter of a day ago explained while I shifted my position on the scuffed orange vac-formed plastic seat on which I had been waiting for treatment all that time. I looked down at my roughly bandaged appendage with its stain of dried blood that had long ago seeped through the fibres to form an oddly erotic Rorshach pattern.

"I wouldn't bother," I returned sarcastically and possibly a little defensively, (as in truth I had been dreading this moment's arrival since first turning myself in and hearing the all too camp nurse's remark of "Superficial, but it'll need a stitch." "I think it's healed on its own."

"I doubt that, Mister Moon. If you'd like to follow me."

I followed meekly, wondering whether I would have been able to keep a straight face if he had given me a true 'Dick Emery': 'Walk this way'.

My five-hour wait had not been in vain. I had begun with a browse through the various so-called 'lifestyle' magazines that I had found littering the colour coded bucket seats of the casualty waiting area, flipping my way through the reams of full colour advertisements for age defying cosmetics and teasing myself with a selection of smug ex-friends and their homes full of useless, but impressive collectable tat. I had given up this game after coming across a four page article that seemed to have been devoted to nothing more than Morris Yussof and his wonderful new home : the house on Spaniards Hill - my house. My home. I had defaced the magazine and moved on to a copy of 'Public Eye' that had obviously been left by another member of the Walking Wounded, as it was far too controversial a periodical to be found amoung the 'Hellos' and the 'Chats' and the 'Gardener's Weeklys' of which the National Health service felt obliged to offer for its outpatient's perusal. Ordinarily I would have been loathe even to touch the cover of such a publication, with its pages strewn with heresay and libel; its mission: to tear down the very fabric of successful society in an attempt to topple the dubiously deserving from their precarious pedestals. It was a magnet to those whose potential had been found wanting and for whom jealousy and bitterness was as essential to their survival as were water and oxygen. I tried not to draw any parallels with my own predicament as I chose this over the racks of self help and pain management leaflets that were my only other option.

"This won't hurt," the nurse lied unashamedly, stripping back my stopgap covering to reveal the flapping soggy gash at the tip of my finger. He aimed an unnecessarily long hypodermic needle an inch or so beneath the wound.

"It already does," I squeaked, as the local anesthetic was pumped into the surrounding tissue. I hauled my mind back to the magazine that I had previously been reading. The cover story had enticed me, inspiring in me an unhealthy dose of morbid revanchism. Somebody had got to Morris ahead of me! Celebrity slayer 'Fawn Kate' - a pseudonym if ever I heard one - had turned her poisonous pen toward my own target, hurling a veritable vitreole, unproveable by few but myself. Kismet ! I thought, as I watched the three-inch needle thread its train of catgut fishing wire into my fingertip. Instinctively I pulled away, even though, true to the nurse's mincing word, I really couldn't feel a thing.

"Don't look," he instructed me, "I don't want you going all floppy on me."

"I can't !" I pleaded, "it's worse if I look away ! I'm a writer, you know - I have a vivid imagination."

"Well, then try to imagine something else," he suggested, winking provocatively in my direction.

I imagined Morris as I had seen him pictured, scurrying along Argyle Street, that ever-prominent beak of his enhanced by a pair of uncomplimentary-mirrored shades. Behind him and slightly defocused were the steps to the Palladium and at the top of them stood a life-size cardboard cut out of the 'actor' in full 'Pterrorbill' costume, as featured in his latest stage role.

The article had been uncanny in its accuracy, though had stopped a little shorter than had my own account, presumably unwilling to deliver names, dates and too much detail for fear of showing its author's hand too soon. I had been handed it on a plate - the groundwork done for me by some anonymous co-conspirator.

I flinched as the nurse cut the thread and in that moment of exquisite pain I made up my mind to defy my principles and take back what was mine.

I ignored the nurse's comment of: "I get off at eight."

It was a little after two when I eventually left the London hospital, and a brighter day than it had been when I had first arrived there a morning before. The rain had passed, leaving a dew fresh scent on the air that instantly cleansed my nostrils of the bitter aftertaste of disinfectant that had impregnated itself on my clothes and in my hair, though I knew that it wouldn't be long before even that scent was supplanted by the acrid taste of twentieth century London.

I crossed the Whitechapel road and skipped down the steps of its namesake station, a plan forming in my mind all the while. I fiddled with the torn out page in the pocket of Frank's coat as I caught the Metropolitan line tube to Liverpool street; rode the central line to

Oxford circus and finally stepped out into the hub of the West end. I was getting quite used to this novel form of transport and was ready to accept that it was probably the most effective and efficient mode of getting between A and B in the city. Perhaps Neve was right. Maybe I was getting too cozy.

Oxford street itself proved to be no more hazardous a challenge to my disguise than had the underground. There I was - an icon of the age - traveling around freely in a crowded capital city wearing nothing more concealing than a twat shaped beard and nobody had batted an eyelid. Was it the fact that nobody expected to see me there, therefore nobody *did* see me there, or was it that they did actually see me, but they just didn't care? Self doubt. Six months previously and I wouldn't even have pondered the choice.

I turned right into Argyle street and followed on down toward The Palladium, smiling to myself as I saw the gaudy hoardings and the neon sign that advertised dear Morris as a 'co-star' in 'Shawn Cocktail : the musical'. I noted the time as two fifty as I stepped up to the first of the row of tellers to enquire about the time of the Wednesday matinee. I was in luck. The programme was not due to start for another hour. Morris would have had to have checked in by now. He would almost certainly be in the building. A sitting duck. I waved away her sincerest of apologies that the performance was long since sold out and asked her in my most humble of affectations whether it would be possible to get a message to a member of the cast. If she recognised me before I gave her my name then she gave no more indication than she had done after she had read back my message.

"Would that be possible?" I asked her again, trying to curb the instinctual sarcasm from my voice.

"I'll see what I can do mister ..." (she looked back to the note that I had handed her) "... Quip."

"Thank you so much," I squeezed through grinding teeth as the apprentice actress with the bigger arse standing than I had imagined on her sitting, disappeared from sight through a low arched door emblazoned with a colour coded seating plan of the Capital's most famous theatre.

I waited in the corridor for a full fifteen minutes, watching the hands of the wall mounted clock tick ever closer toward curtain call. I read every glossy flyer until I knew which theatre was showing which play and on which nights a student concession could be obtained. I scanned the montage posters that ranged the walls, counting in my head how many of yesterday's performers had passed on up to the stage in the sky and noting how many had simply disappeared and therefore been forgotten. Louis Armstrong had played here, back in the forties. And just what had happened to Tommy Steel? The girl had returned to her desk a good ten minutes ago, but had ignored me as if I had been a part of the gilt frescoe. Eventually impatience got the better of me. Scant seconds before the irritating chorus of Tommys 'Little white bull' could get a looping hold on my brain and just as a party of checkered, be-stetsoned, dollar wielding yanks, who had been attempting to bribe her into releasing the royal box to them were leaving, I jumped back in front of the half glass window to press my point.

"Did Morris get my message?"

"I think so," she replied sheepishly, "hold on I'll check."

She dialed a three-digit code into her telephone and awaited a reply. When it came, all I heard was her end of the conversation: "Stage door ? Maddy. Gentleman at tickets wanted to speak to mister Yussof? Yes. He sent down a note? Yes. Do you know if it arrived? Did? Oh … right. OK. Bye."

"Well ?"

"Yes he did get your message, mister..."

"Quip."

"Quip, yeah … but he said the only Sly Quip he knows is …" (she lowered her voice to a whisper and leant in closer toward the glass) "'Bugger off'. I'm sorry," she said, her cheeks flushing with either embarrassment or excitement - I couldn't quite decide, "but I'm going to have to ask you to leave. I've alerted security."

I bit back the insult that she so richly deserved for fear of attracting attention: (the final irony, I know,) and left the theatre.

At six fifteen my alcoholically revived patience paid its dividend. I had parked myself on a municipal bench beside the public conveniences on the crossroads of Carnaby Street and Great Marlborough --a perfect vantage point from which to view the arrivals and departures from the Palladium's stage door. Richard Briers had been the first of the production's recogniseable cast to leave the theatre, no doubt for a spot of luvvy lunch at the Ritz between performances. Several legwarmered and ponytailed dancer types followed him out, crossed the road and skipped past the side entrance to Libertys before disappearing into the throng of distant Regent Street.

Morris was a worried man. When he did eventually appear it was behind those same ill fitting shades that he had been wearing in the magazine article and beneath a Gestapo styled ankle length leather raincoat; its collar upturned and its belt knotted tightly around his waist. The only way that he could have looked less conspicuous was if he had worn a peaked cap with the letters 'SS' embroidered on to it and a monocle. He quite obviously wanted to be seen, though did not want to appear approachable. Nazi garb was probably a fine choice. And anyway - it suited him.

He crossed the road diagonally, stepping between a pair of horn happy black cabs rather than be seen to use the zebra crossing that had been put there in order to avoid such potentially fatal altercations. He ignored the cussing cabbies who, it seemed, had also noted his mode of dress, and strutted on into Carnaby Street, scattering foraging pigeons in his wake. He ignored me, or most likely he didn't see me; so caught up in his own B list aura that he failed to recognise the man who without whom he would still just be 'that specky snide from 4B'.

I followed at a distance. Carnaby Street with its melee of Japanese and American tourists was far too public an arena to make my play. As we reached Beak Street, Morris wheeled left. I overshot the road and continued my stalk from the opposite pavement. The human traffic was thinning by the time he turned into Great Pulteney and a few moments later I saw my chance. I crossed the road and brought myself up beside my old school 'pal', startling him and causing him to career to a halt, his hornbill missing a lamppost by a fraction of an inch.

"Sylvie! What the fuck are you doing !"

"Nice to see you too, Morry mate. So you got my note then ?"

"What do you want?" he panicked, wide eyes staring at me as if he thought I was some common street mugger. "You want money ? Is that what it is?" (He pulled out his overstuffed wallet and tore a wad of crisp fifties which he thrust into my chest.) "Take it!" he blabbed, "Just leave me alone! I'm not even supposed to talk to you!"

"Says who?" I wondered aloud, "Joe Munday?"

"Detective Inspector Prendergast, actually. Along with my agent, my solicitor and yes … Joe Munday."

His eyes darted from side to side, searching for a witness with which to corroborate his planned accusation of assault. He was unlucky.

I produced the 'Public Eye' Article and dangled it in front of his horrified face.

"Put the money away, Morris," I told him; his offer rather stealing my thunder, but sparking the germ of an even more cunning plan, "I didn't come for your money."

"Why d'you do it?" he blabbed, his pale face beginning to redden with those trademark tears.

I laughed, suddenly realising that he thought that I had sold the story to Public Eye.

"I didn't," I said tightly and hopefully threateningly, "but if they're interested enough, then there's a lot more that I *could* tell them, isn't there."

"What do you want?"

"I want you to remember who your friends are Morris."

"You want to blackmail me!"

"No I don't," I protested, "I just want a little payback for all the things I did for you back in the old days."

"This is about the house, isn't it," he floundered, "it wasn't your house, Sylvie, it belongs to Joe. Everything we had was in Joe's name!"

"It's not about the house, Morris; though if you break a fucking thing I'll break your neck! No - I need a favour."

"A favour?" Morris' fear was instantaneously replaced with bemusement. I saw it in his eyes, but his still nervous laughter came out sounding like a hyena on helium.

"A favour," I repeated calmly, noting a pinstriped gent as he turned into the road some way yet behind Morris, "a favour for an old friend who's down on his luck."

"Name it," he said, his confidence returning by the second, "then piss off. And if I ever find out it was you who sold me out …" (He left the threat hanging as we both knew that it would be woefully benign).

"Autographs," I said, watching his forehead ruffle in amused consternation, "to sell. You remember Neve, don't you Morris? Well she

sells memorabilia. Tacky, I know, but it's a living. She'll buy whatever I can get."

"Autographs?"

"Anyone! Anyone famous anyway."

"And that's it ? You'll leave me alone? You'll keep your trap shut if
'Fawn Kate' starts offering you cash?"

"The more you can get me, the less I'll need her money. Oh, and
Morris?"

His eyes narrowed, suspecting a twist, "Don't get any ideas about
selling *me* out either. I know where Dizzy is".

The 'Diz' bit had been a lie of course, though it had been effective
and it had got me thinking. An interview with Diz could be what my
book needed to authenticate its claims.

I made a mental note to check our ex-roadie's whereabouts.

Morris kept his word and over the following weeks four neatly
wrapped parcels had arrived at the Bethnal Green road flat, each
containing an assortment of signed photographs, programmes,
books and posters. Neve had at first been livid with the arrange-
ment. She was, it seemed, less than happy to have her home
address linked with what could be misconstrued as blackmail. I had
placated her by explaining that our potential return could be far
greater than a simple cash payment would have been. Her response
had simply been that it wouldn't 'hurt' him enough. However, a
deal was struck. Neve would calculate a reserve price for each item
and would claim seventy per cent of that figure, regardless of what
I sold it on for. All sales that I made from her existing stock would
net me a non-negotiable twenty five percent of the sale price. My
pitch at Spitalfields was extended to Saturdays as well as Sundays,
leaving me a five day week in which to continue my book.

Public Eye had been conspicuous in their generosity toward Morris,
making no further comment on their previous allegations nor
printing their proposed witness interview that I had been keen
enough to buy my own copy for a chance to read. I felt sure that
this would have concreted Morris' wide assumption that I had
indeed been Ms Kate's mystery source, but it no longer mattered to
my ego. Whilst he thought that I was guilty, then he would contin-

ue to replenish my stock. A full cast signed programme for his musical had gained me an absurd eighty five quid - nearly fifty above Neve's reserve, and a BBC security pass signed by John Peel had taken thirty - almost double its expected value.

In the meantime, like I say, I was still hard at work on my dauntless memoir. I had fleshed out my Morris chapter to include a few other minor defects in my acquaintances disposition with the intention of leaving my audience in no doubt as to his shit bag nature. Having suitably damned the source of my newfound income into perpetuity I had then moved on to Lakhi.

Lakhi Corner was a different kettle of fish entirely. Whereas Morris' and Stephen's exploits could have warranted entire volumes in their own right, Lakhi, the diminutive composer of vaguely eastern origin, had always managed to keep himself and his habits within the letter of publicly perceived morality. Well, almost. He was neither a drinker nor a user; a gambler nor a smuggler - as were the customary rockstar traits of our generation. If he had a single vice, (and few but myself and again Diz could confirm this) then it was of a sexual nature. Lakhi was not what I would have described as a pervert or a deviant and he was certainly not a pornographer nor a paedophile. He was ... just plain kinky. He liked his sex and he liked his danger; and he liked nothing more than dangerous sex. When I say 'dangerous' I don't mean sadomasochistic or any variation on that general theme, it was more the thrill of 'doing it' in 'dangerous places' that turned him on. I sound like I'm defending him rather than attempting to damn him, but then there really was something quite alluring about the idea. He had done it on the Eiffel Tower. He had done it on top of the Empire state building. He'd even done it in a sentry box outside Buckingham palace after some ghastly awards dinner that we had attended in the early nineties. He had done it between floors in an elevator in Hamleys toy shop; he had done it on the stage of the Albert Hall with several thousand people just a velvet curtain away. But it was one particular liaison that interested me : the day when it all went wrong. It was inevitable, of course, that the dirty little bugger's stunt man escapades would eventually net him trouble - we all knew that Joe only hoped that it wouldn't kill him and thus jeopardise our income, though in retrospect I now wonder whether he might have seen the death of our least important member as something of a

145

publicity coup. After all, it worked for The Who, even though it rather knackered the Carpenters.

Tokyo, September 1982, and his most daring fuck to date. Lakhi Corner was never a man endowed with natural prowess or chiseled good looks, so his cohorts have always been plucked from the dauntless army of disposable young groupies whose ordinary, respectable demeanours could so easily be swayed by the thought of a one night stand with a famous face. That particular night's victim had no doubt looked mature for her age, (or so he had later claimed), though I cannot be certain that her youth and that thrill of being caught might not have added a little something to his already bristling libido.

Lakhi's plan, ill conceived in a moment of pre-orgasmic compulsion, had been to attempt carnal gratification while balancing on the roof of the band's tour bus, that Diz had been coerced into driving slowly through the neon lit red light district of the city.

I have to admit, though not publicly, that to have pulled off such a stunt successfully would have elevated my former colleague, even in my own eyes, to the level of 'legendary' without even the need for a spectacular or premature death. But of course, he didn't pull it off. Or at least not without the need for some smart talking and the loss of a lot of Yen on our dear manager's part.

It had transpired that Lakhi; mounting his adolescent accomplice from the rear, had lost his footing and accidentally pushed her off the side of the bus. Luckily she had received a softer landing than she might have done - her fall having been broken by the bonnet of a police car which had been trying to flag down the bus after having received complaints from a coach load of tourists who had drawn up beside them at traffic lights. The girl in question, one Suki Woo, 13, had sustained fractures to both legs, cracked two ribs and received a head injury which had left her an unreliable witness to the evening's proceedings. Lakhi came out of the incident physically unharmed, (though the psychological scarring kept his habits in check for years to follow.)

It was an interesting tale and one that I could quite honestly corroborate, as I had traveled with Joe to the home of the family Woo and had watched as Munday-san had counted out the currency to both the local officials and to the girl's father. I knew it all: dates, times, names and amounts, as of course did Diz, but the big wide world had been spared the sordid details. As I dotted my I's and crossed my T's I indulged my loosely shackled bitterness with a smile that was later mirrored and compounded by my then co-conspirator Neve. It was her that then pointed out the potential collateral damage to the multi-millionaire composer's new career if the Disney corporation; that religiously clean cut operation that would not even tolerate facial hair on its 'cast members' and whose money Lakhi had recently banked by way of advance for his contribution to the soundtrack of their latest cartoon epic, ever found out the perverted truth.

As luck would have it - Lakhi was coming home, albeit temporarily, (if Neve: the showbiz gossip collator of Hackney was to be believed), and I had no reason to doubt her, even though she was predictably unwilling to divulge her source. He was to be in town for one week, starting with his arrival at Heathrow two days hence, to record a pilot for a new music anthology series. The programme, tentatively entitled 'The liggers guide' was apparently intended as a commercial television rival to the BBC's long running 'Top Of The Pops'. Many companies had attempted to steal the Beeb's mantle over the years and all of them had failed. There was no reason to expect this format to be any different. Lakhi was intended as one of three full time presenters. His role would be to introduce, interview and gossip from his poolside in LA, while child star turned 'celebrity-without-portfolio' Georgie Cruz Martin and rock journalist and all round arsehole Jim Reaper would handle the in house reins from London. Recording for the forty minute pilot was set to take place at the London Studios on the South Bank - that place again. The thought of returning to the site of Cameron Shah's last scene filled me with a sense of misplaced guilt, but it would also give me the chance to check on a couple of details from that fateful night that had been worrying me ever since. Perhaps I was getting cynical in my old age, but I don't believe in coincidence. Loathe as I was to admit it even at this late stage, my trust in Neve was ever dwindling.

Chapter Six
"Psycho Bitch From Hell"

It's interesting how a person's life can be defined, retrospectively, by chapter and verse: each part eventually showing a distinct beginning, middle and end; like a series of interconnected vignettes collected together to form one big anthological autobiography. I had never thought along these lines before, but now that I had, it began to make some sense of my life to date.

It was intriguing also to note how the life stories of other's seemed to intertwine with my own, leaving me not as the central player in all that I did, but often more of a secondary character in the larger picture of humankind. Humbling.

I had first met Neve, along with the bulk of the characters that feature in this account, in what from here on in I will refer to as 'Chapter one'. We had grown up together in chapters two and three, before losing touch just shy of chapter four: the part that I like to think of as 'Volume 2: the fame & fortune years'.

Our reacquaintance at the close of chapter five; signified by the death of Stephen along with all hope of reviving the Moonies, could possibly be viewed as an act of fate: a pre ordained thread to be picked up and woven back in to the tapestry of our individual lives, perhaps even a main plot strand that, with the dubious benefit of hindsight could have led us into Volume 3: 'the happy ever after'. (But I doubted it.) Neve was undeniably a catalyst in my life, (and who knows, maybe I was in hers too), but as far as my epilogue was concerned, I couldn't then see her as a likely player from chapters six onwards. We were not going to work out. I had to accept that. We had grown apart. The thing about my chapters theory was that they did not seem to be governed by linear time. One person could experience far more; growing exponentially in the same time period, while another merely vegetates. Neve had missed a whole chapter of my life, but I may have missed two or three of hers, or conversely - hardly anything at all. Our new relationship had started with a bang - perhaps, I now thought, as the result of that long unrequited fuck: an incident that would probably have been better left unresolved after such a long and frustrated respite. We should by rights by this point have evolved out of that initially wary lust, moving upward toward the love and trust tier, but it had never happened. Her skepticism, so evident through those first few days, but which had seemed to evaporate with the drop of her knickers, had returned with the added vengeance of that of a twice-jilted bride.

She didn't trust me - that much was obvious. I didn't know whether her unfounded suspicions were the result of her experience with the late mister Capaldi or of a more personal nature. Perhaps my inherent pomposity was undermining my gratitude? Or perhaps she just wasn't the Neve that I had stitched up back in chapter three.

While she trusted me to run her market stall and, I had noticed, was rarely particularly diligent with the accounts that I showed her, she would stand watch over me every time that I loaded or unloaded my trolley from little Sylvia's locked bedroom. She had watched me, never offering to help me lug my boxes of autographed crap up and down those stairs, into and out of my waiting taxi, almost daring me to pry her secrets. I could see the moment looming when she would ask me to leave her bed and return to the sofa from whence I had come and by this time I almost welcomed it.

But I wasn't yet ready to fly the nest, neither financially nor mentally.

True, I had learned a lot, both from her and from the world that I had found myself in, but I needed a lot more. As each day passed I forced myself to review my ambition to take back what was mine, not just to accept my lot like the majority of the no hopers that I had met down here. Yes - I still needed her, but maybe she also needed me. What if that was the problem, I thought? What if I had been going about it the wrong way? Maybe she did want me. Perhaps I had been a crap shag. How should I know? It was my first and only time after all. I was a selfish git by decree. I knew that. Maybe I had screwed up my chances with her by simply not knowing how these things work. I had been so wrapped up in what she wasn't willing to share that I had completely overlooked what she *had* been offering me! I decided to give it one more try, to put aside those doubts and concerns - stupid that they probably were - and forget about following her to work and searching her home for non existent cabalistic clues.

Two nights prior I had risen in the night on the pretext of a trip to the bathroom and feigned a fall beside the bed. She had stirred in her sleep, called me a pillock and rolled over - giving me the noisy few seconds that I needed to swipe her purse from her jacket pocket and rifle the little brass key from the button-down flap that I had seen her store it in before and after my weekend sojourns. I fingered it now in my groinal pocket. It was warm; as warm as the bollocks that surrounded it. No, *warmer* - as if it were trying to burn its way out of my only good pair of trousers; as anxious to force its way into the lock on the dead child's door as its current cell mate was to slide its way back into the child's mother.

It's ironic how, in all that time without a means, I had been so desperate for a chance to poke around inside the room and yet, once finally in possession of the key - there I was making excuses not to use it. I knew I had the right key. I had tested it less than five minutes after she had left for work that morning; heard the tell tale click of the tumbler and pushed the door open just far enough to release a burst of the musty air that permeated everything within. But I hadn't gone inside. My conscience had got the better of me, plucking the latterly expanded 'what-if-I'm-to-blame' line from my tumultuous mind as an alternative to my more usual 'excuse-for-positive-action' disclaimer.

I had relocked the door and returned to my work, mulling the situation as I had tried to write. This was a nexus point, I knew, and one that I would not be able to pass until I had chosen a path. The time for dithering was over. Lakhi's chapter was finished - all bar a little tweaking and, apart from Rusty's real name being 'Cuthbert Elizabeth' I really couldn't think of anything sordid to tell on our drummer.

I downed tools and collected my stonewashed denim jacket - (the first and only item of second hand clothing that I had ever purchased) from the tie-dyed girl on the neighbouring pitch at the previous Saturday's market. I checked its pocket for change, slung it onto my back and set off in search of inspiration.

I had no idea what I was looking for: flowers; chocolates; a stuffed animal? Anything that might conjure the notion of love and appreciation for my erstwhile friend. I knew that I couldn't spare much cash and Neve did too: that was the beauty of the gesture!

As I passed the newsagent I felt myself recoiling in true comedy double-take fashion. All thoughts of my previous quandary were erased in that split second as I focussed on the cover of the latest issue of 'Public Eye', standing proudly amongst the speciality periodicals - eager to display its exclusive leader over its less informed rivals. Lakhi Corner's origin defying profile loomed down from the cover of the top shelf mag; the telephoto snap having caught him at a particularly vulnerable moment, revealing as it so cruelly did the extra eight years that he had on the rest of us, but which carefully applied foundation usually concealed so well.

'Kinky sex secrets of the Disney composer' read the rather unimaginative headline in scarlet bold, with the sultry promise of explicit detail in red italics beneath it.

I barged the shopdoor, elbowing a shambling pensioner who had been struggling against the door's overly compensative hydraulic from the opposite side; oblivious to my boorish indiscretion - my only consideration the acquisition of another highly improbable act of 'coincidental' plagiarism. Unfazed by the old lady's colourful eastend lamentations I tore the issue from its shelf and began urgently scanning its pages for my own fingerprint.

The names had been removed, of course; in fact, so had any detail of any consequence - presumably by an editor somehow distrustful of his hack's sources, but the sentiment remained intact. Almost word for word!

My brain started dredging its inspirational recesses for plausible explanations, though my heart knew that there was only one likely probability. Neve was a bloody journalist! Of course she was! It was all she'd ever wanted to be ! The only reason that I'd ever studied it was for the chance to spend more time with her. She must have stayed on at the Poly' after Morris and I had left, taken her exams, got herself a career!

Maybe her stint on the psycho ward blew that career. What if 'Public Eye' was her only way back in ?

A lot of 'ifs' and 'maybes', but it was all beginning to slot into place now ! She'd been using me. The shop's Asian proprietor drew my attention to the establishment's 'no browsing' policy and so reluctantly I parted with my three pounds fifty and left the shop heading back in the direction of the flat. Two and two suddenly made five as I cobbled together the collection of loose ends that I had so recently been preparing to overlook in favour of a loosely cohesive motive for both Neve's conspicuous altruism and her precipitous enthusiasm for my work. No wonder she knew so much about the movement's of the rich and famous. The autograph business was just a propitious sideline, made possible by her near unique knowledge of their plans.

But why was she doing it, I wondered? Was it for the money ? And if so, what did she need it for ? She had already told me that the flat had been paid for from Frank's insurance policies. Was it to regain a flagging career - echoing my own desperate position ? This was the more likely, I felt, but neither would turn out to be the case.

I mounted the stairs three at a time and threw open the flat doors, heading instinctively where I knew the answers to be. The time for sneaking and doubting was over. I yanked the little brass key from my pocket where it was threatening to scald my left testicle, rammed it into the lock on the child's bedroom door and pushed my way inside. I scanned the various shelves and the labels on the boxes that I had been forbidden to touch, but nothing stood out. Once again I had no idea what I was looking for, though I knew that I would know it as soon as I found it. The row of dusty teddy bears that sat like the gods of Ragnarok in judgment over my indiscretion sneered down on me; mocking my impudence as if daring me to uncover their master's secrets.

And then I saw it. Poking out from under the corner of the faded 'Forever Friends' duvet was what appeared to be a wooden sea chest. I dropped to my knees and pulled it from its hiding place beneath the dusty old bed. It was locked: sealed with a steel padlock that didn't match the box's obvious antiquity. I spun the chest so that I was facing a pair of rusted rivet hinges. I tested their strength with the edge of the brass key and noted that they had loosened over the years, leaving room enough for leverage. I repaired to the kitchen, then returned momentarily, armed with the screwdriver and the tack hammer that Neve kept there in the cupboard beneath the sink. I wedged the flat edged nib of the screwdriver behind the first hinge and brought the hammer down hard against its handle with a strength fuelled by anger inspired adrenalin. It splintered with the first blow, charging a spark that scalded my unprotected cheek as it ripped from the lid that had held it for god knew how long. I repeated the exercise on its twin, though my rage had abated somewhat with success, requiring two further blows to release the only thing between myself and some answers. I hadn't really known what I was expecting to find, as I said, but by this point my imagination was ready to accept anything up to and including a pair of severed heads. So it was with something of a sigh of disappointment when all I discovered was a scrapbook marked 'Some Young Moon' and a pile of ancient letters. The bottom of the box was littered with dried petals that had at one time been attached to the bunch of headless stalks tied tightly with a frayed blue ribbon that had been tucked under the elastic band that held the letters together. I had picked them up to inspect the handwriting that looked uncannily familiar when I felt something drop into my lap. It was a chain. A chain bearing a locket molded into the shape of a valentine heart, a cheap facsimile ruby mounted at its centre. It was gold plated. I knew this without checking for a non existent hallmark because I remember buying the damn thing from a seaside tat shop some thirty odd years before. The letters were also mine, or at least had been written by me to the girl who at ten years old I had quiet logically expected to marry. The flowers had also been from me, stolen from a graveside behind the church on the green.

I smiled despite myself as the memories of more innocent times drifted back to the fore. I sat down on the bed, the scrapbook in my lap and prepared to peruse my long departed formative years.

As I flipped the stiffened paper pages, passing newspaper clippings and amateur photographs I began to notice the distinct theme that ran through the collection. This was no celebration of the career of one of the countries best loved and most successful pop groups, it was a record of our failures. Every trip, every graze, every minor indiscretion. It was all there. Things that I had long since forgotten. Things that I'd never even known! About a third of the way through Neve's own private Public Eye I noticed a change from clippings to typed eulogies. Was it research, I wondered ? Was she writing her own Moonies obituary ? Predictably my own notes were included, albeit in Photostat form. No wonder she had been so keen for me to write the bloody thing !

On a sudden whim I skipped forward to the section reserved for my own name. My saliva began to burn on my palette as I skim read *my* entry. She had photographs. Pages of surveillance photographs.

Pictures that could only have been taken from within the grounds. Christ! Two shots that could only have been taken from within the house! She had Photostats of my accounts; my bank statement; my bills. She had a list of my credit card numbers; my PIN numbers, even! She had a whole series of photographs of Chelsea, my home visit strip artist. She had her details; her phone number; the names of her husband and her kids! Even I didn't know that!

She had my whole life on those pages, but what had she been doing with it? I had never been done by Public Eye, though with access to this stuff one had to ask oneself 'why not?' Maybe I was to be next, I thought?

I closed the book, my mind then more of a whirr with questions than it had been when I had started looking for answers. My options were still as limited as they had been when I had made the decision to leave the house and my time running ever shorter. Another strategic withdrawal was in order. It took me a few moments longer to gather my belongings together than it took for the minicab to arrive and signal its presence. I stumbled down the last five steps with my rickety fold down trolley loaded to a capacity that far exceeded its manufacturer's specification, trailing nuts and bolts as the left wheel rejected its mooring. I scooped up the spilled boxes, hoping that the cellophane envelopes would protect Neve's pilfered stock from the remains of the previous night's rainfall. I had been in the autograph business long enough to know which were the most prolifically selling stars and had therefore grabbed only those boxes that I felt I could fence quickly. I felt no guilt as I piled her collection onto the back seat of the car, threw in the gig bag containing my clothes, the scrapbook and my own note books before crawling in myself and ordering the driver to my destination.

I hadn't been discreet. The flat looked like it had been hit by a freak tornado. There hadn't been the time or a particular need for subtlety and with luck, I would be far from her retributional snipings by the time she discovered my crime.

I had ransacked her computer files as well as her rooms. Though my experience with modern technological advancements rested pretty much on my ability to use a telephone to call for help, I had watched Neve enough over the past months to have absorbed the rudimentary of 'booting up', 'logging on' and 'accessing' her client directory. Her code was naive in its simplicity, being of course the name that I so nearly shared with her late daughter. I had been presented with a screenful of unintelligible shorthand, none of which I had been able to decipher in the scant minutes that I had had. I had scrolled forward in desperation and had eventually been rewarded for my patience at the same moment that the cab driver had signaled his arrival. I had had time to jot down only three of her regular buyers: A pop memorabilia fanatic, a film buff and a girl with a particular penchant for 'personal' souvenirs. I had hoped that it would not have become necessary to play my only hidden trump, but the situation called for desperate measures.

Thirty-five liberating minutes later we arrived at the gates to my former home. It felt good to be back in civilization again after what seemed like a lifetime in the eastend. I asked my driver to wait, left my belongings in the car and stepped out onto Spaniards road. I followed the twelve-foot wall with its razor wire topping to the point where I had originally made my escape. My luck was holding. Through the ivy and bindweed foliage I could just make out the last rung of the ladder poking up above the defences, where I had left it seven and a half months before.

It was approaching three forty five and dusk was settling over the Heath. This part of the plan I had not sufficiently envisaged. I knew what I needed to do, but not how I was going to do it.

I looked along the deserted street for improvisational inspiration among the fixtures and fittings of NW3. There was very little that hadn't been bolted to the tarmac. Long gone were the days when one could lean a bicycle against a wall and expect it still to be there once your back was turned, or when the local authorities might plant a bench for the use by the weary traveler without first sinking it into three feet of concrete. This was Hampstead at the dawn of the twenty first century.

And then I saw my saviour. Two doors down, the doctor's domestic was dragging two large, heavy-duty plastic wheelie bins out to the boundary line of the property. Dustbin day !

I waited for the elderly groundsman to disappear back to his kennel, checked both sides of the road for prying neighbours, then grabbed the bins and pulled them along the pavement to the point below my ladder. I noticed my cab driver's conspicuous ignorance and imagined myself explaining to him that I had lost my key. I backed the first bin against the wall, then tipped its twin onto its side, relieving it of its foul smelling burden. Unladen, I was able to heft the second bin on top of the first and clamber up on top of the pile. Reaching across the wire, my fingers eventually found purchase on the top of the ladder and from there I was able to haul myself back into what had at one time been my own garden.

Once down it took only seconds to locate my hidden treasure trove inside the old stump. A rather pungent stench of dried urine dominated the area, reminiscent of the first piss of the morning after a heavy night before. The reason why soon became obvious when I noticed for the first time the biggest dog turd that I had ever borne witness to. Shaped like a Tonibel whipped ice cream and balanced with the finesse of a championship freestyle shitter on the very rim of the hollow, my discovery preceded the approach of the most likely artist by bare moments. If there was one thing that scared me more than poverty then it was dogs - particularly dogs capable of turds of that magnitude.

On returning to the cab I finally expressed the breath that I had been unaware of having been holding since the first of four Timber Wolves had bounded into sight. I exchange a laboured banter with my driver, still breathless from my ordeal, and instructed him to head for the first of three addresses that I had ringed in a copy of 'Loot' that I had found in Neve's bedroom.

Chapter Seven
"Self Help"

My malnourished stomach churned both with hunger and nausea as I stepped from the Haverstock Arms and out onto Rosslyn Hill, lifting the collar of my denim and buttoning up against the wind. In my left-hand trouser pocket I tightened my grip around the two and a half thousand pounds in crinkled fifties that the oily little dealer had just given me in exchange for a lifetime's achievements. I had expected more - a lot more! Enough to have been able to at least demo my album, but my bargaining powers were weakened by the fact that even my most recent, criminal exploits had by this time slipped from the collective consciousness. I resolved to stop wallowing in the past and to push myself harder toward a future that I knew I could influence with a clearer mind and a firmer resolve.

Life changes could be very much like the old carpet that was always left in the house by its departing occupants. When first experienced, its patterns could be quite mind-blowing. Each time you see it over the course of the next six months your resolve to change it becomes that much greater, but in time you soon stop noticing its psychedelic whorls and ground in stains; you get used to it; you adapt to it. You start to tell yourself that it's not really 'that bad' and begin to make excuses for your torpor. Before you know it - you've accepted it. This was not the way it was going to be with me. I refused to accept my lot. I refused to become one with the carpet! I wiped my feet on the 'Not-You-Again' wicker doormat as I stepped back into Mrs Beachman's salubrious 'B and B': the result of that first 'Loot 'ad' that I had arrived at two days before. Using Neve's contacts I had arranged to meet the 'pop-dealer' with the intention of pawning my awards so that I could pay the pink haired, unconvincing transvestite the required deposit of two months rent for the use of her grotty little attic room and shared bathroom. I had hoped to have enough left over for me not to have had to resort to the backup plan. Plan B it was then.

Although it wasn't the Heath, I was at least back in Hampstead. I liked it there - it had about it an air of dignity; of civilization: a social austerity akin to the British reserve of the post war forties. It knew it was right and would brook no incursions. It would repel its borders from even the most self righteous of uninvited marauders at all cost. Even McDonalds had been forced to fight for its pitch among the Euro style pavement cafés, and even though the locals had eventually been forced to yield to the American invaders, the cost to the company's pride (they had been forced to dump the obligatory yellow and red plastic façade in favour of a subdued matt black surround) had been a victory that had proved the might of style over consumerism. Hampstead spoke of culture. It had art galleries, antique dealers, art house cinemas, open air classical concerts, designer clothing, nouveau cuisine. Hamsptead had class. Hampstead was home.

I was woken early on my first morning in the attic by the smell of smouldering meat. More than thirty hours had passed since anything more nourishing than a packet of dry roasted nuts had passed my lips, yet strangely Mrs Beacham's breakfast failed to inspire my digestive juices.

I prized myself from my sweat soaked pit and thrust my head into the lime stained basin, yanked on the washer worn taps and allowed the ice cold water to flow across my crown and down onto my face and neck.

It had been some while since I had been able to recall a dream with such perverse clarity and I desperately needed to wash its residue from my mind before embarking on the day. Neve had been in it, unsurprisingly; our unresolved parting obviously still dominating my thoughts. But it was schoolgirl Neve that I had seen: seen talking to Andy and Greg - offering them a briefcase stashed with cash and a pair of tickets to Brazil. It was schoolgirl Neve that I had seen wiring the bomb beneath Frank's car and it had been schoolgirl Neve that I had finally mounted inside the sewer pipe in Leabridge recreation ground and pumped until I had woken up in the state that I now found myself in.

"Mista' Moon?"

I heard, wafting through the smoke and the spit and crackle that

told me where in the house I should expect to find the kitchen.
"Oh, mista' Moon? It's on the table, dear."

I was tempted to feign sleep or even death at this stage, but I needed the energy intake and so reluctantly I pulled on my two day old
clothes, combed my self cut hair and descended toward the table
of doom.

Forty minutes later and following my regular post breakfast ablu-
tion, I stepped back into the real world with my levels revitalized
and my nightmare safely consigned to my memory banks. I still felt
sick though, and the bearded lady's inane prattle had not made this
feeling any easier. She hadn't recognized me, which was a definite
plus - the only thing that I could be grateful to her for. My need to
stay incognito was greater now than ever. I couldn't risk becoming
vulnerable during this delicate transition.

Over the past few days my contrived little beard had come more to
resemble Robinson Crusoe than its intended William Shakespeare.
It had grown thicker and greyer around the chin and cheeks, lend-
ing me more of a 'castaway' look than the Neve styled 'cast off' look.
I had lost a little more weight too, which had redefined my exposed
face, adding a good ten years to my appearance. Ordinarily this
would have worried me, but for the moment it suited my purpos-
es. Besides, it was nothing that a few good Savoy lunches and a
week on Capri wouldn't rectify when it was all over.

I thought about this along with life's other missing luxuries as I
made my way through the tube system to Waterloo. Winter in
London was a long way from Summer on the Amalfi coast, rein-
forcing the sheer magnitude of the task still at hand.

I crossed Upper Ground and headed down along the embankment
toward the London Studios.

As I wandered past the spot where Cameron Shah had taken his
final bow, the thought crossed my mind that perhaps Neve had kept
a file on him too; though quite where the old roué fitted into the
picture would remain a mystery for a while yet. I dismissed these
thoughts for fear of disappearing down an avenue that I didn't want
to pursue at this stage and made my way to the public entrance on
the left hand side of the building. A queue had begun to form,
mainly consisting of teenage girls clad in as little as their anorexic
young bodies would agree to against the subzero December air. I
straightened automatically as I passed the line, (a reflexive

response from a previous existence), but went unrecognized in my transparent disguise. I cheered myself slightly at the thought that it wasn't that they had forgotten me, but that they were probably too young to remember me. I stopped myself from pursuing this line as well, as its inherent flaw was not that far from presenting itself to the scruffy old git that had to prize his middle aged eyes from their goose pimpled midriffs. I tried not to notice that most bizarre of fashion statements: the ill fitting combat trousers, that for some obscure reason had to be worn so low on the hips as to expose the tantalizing glimpse of lace knicker that protruded above every second girl's waistband, as I strolled up to the concierge with as much mustered confidence as my stress worn figure would provide me.

"Pass?"

I began a frantic pocket search for the envelope that I knew I would find above my left breast, then finally produced it with a flourish and passed it to the doorman.

"Has mister Corner arrived yet?" I asked innocently, allowing him to see the name that I had written on the front of the envelope.

"He might have."

"And would it be possible to see him?"

"Nope."

"Do you think it would be possible to get this note to him then? It is quite urgent."

The man of few words drew in his substantial bulk and peered down at me, the shiny plastic peak of his outsized cap obscuring his eyes in the overcast light of the porch. I slid the five-pound note that I had secreted beneath the envelope into view.

"I'll see if he's here," he replied curtly, "Wait over there." He indicated an area of better light that was quite obtrusively monitored by a selection of closed circuit cameras mounted on stalks above the porch. About ten minutes later, jobsworth reappeared and ushered me into the foyer.

"Up the stairs, down the hall, first door on the left."

I thanked him condescendingly, the balance of power having shifted between us. I followed his direction and came to a door marked with a tacky plastic gold star and the name 'Lakhi Corner' written in red fibre tip on the wipe clean board beneath it. I knocked gently.

"Come," came Lakhi's nasal voice from within.

With a confidence of gait that was dissolving with every step I opened the door and stepped inside.

"Lakhi?" I called, finding the 'star's' dressing room apparently empty.

"Right here," came my reply, and as I turned toward the source of the voice a fist connected with my already dislocated nose, knocking me backwards in a cartoon sprawl that sent his horticultural rider of roses and lilys in a spectacular spray in all directions outward. "Spiteful little bastard," he vented, looming over me in a peuce coloured dressing gown with a faceful of panstick and a glass vase raised for attack, "Fuckin' World's gotta revolve round you, hasn'it!"

He seemed to decide against delivering the fatal blow and instead slammed the vase down hard against his dressing table, sending a cloud of powder into the atmosphere and a tumbler of what looked like whiskey onto the floor, "how much did you get, you caterwauling twat? Was it worth it?"

I sneezed from the displaced pollen and sprayed an arc of snot and blood that reached as far as the door, gagging on my scarlet phlegm while attempting to whip off a retaliatory retort.

A broken nose hurts like sodomy the first time around, but the second time ...

"It wasn't ... me!" I eventually managed to spit, gargling in blood as I tried to right myself.

Lakhi swanned about his room like an overrated drag queen on the verge of an impromptu chorus of 'I who have nothing'.

"And I didn't do Morris either, before you start accusing me of that as well!"

Lakhi stopped pacing and, ignoring my protests, slumped into his chair in front of the mirror and began to apply a heavy line of Kohl to his lower lids.

"I'm next, if you don't believe me!"

"Morris reckons you accosted him in the street," he eventually replied without turning to see me pull myself back to my feet, " he told me that you demanded money from him and that you threatened to blackmail him!"

"That's bollocks Lakhi, and you know it ! When did Morris Yussof ever tell you the truth? I never asked for his money. He offered, but I turned him down!"

"And why would you do that, eh? You're broke; living rough, from what I hear - you're a desperado. How much do you want from me, huh?"

"I want your help! Not you're money! 'Same as I asked of Morris!"

For a second I thought that his rage had abated and that he might even have been considering taking my word above that of everybody's favourite compulsive liar.

"Look Lakhi," I prompted in my most considerate of tones, allowing for the fact that I could well have been dying from severe blood loss trauma, "I know who's doing this to us - and I can stop them."

He swung himself back to face me and pointed a shaking eye liner pencil at my face.

"I bet you fuckin' do !" he spat, quite literally, "how 'very' convenient! How much?"

"It's not about money!" I reiterated, though I was lying to myself. I wanted his money; I needed his money and I bloody resented his money - especially as, without my input into his career; without my casting vote that destroyed Neve and made *him* - he wouldn't even have *had* his sodding money! But I wasn't about to let him know it. There was little dignity in scrabbling for autographs from my erstwhile peers to sell for the cash to keep me alive, but at least it had more honour about it than taking handouts from the likes of Lakhi and Morris.

"Yes I'm in the gutter," I admitted with a peculiar sense of pride, as if I was at an alcoholic's seminar about to deliver a rallying speech to my fellow abusers, "and it's a gutter of my own making."

That shut him up, though it didn't garner me the applause that my imagined audience would have heaped on my honest admission, "I don't want your hand outs - all I want is a hand up," (and who could deny me that?) "I'm gonna' work my way out of this Lakhi, I'm going to get my life back. And I'm going to do it the hard way because that's the only way I'm going to learn anything from this."

He could see that I was serious and it seemed to shock him from his former opinion of me. Shit. I had shocked myself as I realized that I actually meant what I had just blurted to him in desperation!

"Are you going to help me out so's I can help us all?" I added for altruistic emphasis.

Lakhi paused in thought and I noticed that he would need at least another layer of foundation if he were intending to pass himself off as human for the unforgiving cameras.

"It's still blackmail," he said, pulling his right eyelid away from his cornea and stroking it with the nib of the pencil that he had previously intended to use as a weapon.

"But it isn't vindictive blackmail," I conceded, as if there was a difference. Lakhi and I had rarely seen eye to eye over our twenty two-year acquaintance, but we had never been enemies. I envied him his luck, but then -who wouldn't? But I didn't hate him. He had often come out on my side in any of a dozen long running disputes between Stephen and myself and had never had a particular soft spot for our friend Morris. And he wasn't a grudge bearer, though I don't believe he has ever been back to Tokyo since the 'incident'.

He smiled at me, a thousand nooks and crannies mapping his leather face and threatening to crack his congealing mask into a dermal jigsaw.

"You've changed, Sylvie Quiggley," he said, turning back to his mirror to study the damage that his facial musculature had rent on his hard work, "You're not the wanker you were. Mortality's done you a favour."

"Trust me Lakhi," I pleaded, my nose still dispensing a constant stream of blood; so much that I was beginning to feel quite faint, "I can turn the tables on 'Fawn Kate'."

"What's the deal?"

"Same as I asked of Morris," I explained, "Autographs - anyone on anything."

I scribbled the address of Mrs Beacham's Hampstead B and B on the back of my spent tube ticket and handed it to him.

"As much as you can find," I said, watching him attempt to suppress another smile for fear of causing irreparable damage to his make up rather than to protect my shattered pride, "It's legal," I protested, "even if it's not moral." Now where had I heard that before?

I made a mental note to remind myself that I had not yet informed Morris of my change of address. It was a huge risk I knew, letting them know where I was staying, but I had no choice.

Lakhi pocketed the ticket then delved into a battered duffel bag that I had not previously seen stuffed beneath the counter. He pulled out a pile of A5 sized monochrome portraits, purporting to be of himself but which bore little resemblance to the man before me. Each one had been adorned with his inimitable stamp and the words 'loving you'. He pulled a dozen or so from beneath their elastic band and passed them to me.

"Do you want to stay and watch the show?" he offered, and my stomach twisted in anger. I calmed myself by thinking that my old ally had not intended the insult that I had translated from this smug suggestion. "We've got 'The Proles', 'Sex-on-a-stick', Rusty's 'Bottom Favours' and 'Nobby Thorts & The Wanquettes'." I stifled a grimace, or at least I thought I'd stifled it, but by the look on his face I had been as transparent as his facial.

"'course not," he replied to his own question, "you never could abide music that you hadn't written yourself. Young upstarts, eh?" he chided, "stealing your glory?"

He opened the door to indicate that my masochistic audience was at an end. "It's a throw away world, me old mucker. Time waits for no man."

Chapter Eight
"Getting Comfy"

Camden Town.

A downhill stroll from the Heath, (all of twenty minutes), and one finds oneself in the heart of the capital's third most visited tourist attraction. There is virtually nothing that can't be bought, bartered or sold in the infamous markets of Camden. From second hand shoes to antique four poster beds; from the latest in rubber and fetish wear to battered bananas on sticks. Two visits will never be the same; neither would they leave you enough time in which to see everything, experience every curio, or sample every succulent delight from the multifarious snack shacks that seem to spring up overnight to be replaced the following week by tastes even stranger than before.

I knew that I couldn't keep the Spittalfields pitch, lucrative as it had become, and so, armed with my regular payloads from Morris and more recently Lakhi, I had adopted myself a stall in the shadow of the old horse hospital antique market at the Chalk Farm end of Camden. It was a lean-to affair: salvaged scaffolding covered with a pea green and white striped tarpaulin roof, tacked down on three sides by bulldog clips and lengths of old tow rope. To my left I neighboured an 'artist' whose peculiar talent lay in the collecting of old iron and his skillful rearrangement of said junk into supposedly useful everyday household objects.

Surprisingly 'the Tin man', as he liked to be called, could not turn out recycled plant pots and cutlery quickly enough - his scrap art selling like cheap cider to a Wino.

To my right I bordered Patch - a teenage wideboy of supposedly Romany extraction, whose business empire had been built by his selling of second hand clothes that he regularly stole from dustbin liners that had been left outside of charity shops.

It wasn't Knightsbridge, but it was cheap and over the two months that I had been working the market I had been able to boost my cash surplus by almost a grand. In fact, taking into account the looming Christmas period, and providing the weather held out as it had done over the past few weeks, I estimated that I would be able to begin recording the album by the spring - having by then completed one whole year in the wilderness. But that year had not been wasted. I had learned so much. I had seen and experienced a side to life that my philosophical lyricising had previously been blind to. The depth and content of this album would surpass everything that I had ever recorded before ! I would come to look on my experiences among the ordinaries as a research project in the years to follow; I felt certain. And as for the book, well ... every story needs a bit of drama and the story of my resurrection now seemed the more exciting prospect than simply my fall from grace and the reasons for my failure.

I couldn't say that I was a happy man, but I was contented. For a while. I had purpose. I had my drive and my ambition back. I had learned to adapt, rather than to adopt my earlier fears of acceptance of my fate. Neve had left me alone. I was sure that she could have found me if she had really wanted to, but she was obviously not as hung up or indeed as mad as I had previously thought. I was safe. I was on my way. And then disaster struck.

"You got a Rusty Rhine?"

"Sorry?" I replied, hauled back into the present tense by a being of sceptical orientation who was wearing what at first glance appeared to be a suit of armour, but which was probably merely some form of orgasm inciting S&M bodysuit.

"Rusty Rhine?" It repeated, "you know. The DJ?"

"Er yeah ..." I replied, smiling to myself at the thought of the Moonies' ex-drummer and his restyled DJ / producer / impresario persona, "How many do you want?"

Now, it wasn't a normal question to ask of a punter in this particular game, but my flippancy was born out of my incredulity that this was the third person to have made this particular request in the past couple of hours.

"How many 'you got?"

I checked my muso file and found two colour portraits of my former percussionist; recent issue - since his famous 'Rusty' locks had forsaken their follicles and he had resorted to shaving his head down to a number two grade and bleaching the remaining shoots to match his seksuka style beard.

I passed them to pinhead.

"How much?"

I had sold the previous two for thirty-five quid a piece, but, deciding that there was something odd afoot in the Rusty camp, I opted to chance my luck. The punter with the pincushion face was obviously not a pauper, judging by the amount of money that it had tied up in facial jewellery.

Maybe Rusty had become Prime Minister over night, I thought, as I plucked a figure from the air: "Fifty quid each," I said, "Ninety five the pair."

"Shit, man," the human dartboard responded incredulously, "the guy's not even dead yet!"

It pulled a wad of twisted twentys from its back pocket and counted five of them into my hand. I fished for a fiver in change.

"What do you mean 'yet' ?" I queried, as I bagged my sale and handed it over with five one pound coins to accompany it.

"You ain't heard?"

"No."

The pierced punter produced a rolled up copy of The Daily Rumour from another hidden pocket, folded it flat for me and indicated the front page headlines.

"Keep it," I heard distantly, as my mind began to accept the days exclusive, "I hope you aint got too much tied up in 'Sly Quips'!"

'SLY QUIP'S SLY QUIP' The leader read in bold black capitals. Beneath it, the page had been divided into two equal parts and pasted with photographs of Rusty and myself. Rusty's profile I recognized as the self same Lichfield that I had been selling all morning, but my own mugshot was a lot less flattering, taken as it was from the security tapes of that Deli that I stood accused of robbing the previous spring.

'Family and friends of millionaire record producer Rusty Rhine, 39, were stunned last night when a special delivery arrived at his hospital bedside from former friend, turned bankrupt fugitive Sly Quip, AKA: Sylvester Quig - (continues 2nd page 4th column) I read, then skipped forward for the punch line: '-gley, 42. An all black funeral wreath was delivered to the £900 a day Squires clinic in Chelsea at 7.25pm yesterday complete with a card bearing the inscription 'Stop hanging about'. The phrase is believed to allude to Quip's 1991 chart flop of the same name - a failure that a source close to the pair claims that Quip blamed on Rhine and another ex member of eighties supergroup 'Some Young Moon', guitarist

Stephen Twenty. Twenty's body was found earlier this year in the burnt out shell of his Maseratti having apparently committed suicide, although police are now expected to reopen the case in light of new evidence.

Rusty Rhine remains unconscience and unaware of his former pal's sick message following his collapse on Thursday evening at a music industry awards ceremony after downing a lethally spiked cocktail of drugs and alcohol. Foul play has not been ruled out. Anyone with information as to the whereabouts of Sly Quip should contact Scotland Yard's serious crime squad on 0171 -'

"Shit." I exclaimed to nobody in particular. I skim read the further details of my own crimes, but skipped the full page celebration of Rusty's achievements. I didn't need another ego battering in the form of yet another of my former colleagues rapturous success stories.

It seemed that I was the prime suspect, and not just in Rusty's case, but now Stephen's as well. It would only be a matter of time before Morris and Lakhi decided to cut their losses and sell me out and both of them now knew where to find me. So much for my giving her the benefit of the doubt. There was only one person who could have masterminded this one and that was Neve bloody Crilly.Panic began to set in. I had nowhere left to go. All that I could think of was getting away from London; finding somewhere to think. There was an answer to all this, I knew, but my head was too full and too factious to flag the obvious solution. I left my stall and my stock and jogged out through the Saturday morning hustle, eliciting yelps and threats from the browsing public as I rebounded off of their shopping bags in my haste. I ignored the abdominal stitch and the dry sting in the back of my throat, not daring to slow my pace until I had completed the uphill mile back to the house.

'Tranny' Beachman was not at home when I arrived and thankfully 'her' copy of The Rumour still lay untouched on the door mat. I took the stairs two at a time, flagging by the second tier; opened my door and then locked myself in. I took a paranoid peek through the moth eaten nets at the road beyond, but could see no sign yet of the S.W.A.T team. I pulled my gig bag from beneath my rickety hospital surplus bed and started cramming it with what I had left. It wasn't much. I pulled the envelope that I had stuffed with cash from under the loose board and finally, the scrapbook; though

what use it was to me now I couldn't begin to contemplate.
This was fast becoming a habit.

"If you don't mind me saying so, Sly old chap, you look like shit."
I woke with a start, half expecting to see a truncheon raised above
me, as had been the content of my fitful night's dream. I took in
my incongruous surroundings in a sweep and tried to focus on the
bearded and bedraggled figure above me. My head ached from
alcohol abuse and I was unable to recollect any precise details of
the previous night's journey. I could remember leaving the flat,
buying a bottle of homebrand ... and heading north.
"It is you, isn't it?" the tattered tramp persisted, squatting on his
haunches to stare just a little too closely for my comfort. I pulled
myself up and away from his stench.
"Where am I?" I asked, as I tried to massage some feeling back into
the arm that I had been sleeping on.
"You're on my bench," he replied, a little too indignantly for a man
of his standing.
I squinted back at him, the breaking dawn stinging my eyes as the
winter sun began its gradual incline above the distant trees. I had
to admit - he did look familiar. The hair was a lot longer and had
become matted at the collar. His face was filthy and he stank like
the stagnant urinal in the band enclosure at Glastonbury, but his
clothes; though tattered and frayed, were still obviously of a finer
quality than anything that I had possessed since we had last met.
"Albie?"
The soiled vagrant coughed effeminately.
"Highness is the term I believe you're thumbing for, subject."
"Still think you're the Prince of Wales, then?" I mocked, dusting
myself down and scanning the horizon for recogniseable land-
marks.
"No, I'm the fucking queen!" he spat, and for the first time I began
to consider the possibility that he might have been dangerous.
"Where am I, Albie, sorry: highness?"
"You're on my heath, dear boy, but I'll let you off. Royal pardon and
all that. I've telephoned your social worker for you. Delightful
woman. Says she'll soon have you back on the ward -"
"What the fuck are you talking about, loon?"

"Miss Crilly," he replied, flashing a crisp, white calling card similar to the one that Neve had given to me after the funeral. "She said she thought you might show up here," he said.

"I'm still in Hampstead?" I panicked.

"They've been looking everywhere, old chap. Seems you've caused something of a stir this time."

My gigbag sat beside me on the bench, its clasps undone and its contents rifled.

"What've you taken?" I demanded, pulling myself to my feet and urgently searching my remaining acoutrements.

"The money ? Where's my -"

I failed to see the swing that caught me off balance and cracked the already weakened bridge of my poor nose, sending me rolling backward across the broken back slats of the bench. I don't remember losing consciousness nor indeed regaining it, but by the time that I had righted myself, my attacker was nowhere to be seen; the heathland empty of all, but birdlife and rabbits.

I retreated under cover of the nearest thicket to take stock of my worsening situation. All that I had struggled for - all the indignities! All for what? All I had left was the bloody scrapbook and a bagful of secondhand clothes. I had come round in a circle - from nothing to nothing. The last time that I had been here I had been attempting to toast myself, but that mad little vagrant had saved my life. Over the last couple of weeks I had found myself wanting to thank the little bastard for giving me a second chance at life.

I suppose it all comes down to how one values one's life. It could be argued that his actions back in April were priceless; because my life could never be quantified by cash. He had taken everything that I had. Ought I still be thankful that I was alive because of him? I could feel my ruminations heading dangerously toward some kind of straw clutching religious experience and pulled myself together. Stay bitter, I told myself, harness that anger. It would be an essential motivation if I were to avenge myself of my nemesis.

From my hideout in the trees I knew that I would be able to see her coming and make good my escape whichever way she chose to enter the Heath. Or I could kill her.

And that was when I noticed the paper. Sticking out from beneath the scrub was a damp and thumbed copy of the 'Rumour on Sunday'. Yet again it had been the headline that had caught my eye 'RIP RUSTY RHINE'. Jim Reaper, as sensitive and tactful as ever. Reaper was the lowest of all forms of journalist: the media correspondent. He was a weasel; a germ, and as his name suggested - a harvester of souls. His moniker was synonymous with the kind of story that I knew I was about to read. He was a destroyer of careers; a despoiler of lives; probably most famously that of the late lamented Henri Blutoe himself, (an act that had even seen him immortalized in the filmed version of Blutoe's autobiography.)

He had given over a third of his Rusty article to a factless slandering of myself, all but pinning the blame for Rusty's mysterious death on myself and the premature tribute that I was accused of sending him. It was a call to arms: a challenge to every other gutter publication to start raking the muck. I could see myself with the social standing of Gary Glitter within the month !

I supposed that it was inevitable, the scandal hungry public liked nothing more than to claw back their over achievers when they were found to be less than perfect individuals. And there were plenty of imperfections here for them to chose from. One only had to look at Neve's scrapbook ... and then I saw it!

I pulled the overstuffed bible of Moonie inadequacies from the bag and placed it in my lap, carefully turning its pages until I arrived at Rusty's entry. As with all of us she had an extensive selection of Rusty surveillance shots, inside and outside of his Bedfordshire folly. She had detailed movements and personal observations. She knew his poisons. She knew his dealer ! Name and number ! How hard would it have been to slip ... no. Surely she couldn't have. Could she ? Could she have murdered him in cold blood just to get at me?

I could hear voices. I looked out over the heath and saw a squad of uniformed police spreading out to begin their search. As I stood up, some of the looser leaves slipped from the book and as I stooped to recover them I found a whole page dedicated to Diz. There were photographs - some taken with a zoom lens if I wasn't mistaken, outside the gates of Wormwood Scrubs. So he was out ! There was an address in Balham; even a number.

Trying not to disturb the local wildlife I used my two hundred yard shielded advantage to slip through the trees in the direction of

Kenwood and the ponds.

For as long as I can remember I have been driven by ambition. Not money. Not fame. And definitely not by sex. Whenever my world has been dogged and uncertain I would set myself yet another improbable goal.

The first one that I can clearly recall had been the aquisition of Neve Crilly's heart, followed quickly in adolescence by the aquisition of her body - ambitions that had only recently been achieved (and even then only at a price.)

Having decided early on in my life that I was unlikely ever to reach these goals, I set myself another: to be more than the sum of my parts; to be better than that which was expected of me. Looking back on it now I am somewhat saddened to have to acknowledge that a great deal of my energies have been spent in trying to impress Neve Crilly. And in order to satisfy this wanton sexual desire I have allowed myself to become embroiled in my own hypocritical obsession with money and fame.

I thought I had ambition. I thought I had purpose. But who had I been kidding ? And take away the catalyst to my achievement and where have I to go ? What had I been doing ? For the first time in my life I now realized the utter pointlessness of my existence. I'm glad that Albie saved my sorry delusional life - even if it was just so that I could learn that ! I am like everybody else on this planet. Ordinary; possessed of nothing greater than that primal urge to survive.

I don't really know why I bothered to go after Diz at this point or what I was hoping to achieve, but I had to keep going. Instinct told me to survive and in order to do that I had to know what it had all been for. You know - the meaning of life?

I watched the taxi's tripometer tick through the numbers while we sat in the mire that was rush hour Euston. At this rate, I thought, I would have to get out well before the river. All I had left was the loose change from Camden. Albie must have taken my wallet while I had slept off my binge the night before. I tried to focus on my plan, such as it was.

They were in this together, I felt sure. That was how Neve had known the dirt before I had written it down. So why had she been so keen for me to persue the book? The only reason that I could think of was that she had intended her role to appear purely passive. Had it been that simple? Prove my bitterness toward my former associates and I would have motive for her crimes?

But how much had they manipulated and how much of my demise had actually been of my own doing? Neve had had copies of my accounts. She would have noticed that Andy and Greg were in above their bent little heads, as should I have done if I had taken a little more interest in my personal finances. Had she blackmailed them like she had intended that I do to Morris and Lakhi? I couldn't rule it out. And what was the ultimate plan? Was she intending to top the whole band, then blame it onto me?

A thought struck me just as the traffic broke and Marylebone Road became Portland Place, and by the time we had reached Regent Street I had the scrapbook back in my lap and Stephen Twenty's entry open and digesting. She really had had it in for Stephen! She had more detail on her teenage lover than MI5 would have needed to have put him away twenty years earlier. Certain texts had been highlighted in blue marker and alluded to a whole stream of miniature photographs. Stephen had had a lover, it seemed. Well, big deal ? He was as famous for his love life as he was his riffs and licks, but it appeared from Neve's surrupticious investigations that this one was more than just a showbiz-column fling with a spotlight starved socialite model. She had intercepted his mail! She had followed them around! There were copies of love letters. There were holiday snaps. There was a name: Carrie Sewell, an address in Camden; a home number, a mobile and a work number as well! But by far the most interesting detail was that Neve had been taking money from Stephen to keep her mouth shut. I thought back to the suicide and the 'Rumour's' revelations of Stephen's missing money. Stephen's wife had never been happy about his affairs, but then she had made him sign a precedent setting prenuptial that she could have exercised at anytime. She hadn't left him, because Stephen had always managed to convince her that the bimbos had meant nothing to him, and anyway - they kept him in the public eye and bringing in the lucre. But this affair was different. Stephen had been in love. And if Neve *hadn't* ruined him, then she would have done.

So maybe it *had* been suicide. Or maybe it had just suited her plans at the time for it to have *looked* like suicide.

The whole journey took me seventy five minutes and left me with a paltry one pound seventy to my name. But I no longer cared about the money. Lochinver street was just off the Balham high road.

I paid my dues and made my way up the concrete steps toward number twenty seven. My heart was racing as my sweaty finger pressed the bell. Diz was not a slight man. All I had in my favour was the element of surprise.

I tensed as I heard the clang of two security bolts being withdrawn and steeled myself for the attack as the flimsy plywood door jerked open. In a sudden rush of conjoured adrenalin I barged the door with my shoulder, forcing it inward a full inch before it snagged against its brass chain. I reeled against the blow which had sent a shockwave of pain in all directions south of my shoulder blade. As I coiled forward in convulsion, cursing crudely under my breath, a furry, tatooed arm lunged forward from within, grabbed me like a minnow in a net and hauled me into the dank, fetid hallway beyond. In a well rehearsed manoeuvre; made easy by the utilization of that element of surprise that I had so royally fucked up myself, the grip was released and I was slammed hard in the chest against a flimsy dividing wall, then nailed by my neck to the plasterboard by my attacker's elephantine fingers and thumb.

"Sly?" The Neanderthal exclaimed, somehow recognizing his former employer through my abstractly rearranged features: a disguise that had fooled just about everybody else including myself, but obviously not Diz.

"You're ...ch...ch...choking!" I managed through numbing lips.

The ex-con' roadie who now looked more like some kind of experimental human / ape hybrid than ever before released his grip on my throat and I dropped like a fledgling sparrow on its maiden flight. I didn't know how much more of this punishment my body could take. My once regularly pampered skin was now scarred, bruised and dented far beyond mere exfoliation repair and my whole skeleton throbbed in much the same way as I would imagine a football to feel after an FA cup final. (If of course a football was sentient, which of course it wasn't.)

"What the fuck 'you doing here? How d'you find me?"

I coughed into my hand, droplets of blood spattering my fingers as my now Negroid nose began to weep again.

"How d'you *think* I found you!" I fished.

"She didn't tell you?"

"Who ? Neve ?"

Diz led the way into the kitchen and I followed him in. The sight that greeted me made me realize that I still had a long way to fall before I reached rockbottom. Apart from the collection of over flowing bin bags, each exposing their contents of decomposing curry in silver foil dishes and ash filled cans of cheap beer, every available surface was stacked with video equipment in various states of disrepair. The stench of rotting food was almost over-whelmed by the heady smell of fresh solder. It was then that I real-ized Diz's unique contribution to Neve's misconceived plan.

"You don't look too good, mate," Diz noticed, wrenching the ring-pull from a tin of 'Special Brew' (although by the rusted state of the tin I doubted that is tasted very special.) "D'you want one?" He asked, offering me the can that he had only just swigged from; the fallout from which could still be seen bubbling in his silvering beard, "or I 'got some smoke in the other room?"

"Just tell me what she's got planned," I spat, my confidence return-ing now that I had seen that prison life had not changed my old friend as much as I had worried that it might have done.

"Ah shit, man! I don't know. 'Aint nothin' t'do with me!"

"You fitted all our security systems, Diz ! Who else would've known how to bypass our alarms?"

"You can't prove -"

"No, I know! You were banged up at the time! Perfect alibi! Why d'you do it, eh? What did I do to you?"

"Five years, man! For something I never did!"

"I didn't do it to you!" I shouted, with blood trickling off my chin, "I stood up for you in court! I was your character witness!"

"I still went down, Sly. Five years of my life!"

"She's ruined me Diz! And she killed Rusty!"

"I know! I know! But what can I do? All I did was show her how to do it. I didn't actually do nothin'!"

"She offered you money?"

"Yeah! I fuckin' needed it! I didn't have nothin' to come out to !"

"How did you meet her? You never even knew her."

"She visited me in the scrubs, didn't she! She said she was an old girlfriend of Stevie's. Said she wanted to get back at him! Why wouldn't I have helped her? She said she was gonna blackmail him. Said she'd pay me out of what she got off him!"

"And you told her all the stuff about Morris and the drugs? Lakhi and the geisha?"

"She already knew that."

"From where?"

"How should I know?"

"Only you and I knew that stuff, Diz."

"And Joe."

Joe! How could I have been that stupid ! I thought back to that lunch at the Savoy where Joe had broken the news to me that the Munday corporation would not be renewing my contract. The company that I had helped him to set up; the company that, without my talent at its creative helm, would have never got off the ground - were dropping me! He had pleaded with me not to cause a scene. He had a reputation to consider. He hadn't seen me cause a scene! He hadn't seen that guacamole coming either. We had traded insults as if the bottom was about to fall out of the market in swear words. I had threatened to kill him. I had promised to kill Stephen and Rusty too. And he had promised to ruin me before the century was out. It was now December 15th 1999. So who was using who? What did Joe possibly have to gain from Stephen and Rusty's deaths? They were his stars; his cash cows: his license to print money.

Diz had pulled a musty smelling kahki kitbag stenciled with the legend 'Some Young Moon' in white emulsion from beneath a pile of assorted rags. I had followed him from the kitchen to the living room, (though by the state of it 'living room' was something of a misnomer, as no earthly life form could possibly have 'lived' in the squalor that I had found myself in.) He had begun some kind of spontaneous spring clean as I had been ranting at him. I tried to focus his attentions on the problem in hand. My problem.

"You've got to come to the police with me, Diz. Tell them what you know."

"You jest!" he giggled, stopping to pick up a crusty grey sock from a stereo turntable which he duly sniffed, then discarded. "Why would I want to do that?"

"To get me off the hook," I explained emphatically, "to help me get my life back; to save everyone else's lives!"

He laughed out loud and I caught the blast of his nicotine stained, decaying toothed breath. I watched him knot the cords of his sack and sling it over his shoulder before I realized that he was intending to do a bunk before my very eyes.

"Hey, wait a minute," I said, attempting to hold the man giant back as he pushed past me and out into the hall, "You can't just leave me to it ! I need you. You've got to help me!"

Diz turned back to face me, one monster hand resting on the front door latch.

"You want me to go to the police and tell them that I sold the plans to your houses to a mad woman, but it's OK 'cause me mate Sly didn't really do nothing wrong after all?"

"Something along those lines ..."

"Wake up Sly, man! You're not the millionaire popstar living in a mansion on the Heath and dealing with your nobody employee now. You're down among the ordinaries. You're one of us ! Face it. You're no bigger than me, now. In fact," he emphasized by poking me in the ribs with a bloated finger, "you're smaller than me!"

He opened the door and checked both directions on the landing before stepping out. "I wish you luck old son, but you're on your own."

I watched him go : my only chance of coming through my hell quickly disappearing before my eyes.

I gathered up my few belongings and did a quick reconoitre of the flat to see if the big man had left anything that might be of any use to a down and out like myself. I checked the fridge, but decided that I wasn't that hungry just yet. I availed myself of the facilities, such as they were, but was unable to work the flush. Deciding that under the circumstances nobody was likely to notice my solitary hygiene faux pas, I closed the flat door and headed back along the landing in the direction of the stairwell. I couldn't think straight at all ; my mind a blur of plots and counterplots. Paranoicly I pondered the folly of leaving a pile of genetic waste material floating in the bowl behind me. Could they check that kind of thing in the same way that rapists could be identified by their semen ? Could they be tracking my movements, I wondered? And what would Reaper have made of that story ! 'Sly dump traps Sly blackmailer!'

As I turned the corner that would lead me onto the first floor landing my heart sank so low that I almost expelled it from my arse.

I didn't need to check the body for a pulse. Nobody alive would have been able to lie that still while losing that amount of blood to the macabre scarlet waterfall that was cascading down the last few concrete steps. In the scant minutes since I had last exchanged words with my ex-employee, he had managed to gain a brand new orifice - this one wider and cheesier than the grin that was etched onto his other lips in some kind of rictus gurn.

I was glad then that I had taken the chance to relieve myself before leaving the flat.

Chapter Nine
"What Price Immortality?"

I watched from the bar as Joe weaved his bulemic frame through the shoulder to shoulder punters, crossing the sticky dancefloor and heading toward the cluster of little round tables on the far side of the auditoreum. He looked like an anorexic Neil Armstrong as he bounced across the sprungwood floor in slow motion, reaching Neve's table one step ahead of the tidal surge of bodies as they pressed forward toward the Fiddler's raised stage at first sight of the evening's support.

Neve turned her head as she felt our manager's bony fingers brush against her shoulder as I had seen her do so many times in this memory. She smiled: that coy, bedeviling smile that I could remember nothing past. She inclined her head toward Joe's lipless mouth, digging her finger into her free ear to drown out the squeal of feedback from the unsoundchecked amateurs that were by then pogoing to the strains of their opening gambit.

Her smile gave way to a frown as her brain began to digest Joe's typically blunt and tactless dismissal. She pulled away slowly, her face a canvas of betrayal. She said nothing, but she looked out across the dancefloor and saw me watching, all awkward and exposed. Our eyes locked for what in real time must have been a fraction of a second, but which in the eternity of my conscience I now know had never been broken.

"What did she say?" I asked as Joe returned to the bar; that smug, self satisfied leer that he usually reserved for journalists and interviewers blighting his otherwise misleadingly benign features.

"She was fine about it."

"What did you say?"

Neve's half empty glass sat spotlit on the table that she and her mates had recently vacated.

"I told her to go back to college," he replied out of the corner of his mouth as he sparked a fresh cigarette in the crook of his lip, "Writing's where the money is, Sylv. I told her I thought she should stick to what she's good at," He chuckled as he exhaled sharply, breathing smoke into my already fume weary eyes.

"I said she'd be making money long after you lot are dead and buried and -" (he laughed at his own jibe) "If she played her cards right she could even make money out of that !"
Joe's final line now reverberated around my skull like a taunt from a playground bully.

A pair of rust hued, tarpaulin draped refuse scows dipped beneath Wandsworth bridge chugging gracelessly down river like nautical pooh sticks. I followed their progress from my parapet on the bridge as they traced the gentle curve of the Thames, on their way to one of the gull infested landfill sites out past the Isle of Dogs. I mused as they passed the four defiant stacks of Battersea's long defunct power station; obsolete, yet splendidly arrogant in its redundancy, like two sets of giant fingers flicking the 'V's' against a world so bogged down by its own beuraucracy that it had made it impossible for it to destroy this useless monstrocity in order to make way for the progress that had rendered it useless in the first place.
I thought back to a time when this image would have been a metaphor for my own shambolic existence; a time when I believed that past glories could never be toppled by future failures.
But I have learned over the past year that nothing is permanent; that nothing can be taken for granted. The World might still be there waiting for you when you open your curtains each morning, but then again - it might not. And neither was the past as static and rigid as a dust covered history book in a school library. It is as fluid as the present; as rewriteable as these memoirs. If Neve's plan, or Joe's plan for that matter, was allowed to run its course then all of my past achievements would soon amount to nothing. One only has to look to Gary Glitter or PJ Proby to see how a man's contribution to the world can be singularly removed from history following a mass media scandal like the one that they had planned for me.
Two choices hung before me like jeering demons vying for the copywrite to my contaminated soul. If I were to die now, before

they had a chance to kill Morris and Lakhi, then I would probably be considered another victim and exonerated in my absence, achieving the immortality that I had always dreamed of.

Option two was no less a sacrifice. I was forty three, almost. I was only half way through my life. How badly did I want to continue that life ? How much better could it get ? Could I learn to live with second best ? Whichever choice I made, I knew then that I could never be Sly Quip again, or Sylvie Quiggley for that matter.

I could disappear; start a new life somewhere else. An anonymous life where nobody would think to look for me. Down here: Down among the ordinaries. And who knew: maybe one day I might even find my nirvana, where I least expected to find it.

The man with no name opened his battered gigbag for the last time and mulled over its contents. It was all that was left of his dream; of his life. He flipped through the pages of his notebook, replayed the last few seconds of tape on his Dictaphone, smoothed the creases of his leathers and refastened the broken latch on his Leichner make up Kit, (which head leaked powder all over the other contents of the bag). He closed the lid and kissed it mournfully, like a good catholic son would kiss the forehead of his mother's corpse. He clambered up onto the railing and teetered precariously in the rattling wind. He peered down at the bepling surface of the filthy river below and stayed for a moment as a tiny police launch battled against the tide to disappear beneath the bridge.

He was reminded of a news report that he had seen as a boy of the maritime burial of sixties popstar Paul Raven, less than a mile further down stream. His own demise would be a far quieter affair, but would share one important factor ...

Epilogue:

"Mister Munday will see you now," said the preened and pouting little wannabe someone, whose employment at Munday Towers was presumably the lowest indignity that she was prepared to suffer in her quest to be 'spotted' and catapulted to success by the millionaire mogul himself.

Neve smiled down disparagingly on the girl and made a mental note of her name just in case she ever did make it past the casting couch, and clipped her way along the marble floor toward the arrogantly grandiose granite edifice of Joe's office.

She knocked gently, yet still managed to chafe her knuckles against the rough-hewn slab that served as a door. She heard the electronic lock disengage itself with a sonic boom and waited until her entrance was bidden. She stepped into what she had come to think of as the devil's domain.

"Neve!" The shiny domed impresario greeted, with skeletal, satin clothed arms spread wide as he sat on his gilded throne behind his graphite desk.

"Joe," she replied curtly, resisting the demeaning, yet infuriatingly compulsive urge to curtsy to her effete benefactor.

"Good news, I hope?" he bellowed from across the unfeasible expanse of leopard skin carpet. He gestured for her to sit in one of a number of high backed wooden chairs that appeared to have been hand carved from a single tree by a madman wielding a chainsaw.

She walked toward him and took the seat nearest the desk.

"They've found his briefcase," she said, "the one that he used to keep his mementos in. It washed up on the gravel beside Chelsea pier with one of his winkle pickers."

"But no body?"

"No. But he's finally been listed as 'missing presumed dead'."

Joe smiled broadly. Lasciviously even.

"Of course, they'll never find a body," she said, "Oh, there'll be plenty of possibilities and endless 'sightings', but they'll never find him."

He stood up and walked around his preposterously oversized desk, stopping to rest his arseless legs against its rock blasted edge beside her. He folded his arms across his pigeon chest and closed his eyes momentarily.

"Perfect," he finally rewarded, and she caught a breeze of his fetid breath, "you performed like a dream, my dear. I always knew you'd succeed in life where others would fail. You've got more inside that head of yours than all of them put together."

He hoisted his fragile, shiny body up onto the desk and strutted across its top to peer out of the picture window that comprised one whole wall of the football pitch sized office and from which could been seen sights as far spread as Canary Wharf and the telecom tower.

"Every record company needs an enigma," he continued, "much as it needs its suicides and its murder victims. We all need our Marc Bolans and our Buddy Hollys, our Kurt Cobains and our Glen Millers."

"I'm sorry?"

"Sly," he enlightened, "'missing-presumed-dead'. He was useless to us alive - long past his sell by. And Stephen Twenty's sales have never been so high! Rusty, of course, was becoming a bit of a liability - getting a little too interested in the business side of the operation. But missing at sea. Missing at sea ! What a gold mine! The book rights are yours, of course, nobody can ever prove you didn't write it. I'll publish, naturally, but you'll make a mint, dear."

"And you'll milk every last drop out of 're-issues' and 'best-ofs,' no doubt."

"No doubt. Well done Neve. I couldn't have thought of a better plan myself."

"Oh I'm sure you could if you put your mind to it," she whispered as she left the room, having picked up the golden envelope with her name on it that contained her bounty for the delivery of Sly Quip.

They had been as close as siblings. Once. But then, who said that siblings had to like each other ?